ROSIE LETS HERSELF GO

A ROSIE LIFE IN ITALY
BOOK 6

ROSIE MELEADY

ENVY PUBLISHING

Names have been changed, as have places, some situations and timing.

Thanks to:

Elizabeth Reed and Lucy Hayward for their editing skills. And Marco Marello for the cover.

For all the great people I have met at retreats and workshops.
Especially the Qi-Gongers, Vulva Huggers and Ghostbusters.

PROLOGUE

I'm sitting in the dappled light of old holm oaks, my head back, face to the sun, my sunglasses on, with a gorgeous-looking tanned man, brown eyes, close cut, white-blond hair and stubble that is just about long enough to be classed as a beard. I've noticed he has removed his wedding ring from his beautiful, strong hands.

He doesn't speak English. But we don't need words. Hand gestures, facial expressions and some laughing are all we need as we make music together in the secluded spot we found in the sacred wood. I met him yesterday and like the others I have met this year, I may never see him again, but we have shared intimate things we have never done before, not even to ourselves.

A couple of hours before, I was like the stereotypical deranged woman in the corner of a stereotypical old psychiatric hospital scene of a movie; screaming the loudest I have ever screamed, and laughing hysterically until I sobbed so hard I thought I could never stop, before screaming again but more guttural with anger—because the dead told me to.

1

"Okay, so let's make a list," I say to Ronan, who is sitting on the sofa, while I lie down on the floor, inhaling the scent of sandalwood. I came into the Tranquilla Room intending to do yoga. Ronan uses the room for meditating and over the months the scent of incense has seeped into the cushions, books, woodwork and sofa. I always wanted a house that smelled like this. Other rooms downstairs can smell of dog and burnt dinners, but not the Tranquilla Room. This is to remain smelling magical.

Ronan eyeballs me. Even after thirty years, me announcing the need for a list is like me saying, "let's figure out a way to start our own country."

Granted, my lists usually mean something major for him to do. They start off with me being very enthusiastic, then me disappearing to write, and leaving Ronan to do the manual labour.

I try to soften the blow.

"A five-year plan."

He looks a little less affronted. He knows my five-year plans can evolve and change every couple of months, whereas a list can be a to-do list for the next few hours, days, or months. The only lists he likes are grocery shopping lists. It saves him having to think about what to make for dinner.

I used to do ten-year plans, but as we get older, five-year plans are only needed. We don't need to take schools, kids, work or mortgages into consideration anymore. Five-year plans are less stressful and less scary.

The last four years have been a shit show of greatness and devastation. We, like the rest of the world, kicked it off with Covid, unable to reach family or get family to us. I lost two of the men I loved most in the world, my mam came to live with us twice before enthusiastically moving into a care home back in Ireland (away from my cooking), my kids grew up and both moved to a different country to us. But on the flip side, we bought a villa in Italy, renovated it, I became a full-time author and Ronan retired. We are in good health and both of our adult children are independent and doing well–actually better–without our interference. If it wasn't for the grief, I'd be living our perfect ending. But I am far from an ending yet.

"A five-year plan?"

"Where do you want to be in five years?"

"I don't know," Ronan says, sounding like a grunting teenager.

"Well, do you want to be in Ireland, or here, or near the kids in the UK?"

"I don't know."

This is getting frustrating. "Okay, if someone gave you a million quid to buy a house, where would you choose?"

"A million? You'd probably only get a semi-detached in Dublin or the outskirts of London for that."

"Okay, a billion then."

"That would be a lot of money to manage. I'd probably give it away."

"Oh, for goodness' sake, that is not the purpose of this exercise, Ronan. What I mean is, if money was no object, where would you live?"

"I don't know. How about you?"

"I haven't given the next five years much thought, that it is why we are having this discussion, to create a plan so we can get where we want to go." I put my pen and notebook down and lie back on the floor again.

I've never not had a plan. Without a plan, life just ticks along, and the next minute, you are ten years older and have done nothing different other than age. Well, that is my fear. I've always filled my life with urgency in case time runs out, and now that I'm getting older, it's all the more reason to plan even more carefully to make life work for us.

"I'd like to work on the garden and get it finished," Ronan says.

"Hmm, good idea. They say a garden takes five years."

"There you go. That's my five-year plan. Now, what do you want for dinner?"

"That's it? That's all you want to do?"

"Well yeah. There's a lot to be done. The grass alone needs to be cut twice a week and by the time I fix the lawnmower each time to do it, half a day is gone."

"We'll write 'create a beautiful garden' on the list, I mean plan. But I was hoping we could create something more extensive, rather than just fixing the lawn mower and cutting the grass twice a week for the next five years."

"Like what?"

"Well, if we want to create the garden, that means we are staying here in Italy, in this house?"

"I suppose it does."

"And if we are staying and not selling, we need to get the house to make money so we can continue to improve it. If we rent rooms and do retreats, then the house could pay for itself."

"We discussed this before, when you were coming home from your shitzu retreat."

"It was Qi Gong. A Qi Gong Retreat."

"Yeah, well whatever, I'm still up for the idea. You could put that on the plan. How many rooms would we need to rent out? What will we charge? I'll put an ad up on Airbnb and we could take bookings starting in May. We'd need the garden done."

For a man who had no plan two minutes ago, he is now flying too fast for me.

"The garden will take five years."

"The garden doesn't need to be fully grown to rent out rooms or run retreats. But we'll need to do the front garden."

"The front garden will be the last thing done. It's a bloody mess Ronan." The only things that have managed to grow in the front garden are brambles. I can't figure out what to do with the north facing, narrow strip, we call a front garden. So I just avoid it.

"True. We could still rent without it being done—good to keep people's expectations low so they are not expecting too much inside."

"We mightn't get too many bookings with that philosophy."

"We'll get it done before we have people staying in the summer," he says confidently.

"It will take months. As will the back garden and all the other stuff we've got to do."

"I know."

"How many months do you think are in a year Ronan? You are talking about doing all this work before opening in May–that's six months away."

"Oh."

"I don't even know what we are offering."

"Well retreats. You have done them before."

"I've taken part in one and run one–which was great, but I don't know how it compares to other retreats out there. Will people expect a pool? Will we like having people in our home?"

"Well, there is only one way to find out. To start."

"We can't advertise rooms or retreats, take bookings and then realise we hate it, or the house isn't suitable. And there's so much clutter lying around. And we need beds and furniture. So much to do. We need to make a list."

Ronan's giving me that eyeball thing again. So I correct myself and state, "A plan."

I lie back flat, breathing in the sandalwood, not having done any yoga yet. I might just lie here and think instead. Yoga seems a bit energetic and my body has not felt energetic for a long time. Someone told me, imagining stretching is as good as doing it. At this moment, I am choosing to believe them.

It's not just me feeling drained, Ronan is feeling it too. Completely zapped of energy. I get up off the floor with difficulty, having thought about doing yoga for long enough, open my notebook on the coffee table and draw a timeline.

"So for the next five years, we want to stay here in Italy, and get the house to pay for itself. Right?"

'Five-year plan,' I write at the top of the page and underneath, 'Stay in Italy.'

Followed by; 'Create a beautiful garden.'

'Fund future house improvements by renting rooms and doing retreats.'

Lying on the floor gives you a different perspective of a room. The cuckoo clock hanging above the TV is ticking. It was only hung there temporarily because of a spare nail and has not been moved in the two years since. It needs to find its place and I need art on the walls.

We are at the stage in our house renovation where we can look at the details, rather than which walls to knock down. Each of the twenty-two rooms now need to develop a personality and a purpose.

Until recently, I thought how everything we did to the house would affect the resale value. With the plan that when finished the renovations, we could sell the house, give our daughter back her investment with a healthy profit and we could buy a smaller place with our cut. Since we have decided to stay, I feel like it is our place. I don't want to do up the house for the next person to live in. I want to live in it and make it ours.

With the additional decision to run retreats in the house and open it up for strangers to come and stay in–it needs to be adapted for that purpose as well. I feel a pressure building, a deadline; to get the rooms and the garden looking good.

I am no interior designer, but I have to say, the furniture stores in Italy seem to hit two extremes; expensive, old style, heavy, dark furniture or cheap, put it together yourself, factory made furniture. Neither fit with the look or style I want to create in the house. I want the house to have clean lines and uncluttered, but it also needs to be so cozy guests won't want to leave. It needs to be a haven of tranquility, where people will come to create and find their passion for life again. Like it did for me.

In red ink I add "Find good quality, beautiful furniture," onto our list.

I wander out to the garden with a cup of tea. Last year's grief for my father and brother made me dig and weed fanatically for hours. The flower beds I created, along with the beautiful courtyard paving Ronan lay the summer previous, have the back garden looking like something other than overgrown scrubland. Sections of it are starting to take shape.

I sit with my tea at the extendable garden table. I expected it to host family type meals surrounded by twinkling fire flies and fairy lights, backed by the sound of cicadas and toads. Like the night in La Dogana eight years ago for Mam and Dad's sixtieth wedding anniversary. But it has never happened in our court-yard, the extendable table has never had the need to be extended..

Mam is comfortable in her nursing home in Ireland, she won't be coming back to Italy, and I can't share Italy with Eileen, my older sister, who would have been due to retire this year at sixty-four. She had planned for her retirement so well, but she only got to the age of forty-six. My Dad and James are gone too, in a short time of each other. My heart still aches so much for them both. All the elders of my clan who I wanted to share my table in Italy with will never be here. I need a different image to hang my vision of my life in Italy on. I need time to restructure how I envisage my future.

Several times I have attempted to do plans and sketches for the garden, but I can't seem to develop an overall look, instead I am happier doing one patch at a time. Friends have been generous with cuttings and gifts of plants during my times of raw grief over the last couple of years.

I think back to the back pain and callouses I had, having just finishing planting a batch of plants and then a friend would arrive with another box of cuttings.

"I brought you some plants."

"Oh, bloody hell!" Feck, did I say that out loud? I didn't mean to be ungrateful, but all I could think of is, "Really? More plants?"

I planted their generous donations randomly, forgetting what my friend told me they were and what size they will grow to. I did the same with the cuttings and plants friends gave me for my birthday, and the twenty-eight faded packets of seeds I had collected from shopping expeditions, with great unfulfilled intentions, at the beginning of each spring for the last five years.

For every plant donation or gift, I'd battle the weeds and brambles and clear a patch. Dig the holes required, battling the roots of old trees that no longer stand. Fill in the snake holes and avoid the scorpions. After fertilising the area with expensive organic stuff, I'd carefully tip the plant from its pot and bed in the surrounding soil.

My nearly grown back nails would break again and no amount of soaking or scraping removed the ingrained dirt.

For at least a month after each planting, my daily workout included carrying two full watering cans per plant down the garden.

It rained, then sunshine. Then rained again. Alongside the plants, the weeds took advantage of all my hard work.

Then, one fine morning Ronan, would go out with his strimmer and whack not only the weeds, but all the plants I had carefully planted and nurtured down to the roots because, "they all look the same" to him.

This happened after every planting session.

I'd then spend a week, and a small fortune, tracking down and replacing the same plants so that the friends who gave the originals to me wouldn't be upset. And the process of digging and planting would start over again. All I could do was hope that some might survive the next round of impromptu strimming.

But the time had come. I was now ready to organise the garden.

I go back to my list and add:

'Get rid of rubbish in the garage.'

Ronan winces. He knows I'm referring to the roofless shed to the front side of the house. It is filled to capacity with rubbish left since before we bought the house, broken wood wormed furniture, and junk left by the first set of builders. All thrown into the shed until we have time to clear it. I have been asking Ronan to tackle this for three years. But instead of tackling the stacked rubbish, he added to it every time we cleared a room. "I'm just storing it there until we get the pass for the dump," he'd say.

I'm about to add 'Get pass for the recycling dump' when I notice what Ronan has added onto the list.

Beside my to do of 'Find good quality, beautiful furniture,' Ronan has written; 'Including an old-fashioned roll-top desk where Rosie can write her best-selling novels.'

I smile, remembering how writing the first A Rosie Life In Italy book dredged up things I had forgotten. Including how as a teenager, I thought all I needed to become a best-selling author was a roll-top desk, candlelight and a quill and ink. Maybe someday I will get one, and I will sit at it and write all the books in my head patiently waiting for their moment.

2

I t's been raining for two weeks—it's good for the crops and lake and we know it will stop soon and the sun will come out, not like in Ireland.

I never owned an umbrella in all the years I lived there. As soon as you walk out the front door on an average day in Ireland, you are soaked with rain by the driving strong wind. An umbrella is useless. Either that or you are frozen to death. The weather and lack of sun was one of the main reasons I left Ireland for Italy. I have no memory of people wearing sunglasses when I was growing up in Ireland in the 70s. If you wore sunglasses, you were full of yourself or blind. Then Madonna arrived on MTV and we all got Madonna shades, like when Don Johnson arrived and the lads wore Miami vice suits in pastel shades with slip-on shoes and towel socks.

It's probably just as well, if we had good weather in Ireland we probably wouldn't have produced all the musicians and writers we did, as we'd have been outside enjoying ourselves rather than sitting inside telling stories to each other and being creative to save ourselves from boredom.

The day after the last heavy downpour, I go out to the garden and start working on clearing ivy from what was once a garage. It is an eyesore at the front of the house which I have got so used to looking at, I have become blind to its ugliness. But now, thinking of hosting people at our home, I am seeing it through new eyes.

I'm prepared for a shower of insects while pulling the ivy off, or at least a snake or scorpion, but there's no scary stuff. The ivy has become thick and has dug into the mortar so much it has loosened the bricks, but the wall is only chest height, so there is no fear of them falling on my head, only my toes.

"Is ash good for the ground?" Ronan comes out holding a metal bucket of ash after cleaning our large open fireplace. Since the flue in the chimney was replaced and smoke is no longer seeping into the house through the walls, making the entire house look like an opening scene from an 80s pop video, we have been enjoying log fires every night.

"If it is wood ash, yes, you can sprinkle it on the flowerbeds."

"I've never really done gardening before; I'm really looking forward to getting into it this year." He goes off to sprinkle and I go back to my ivy whacking.

"Signora," a man calls from the gate. He's grey haired, well dressed, wearing a scarf tight around his neck tucked into his zipped-up puffer jacket. The dress code for every Italian from the first of September to mid-April even if the temperatures go up and it's sunny. I'm in short sleeves and sweating.

I think I recognise him as the son of the couple in their nineties next door. I have never seen the son up close, but he has from time to time stuck his nose over the fence and inspected the work Ronan was doing without any words or animation on his face.

I stick my hand out through the metal bars and introduce myself with a smile. He looks at my hand and shakes it weakly with some reluctance.

He speaks Italian, and as usual my brain panics and tells me I do not understand this language and I just hear white noise. Focus. As he waves his hand in the direction of the grass near the neighbour's, I understand "The grass. Cut." I get a flashback to the day we bought the house and Uncle Francesca issuing me with the police number of the officer I need to contact, to discuss the complaint of the neighbours about the grass needing to be cut.

The grass is not long. It was only cut two weeks ago, but the continuous rain since, with the warmth of the sun, has made it grow faster than usual. However, it is too wet to cut.

"I was born here," he waves his hand to the side.

"In this house?"

"No. Here in this town. And I take care of the garden." He gestures next door. "When will you cut the grass?"

"My husband to cut... but rain..." I answer in Italian.

"When will he do it?" he demands.

I look at him. I don't know how to say "Mind your own business" in Italian.

"When?" I repeat back to him in disbelief.

"Yes, when will your husband cut the grass? Today, tomorrow, next week?"

The gall of this guy. It's then I notice the skin on his neck behind his scarf is like a ploughed field. The wrinkles and the liver spots on his thin skin give his age away to be at least late seventies. He is not the son of next door. So now I am even more confused. Silence is the best option.

"You don't understand?" he states.

"No."

"I cut the grass for you. I am a gardener. Also, for next door."

Ahhh, now I get it. He is offering his services.

"Eh no, my husband will do it."

"When will your husband do it?"

"When it stops raining. We have a lot of work to be done in the house and in the back garden first."

He tuts and walks off.

Ronan calls from the back garden. He has made me a cup of tea.

"The audacity of some people," I say, taking a seat beside Ronan on the bench he created from the single piece of olive wood we took from Dogana. Now it rests in its own perfect place under the hazel tree.

"Did you see this article in ANSA?" Ronan holds out his phone to me.

The news article is about a 103-year-old woman who was

caught driving an uninsured car at night with an expired driving licence in the northern region of Emilia Romagna.

The officers dispatched to the scene were "surprised when they discovered the year of the driver's birth", according to a police report. Giuseppina Molinari, known as Giose, was born in 1920. She had been driving to Bondeno near Ferrara to meet friends and "probably" got disoriented in the dark and lost her way, police said. Molinari's licence expired two years ago. In Italy, drivers over 80 years old, must undergo a medical exam every two years to renew their licence. Molinari was fined and taken home by police.

"I will buy myself a Vespa," Molinari told a local newspaper. In the meantime, she plans to visit friends by bicycle instead. Ferrara's mayor hailed her approach to life. "I would give Giose a medal rather than a fine," he said. "It's not common to have such inner strength, and it gives me hope for my own old age!"

As I finish reading, I become very aware of a weird constant buzzing noise.

"Where is that noise coming from? Is your phone vibrating?"

"Well, it's not my phone cause you are holding it in your hand."

"Oh, yeah." I hand Ronan back his phone and follow the buzzing sound to the other side of the tree, where it is still the same intensity. I look up and there is the source. Hundreds of small bumble bees bouncing from one to the other of the thousand catkins dangling like yellow felt earring on the hazel branches.

"You're doing a great job of stripping the ivy off the wall." Ronan says, admiring my work and the old stone wall I've uncovered while handing me back my cup of tea before it is forgotten, like so many teas before it. "I thought you had edits to do for your book?"

"I do. But I'm procrastinating—that's why the ivy is being slashed. I am about to start on the other side. I think there is a tree under that clump." We both stare at the tall ivy monster we've gotten used to looking at, standing beside the shed full of rubbish as if he's guarding it.

"Before we begin to plant the front garden, we need to clear it. Will you clean out the garage?"

"I will."

It's the same response he has been giving me for three years. I wasn't expecting a different answer.

"But I need to do some strimming today."

Strimming is Ronan's new way of procrastinating about clearing the inside of the garage. Not having a permission card to use the town recycling dump was our excuse for a long time not to attempt clearing the shed. We went and got the card from the office two towns away a couple of weeks ago, but we still have not been to the dump. The eyesore of the shed remains the first sight that greets everyone who comes in through our gates.

In the meantime, I begin work on the outside of the ugly, dilapidated structure.

Carefully I cut the thick stems of ivy growing from the foundations which have, over years, wound their way around everything in their path. I discover old window frames with full sheets of glass buried under it between the shed wall and tree trunk. Once the base of a stem is cut, a few tugs with my gloved hands pull away huge clumps of the ivy monster's body and limbs. Other pieces come away from the tree trunk easily, revealing a bark of shimmering creamy silver on a perfectly straight trunk.

"Wow," Ronan says bringing me out another cup of tea as two hours have passed easily. "What is it?"

"A tree." I say, squinting up at the majestic branches.

"I know it is a tree. But what type of tree?"

"I don't know, but maybe this will give us a clue," I say, plucking one of the green bum shaped fruits now dangling freed from the ivy. Breaking the fruit in half gives us no further clue. It doesn't look edible.

"It's a beautiful tree. Let's just leave it at that."

The leaves dance in a nonexistent breeze, as if saying thank you for their newfound freedom.

"I'm going to start strimming now," Ronan declares again.

"Right. I'll leave you to it." I have done enough physical work for one day and I can no longer use ivy whacking as an excuse for my own procrastination from the editing waiting to be done. "But before you start strimming and I start editing, I'll just show you where not to strim." This is my new trial control method of saving my plants from the threat of Ronan's strimmer. "You need to avoid the flower bed," I say, pointing to it, or at least where the flowerbed used to be.

"Oh my god, what happened to the flowerbed?" I can no longer see the plants. They are buried under mounds of white and grey ash.

"What's wrong? You said ash was good for plants, so I emptied the big steel bin we've been using for the ash all winter."

"Bloody hell Ronan, no more ash. The place looks like Pompeii."

I can't deal with the mound at the minute. I really need to get some work done.

"Just strim grass verges, don't strim this flowerbed or near the hedging or bamboo I've planted." There is nothing more I can say. It's time for me to hide as I always do when Ronan is strimming. It's not only painful to watch him cut through precious plants but also dangerous, as pebbles and sharpened sticks in the way of his path of destruction fly in every direction.

After getting a satisfactory amount of editing done, I have an early night. But I am woken by the sound of a man's voice passing our gate. It's unusual to be woken by someone on the street being too loud after too much to drink. It hasn't happened before. But the guy isn't shouting abuse or having a drunken brawl, this is Italy. He's belting out a slurred aria in deep notes—He's opera singing.

3

Ronan is definitely a night owl. My 87-year-old mother, who is resident in an assisted living home back in Ireland, is more of a mid-morning mongoose. I don't call her after 8.30PM or before 10.30am. There is a potential of her being fast asleep between both times; she's always loved being in bed. When eight of us were living in our little family bungalow, her bed—a big iron frame, with decorative detail lost under thick layers of gloss white paint,—was her hideaway, where she'd go and read; unless there was a party of course, which was a regular occurrence.

Her love of parties hasn't stopped. Finding a lively nursing home was important when we started looking for a place. She needed somewhere to go to live in, not somewhere to wait for death, like some we visited.

I call Mam. It's 11am, and she seems groggy. And her voice choppy.

"Are you okay?" I'm hoping she's not getting a cold.

"Yes, I'm fine, just having a lie in after my breakfast."

"Your hair is nice."

"I got it done yesterday for the party. It was getting straggly and awful looking."

Mam's hair is never awful looking; a brush and a can of hair spray is always at hand. Whereas I can forget to brush my hair for several days.

"Last night we had a cocktail night with a bit of singing and dancing. We all had to wear pink, so I wore that pink dress we bought when you were over. There was a fella in making the cocktails and he asked me what I wanted. I told him I never had drank cocktails, just whiskey, so I said I'd try one.

"I says to him 'what's that one?' And he said 'That's Sex on a Beach' and I said to him, 'I've had that already, what's the other one?' and he said it was.... I can't remember now... It was some kind of banger?"

"A Harvey Walbanger?"

"Yes, that was it. So I had sex on the beach with the banger and added my whiskey. We had a good night. But I've a bit of a headache today and my voice is gone from singing."

"What's on today?"

"Mass."

I don't think Mam will come back to Italy for visits; she hates the food and the hot weather and all the travelling is too much for her. She's very comfortable in her private room with her balcony garden and going to the activities and the live music sessions the nursing home hosts, with her new friends there amongst the residents and staff. And thanks to video chat, we talk every day and I go to visit every eight weeks.

Unlike Ronan or my mother, I am a morning person. I love getting up early and opening the shutters of the ground-floor windows like I am in Downton Abbey—not one of the Downton ladies, more like the housemaid.

Later in the day, my vibe tends to be the worn-out-gardener. When friends stay, I have a touch of Mr. Carson, the butler. When you buy a reno project, you never have time to sit and take it all in without feeling guilty, as there is always something to be done, some role to be played.

We have inner shutters and outer shutters. Inner shutters are so much more practical than curtains. Today, as I open them, sunlight beams in and darkness instantly melts away, I am looking at each room differently. The walls and ceilings are painted crisp colours and the coatings of dust are now manageable with a cloth rather than the need for a shovel. But each room has something needing to be done before we have paying guests; whether it is window shutters to be painted, a light to be fitted, or furniture to be installed.

Painting the outside shutters was the first DIY job I started on the house when we bought it four years ago. There are thirty-three windows and most have two shutters. Getting new shutters would cost nearly one thousand euro per window—it would be cheaper to install air con through the house.

I had originally started painting the shutters a pale blue, like they are in France. Having sanded and painted three sets of outer shutters blue, I decided they should stay the classic Tuscan green because, well, they look better. The light here differs from France, and the stonework is different too. Last summer, with great enthusiasm, I repaired and painted the shutters green on the side of the house facing the driveway. So now, I have one side of the house with green shutters, and the other, less visible side, with blue shutters. There are still some shutters on their sides on the balconies at the front and back of the house waiting patiently to be painted any colour.

Some shutters have completely disintegrated and can't be repaired, having fallen from the house before we arrived and smashed on the ground. Now and then I find a shutter slat in the garden.

The outer shutters I have repaired and painted are purely for decoration, strapped together with bits of wood on the reverse.

There always seems to be something more important to do than paint and repair shutters. But this year I will paint the shutters.

I add 'Paint Shutters' to my To Do list.

One room that does not need work is the main bedroom. It's the most pretty with its double aspect windows and free-standing bath in the corner against the exposed stone wall.

After renting a house for two years with only a drippy shower, one of the first things I got when we bought our derelict villa was a bath. It was stored in our campervan for six months before it could be installed.

I wanted a bath so badly; I had a whole Pinterest board entirely dedicated to baths I'd drool over. I got the one I lusted after most; a slipper shaped double ended bath which was eventually installed in our bedroom, like the decadent photos in luxury home magazines.

"It looks nice, but you'll never use it," Ronan said as the plumber installed it into the corner of the bedroom where I planned to have candle nooks inset into the wall and a large fern plant to give it a tropical feel.

"Of course I will!" I said, appalled at Ronan's non-appreciation for the effort I had gone to, to ensure I got an extra-long version with deep sides so he, my tall husband, could enjoy and understand the benefits I hungered for from having a relaxing bath.

It's now three years later and after posting the before and after pic of my bath, four comments ask "how often do you use it?"

"All the time," I want to say—if they mean as a laundry basket. But to actually bathe in... it makes me choke to admit, never.

I will not be defeated. So I fill the bath. I put in the special seaweed someone brought me as a present all the way from Ireland. And the special bath oil our daughter Izzy gave me for Christmas. I know it was expensive. I only add a cap of it, saving it, making it last. But then I think about how many years it would take me to use the oil up at the rate I use the bath. It would be about forty-three years I calculate, so I decide to be extra generous and throw in an extra big dollop. I convince myself that the room smells great. A bit sweet and flowery for me, like I'm in the doorway of a candy store.

I hover beside the bath, dipping my toe in.

Okay, I need to be honest here, there is no dipping. The height of the slipper sides requires me to throw my leg over awkwardly and my foot plunges into the depth of water that didn't seem that hot on my hand but is too hot for my foot, which is now turning a pink scalded colour. Grabbing at the hose while trying to keep my balance, I whack on the cold water and hose my foot under the cauldron hot water before it and my lower leg begins to melt.

After some minutes and the bath filling up beyond its halfway point, I feel confident enough to swing my other leg in while gripping onto the sides. I still have the cold water running, but this leg adapts quicker, so I turn off the tap. I crouch down and then wonder how I have had baths in the past. Surely it is not a skill that you forget, but apparently I have.

I am unsure how in the past I got my legs from squat position to outstretched in front of me in a smooth, elegant fashion. Of course, the last time I had a bath was before I had two frozen shoulders and had gained an extra twenty pounds. Also, this bath is of a contemporary style with a flat base, so there are no curvy sides to use as a slide.

I decide to just go for it. Hold on to the sides and sit back....

It's like I've turned on a wave machine. Water surges forward before swishing back. I let go of the sides before my spine meets the back of the slipper, but the slipper is now a slippery oil slick and I immediately slip down as the second, bigger tidal wave comes crashing back. I had not considered that a bath where my foot taller husband could stretch out, would be a foot too long for me. I can reach the end with my feet, but not enough to push myself back up.

I'm going to friggin' drown in my bath. Or choke on the seaweed that has now slapped me in the face.

I grab for the sides and yes, I can reach them, but I have no traction to pull myself up.

The sweet, sickly smell of the bath oil has mingled in the warm summer heat of the room. I might vomit or faint as it's becoming quite overpowering. I need to get out of this.

I wait for the wave machine to calm. There is nothing I can do other than take a chance and try to flip over. That sounds elegant. If you ever saw them trying to get a beached whale back into deep water that would better way to describe the image that I don't really want you to imagine as I hold on to the side with both hands and try to remain kneeling in the oil slick.

I reach cautiously and pull out the plug and wait for the water to drain. Luckily, there is a towel in arm's reach. I grab it and use it to give grip to my hands, knees, feet, elbows as I clamber and cautiously climb out.

I look like I have been in the sun for five hours without sunscreen and I feel like a gull after being rescued from an oil spillage. The oil created enough of a barrier that no water has gone near my body, so there is no need to dry off.

After fifty-two years, I realise I hate having baths. I just love the cozy comfort, the idea of having a bath invokes.

I slip on a dress, shake my hair out and go downstairs.

"Did you have a nice bath, Love?" Ronan asks glancing up from his book.

"Yes, great, thanks. You should try it."

"Maybe someday. I'm going to the supermarket for dog food. See you later."

But later comes just two minutes after. Ronan comes back in from the driveway looking rattled.

"Someone broke a window in the car."

4

I look at Ronan in disbelief.

"The back window of the car is smashed."

As if neither of us believe what he is saying, we both go out and check if it really broken. It is not just broken but shattered into tiny turquoise diamonds on the ground beside the car. There is nothing inside to show someone threw something at it.

"It wasn't locked, so it's not like they needed to break the window and there was nothing in it to steal. Could someone have been sleeping in our car and kicked the window out because they got trapped inside?"

What would Daisy, the sleuth I write about in my cozy mystery series, do?

"What happened different yesterday to other days?" I ask retracing the previous twenty-four hours.

"There was that old man who came to the gate about doing the garden. He was pretty pissed off. Maybe he's crazy and came back yesterday and smashed it."

I search the gravel around the car, but there is nothing there to show what it was broken with.

"No arrows?" Ronan says, holding back a grin. He's rekindling a memory of when we lived in Ireland in a nice little house in the countryside with a sizeable garden. Ronan fancied himself as Robin Hood and had bought himself a compound bow and target. While loading the bow one of the first times and last times he used it, his finger slipped, and the arrow took flight at top speed towards the neighbour's big house next door. Thankfully, the neighbours were out. The arrow left a perfect small round hole through their triple glazed window.

"It's so small. Perhaps they won't notice?" Was Ronan's first response.

"They might not immediately notice the hole, but I think they will notice that," I said as we both cupped our hands and looked through the window at the arrow perfectly lodged firmly in the centre of their wooden kitchen dresser on the other side of the room.

Thankfully, they were very understanding neighbours and focused on the positive; while cleaning up the glass, they found the TV remote control down the back of the sofa that had been missing for four months. Ronan took the bow back to the shop and paid for a new window with the refund.

"The opera singer!" I say, thinking back on what else different happened in the last 24 hours. "The guy singing last night. Perhaps he reached a note so high I couldn't hear it and it shattered the window."

"I'll take it to a garage and see about getting it fixed."

Ronan says looking at me in the way he looks at me sometimes, unsure if I am joking or if I have lost my marbles. He heads off on his mission for dog food and a car window.

While cleaning up the glass, Shelly, our English neighbour and now dear friend, passes on her new electric bicycle and stops for a cuppa.

"Maybe I should go on a health retreat?" I say to Shelly, handing her a mug of tea.

"Are you intending to run health retreats?"

"Maybe. I'm thinking about health retreats for perimenopausal women. We could all do with more information and support getting through all the crappy symptoms, like brain fog."

Brain fog is something I now understand and recognise. I've been reading lots of research about perimenopause and realise how much it has been affecting me.

About six years ago, I developed a frozen shoulder. Six months later, the other shoulder also froze. For two years, I struggled to put on my coat, bra, brushing my hair or getting up off the floor. I saw doctors and physiotherapists in Ireland and Italy.

"It happens to some women when they get to about forty-five years of age," I was told repeatedly.

"Why?"

"No one knows, it just happens," was the general answer I got.

I'm no genius, but did no one in the world of medicine link the age range, frozen shoulders and perimenopause together before now?

If one doctor had suggested, "Perhaps you are in peri-menopause?" I could have at least educated myself a little as to what was happening to my body. The same thing that happens to every woman in every country who has lived and got to the age of fifty. But I had never heard of the word perimenopause; not until about five years ago when I was in the back of a taxi in Rome going to a film festival with my friend from Derry, with my frozen shoulders and the odd hot flush.

"Sounds like you are hitting perimenopause. It's a right curse."

"No, I'm too young. I haven't reached menopause yet."

"Not menopause. Perimenopause. It happens for years before menopause."

"What? There's another thing we women have to deal with?"

"Aye."

And that is how I got my female health education about some-thing that was never spoken about. Probably because there was not a name to it. Throughout history, the symptoms were referred to as; all in her head, being over dramatic, hysteria.

I feel lucky to be part of a generation that knows much more about our bodies and how to look after our health. Our parents and grandparents knew way less, such as the dangers of smok-ing. My parents' generation didn't know it was bad for them until they were in their thirties.

As a kid, when staying with my cousins, we'd go on Sunday drives across the Wicklow Mountains. Four of us squashed into the back seat, all the windows closed and my aunt and uncle in the front seats, chain smoking.

We'd stop for a picnic of diluted orange squash or red lemonade and jam sandwiches. These would slosh around in our stomachs as we went up and down the hills of Wicklow without seatbelts in a car with very little suspension and no power-steering while we inhaled the country fresh air laden with John Player Blue cigarette smoke.

One Sunday drive took us to the beach for the day, and while my relatives' sallow skin tanned, my blue whiteness turned to cerise pink. When we got home, I vomited and shook most of the night. As soon as the sun rose, I dragged their house phone from the hallway into the sitting room so not to wake anyone, and called my mam to come collect me. Looking back, I obviously had sunstroke, but sunscreen didn't seem to exist when I was a kid and staying hydrated wasn't a term ever used. I don't think I drank a glass of plain water until I was in my twenties. Water was used to dilute orange squash or blackcurrant.

I remember when I was about ten years old watching an interview on The Late Late Show. The host Gay Byrne asked in his patronising, disbelieving way, as only Gay could do; "You are going to bottle Irish water and sell it? And you believe people will buy it?" The guy might as well have said he was selling tins of air. The entire audience was in convulsions of laughter. The guy being interviewed had just started a company called Ballygowan Water.

So besides having secondary smoke inhalation, sunburn, unacknowledged sunstroke and never drinking water, I had a very healthy childhood. We ate good home-cooked meals, never processed. And if we didn't like it, there was always bread and jam as an alternative, but not on weekdays. Mam needed the whole loaf for the lunch sandwiches the next day for Dad and the five of us.

Ever since I found out I have arthritis in my spine, (thanks to the X-ray I had to confirm my scoliosis), I want to find out if I also have osteoporosis.

I don't think Italians have an issue with bone health; they get lots of Vitamin D and walk up and down steps and hilly towns all the time. There doesn't seem to be a long waiting list for hip replacements, even though they have the second oldest population in the world.

When my mother was staying with me here in Italy, I took her to the doctor to get her hips and knees checked before going back to Ireland.

I tried to say in Italian something that translated into "Will her knee and hip joints need help?"

"Yes, smoking cannabis can help with pain relief. It needs to be medical marijuana. Not the type you buy on the street," the doctor said in English with a knowing smile at me.

Do I look like a pothead who buys illegal drugs on street corners?

He was doing that thing people often do when they see my long grey, hippy style hair; they presume I smoke pot.

I checked my translation app. It had given me the word 'gli spinelli' for joints. The type smoked, not knees and hips.

"I can write a prescription?"

"No need," I said.

He smiled again.

Oh, bloody hell, now he thinks I have a stash at home.

I stopped trying to be clever with my effort of Italian and just spoke in English.

"No, I mean, it's not what I was asking. I was asking if she needs to get her joints, as in hips and knees, seen to when she gets back to Ireland."

But he was not listening. Mam was gabbling away at him about my crap cooking and how she buys a tin of pineapple to put on her pizzas and doesn't drink coffee, and what an awful place she thought Italy was. Luckily, he didn't seem to be listening to her either while he was busy writing the prescription.

I have since found out the use of marijuana has been decriminalised in Italy. Those who partake no longer face legal consequences. However, the possession or sale of cannabis is illegal and can be punished by penalties. For instance, if caught in possession of cannabis in Italy, a person can lose their driving license for up to three months.

However, a doctor, dentist or vet can prescribe medical cannabis in the form of capsules, resins, eye drops, suppositories, creams, gels, edibles and syrups for glaucoma, chronic pain, anxiety, multiple sclerosis, nausea, Tourette's. Anything really.

For some diseases, the health system will pay most of the fee. All medical cannabis prescribed in Italy is produced by the Military Chemical Pharmaceutical Plant, or else imported from Canada or the Netherlands.

"My joints hurt too. Maybe I should get some?" I said to Dr. Chicken.

He looks up from his prescription writing. "Losing some weight would help. It is easy to do."

Seriously? Did that skinny 35-year-old man just say to me, a perimenopausal woman, losing weight is easy to do?

I ignore him.

For the past twenty-six years I have been trying to lose the 'baby fat'. Two years ago I lost five kilos doing an hour of daily exercise for a few months, but I gained it back and three more kilos on top of it. The same thing happens every time I lose weight over time. As soon as I stop doing whatever it is I am doing to lose it, I gain the weight back plus three more kilos. It's like my body says; "Oh thank god, we got that lost weight back. I don't know what happened there, but just in case it happens again, we will throw a few more kilos on just as a reserve."

I don't eat an unhealthy diet—no preserved food, no sweet drinks. No takeaways—as there are none in Italy—at least none where I live. My downfall is I don't exercise. Writing is a solitary occupation and involves sitting for long periods of time.

"Maybe I should try out one of those retreats where they starve you for five days and you come back looking fabulous?" I muse to Shelly.

"I think people say they are going on them when, in fact, they are really going on a cosmetic surgery holiday. Maybe just feed your retreat guests water and bread and call them weight-loss bootcamps? It would cut down on costs."

Shelly usually comes out with good ideas. I don't think this is one of them.

Ronan is back and looking coy. "I was thinking about what you said about what happened different yesterday and I think I know who broke the window."

I stall mid lift of my tea mug, just like on any good mystery. "Colonel Mustard, with a candlestick in the driveway?"

"No. It was me, In the garden with the strimmer."

Of course.

5

Autumn in Italy is one of my four favourite seasons. It's like the heating switch has been turned off outside. Sunsets are spectacular. The garden has a profusion of edibles: grapes, hazelnuts, plums and pears.

Green and brown stink bugs are crashing everywhere. It's like they were given wings, but the flying control mechanism never evolved in their brains. When one comes into a room, you can hear its wings loudly buzzing, but not like mosquitoes. You can hear that these are wings carrying something too heavy for them. Then, thud, it hits the wall. It starts again buzz, buzz, buzz, thud, buzz, thud. That's a stink bug's life. I feel for them.

The beautiful blue plumbago a friend gifted me is still flowering, as well as the roses I planted last year. Dark purple and green olive drops hang from the lines of olive trees like shiny mini Easter eggs.

I've offered to help Blodwyn and Ivor with their olive harvest. They can do with some extra sets of hands since Ivor fell off his ladder when pruning the trees and injured his back, so thankfully he will not be out in his kilt up the ladder while we are harvesting. Shelly and Ruth come to help too.

"Set your feet so you don't tread on the olives and just run your hands along the branches and they will easily fall onto the nets." That's all the instruction needed for olive picking. The autumn sun is warm, the scent of mint rises from under my feet. I step carefully so not to walk on the olives.

"So, how was your week?" I ask Shelly, who is on the opposite side of a tree. Shelly's response undulates for want of breath while sawing off a rogue branch. "I went to Castiglione for a rogering. Have you been?"

"To Castiglione for a rogering?"

"To Roger for a cleaning? The English dentist? He's been in Castiglione for thirty years and his 101-year-old mother lives above his clinic. His partner is his assistant."

I am still a little too far to hear her clearly.

"Molly likes to sit on patients while they are getting treatment. She just jumped up and Roger asked if I was okay with it. I wasn't too sure at first."

"Bloody hell!" are the only words my over exerted lungs can propel out as I pick up the fallen branches and carry them to the fire area, "Is Molly his assistant or his mother?"

But Shelly hasn't heard my question, she just continues.

"I think she is the same breed as your Looney, or maybe a Malteser? Is that what they are called? You know me, I'm not a dog person, but she started licking my hand. It was really comforting while I got my teeth cleaned."

"Oh, Molly is a comfort dog? How cute. I might make a booking. A dog on my lap during dental treatment would ease my fear."

Escalators, heights and dentists are fears since childhood, along with quicksand and self-combustion of course, but I've gotten over the last two. My visits to a dentist in Ireland have always included sedation, even for a cleaning. If I am to stay in Italy, I need to find a dentist I can comfortably go to. So I think I might book a rogering, with Molly the dog, not Roger's partner, sitting on me.

Olive picking is easier and more pleasant than grape picking. There are no insects hanging out, guarding their fruit.

I share this observation with my group of women friends as we work together harvesting. "Talking of insects, does anyone else get moths in their food cupboards, followed by spiders with bodies that look like a rosary bead?"

"Ah, yes, pantry moths. They get into everything and lay their larvae," Blodwyn says. "You need to put a bay leaf in the jars to keep away the moths and lavender in the cupboard to keep away the spiders."

"What's your favourite insect?" Shelly asks, like we are kids in a playground together, not a group of middle-aged women.

We all have a think. Some say the obvious butterflies and bumblebees. But Blodwyn says, "Fireflies. They are amazing here in the olive grove during the summer. It looks like a scene from *Midsummer's Night Dream*."

"Well, that is a good sign. They can only survive in extremely balanced ecosystems, where they can find snails, their favourite food. There have been a tonne of snails this year. Has anyone else noticed?" Ruth says.

"Did you say fireflies eat snails?" I can't imagine the tiny fairies in my garden munching on escargot.

"Yes, their mouths have adapted to being able to penetrate the hard shell of the snail to eat it."

"Ugh, you have put me off them now," Blodwyn says, carefully gathering a net under a finished tree, encouraging the plucked olives to tumble and gather in one spot. "Although in the old days in Wales, they used snail juice for any ailments in the eyes. The logic was that the eye was wet like the snail juice."

"Snail slime is becoming very popular in anti-aging serums and creams," Shelly says, lifting the other side of the net and together with Blodwyn, they pour the olives into a cassette.

"Oh, there's nothing new about it. Snail slime has been used for anti-aging since ancient Roman times. It's also great for wound healing and melanoma and skin regeneration after radiation therapy," Ruth says.

"Maybe you should set up a spa with baths where snails slither all over guests for health and beauty benefits on your retreats? You could make a fortune," Shelly suggests.

I'm still trying to think of unique experiences to offer guests, but I don't think snail slime is one of them.

"In all seriousness, Rosie, how about doing menopause workshops? You educated me about stuff I never knew, and all the latest research. And I've seen Menopause Coaching advertised online. Maybe that is something you could do. You'd be really good at it," Shelly says.

"Have you finished your Qi Gong instructor course yet?" Ruth asks me.

"Not yet. Another couple of months to do."

Three hours pass quickly chatting. There is nothing as blissful as having tea and a packed picnic sitting on the olive nets in the warm autumn sun, with the scent of crushed wild mint rising from under where we sit.

I can see how the benefit of women working together in the fields or by rivers was in the old days for the exchange of essential life information; in one afternoon I've learnt how to deal with the moths and spiders spoiling the food in my cupboards, and I've learnt a new use for the snails in my garden.

That evening I fall down the rabbit hole of looking up snails involvement in beauty regimes during Roman times.

A Roman woman's skin was closer to olive than ivory, so they went through the process of powdering the face. This involved the use of chalk powder, crocodile dung, and white lead to whiten their entire face. Ovid (that old beauty columnist) described a mixture with which to lighten skin colouration:

Two pounds of peeled barley and an equal quantity of vetches moistened with ten eggs. Dry the mixture in the air, and let the whole be ground beneath the mill-stone worked by the patient ass. Pound the first horns that drop from the head of a lusty stag. Of this, take one-sixth of a pound. Crush and pound the whole to a fine powder, and pass through a deep sieve. Add twelve narcissus bulbs which have been skinned, and pound the whole together vigorously in a marble mortar. There should also be added two ounces of gum and Tuscan spelt, and nine times as much honey. Any woman who smears her face with this cosmetic will make it brighter than her mirror.

Some other intriguing beauty regimes included taking baths in ass's milk for the skin, used by Queen Cleopatra in Egypt; swan fat and bean meal were used to treat wrinkles, and the ashes of snails could supposedly cure freckles.

However, Ovid claims that before physical beauty care begins, a woman must perfect her manners: the manners, or personality, will lure the men in and—after beauty has waned—keep them.

I'm not sure if I'd want to keep them if I had to go to so much trouble to 'appear' attractive to them in the first place. I would never have survived in old Roman times; washing my face in the shower is as far as my beauty regime goes.

I go down another rabbit hole and end up signing up for a menopause coach training course. It's more out of curiosity than anything else. Shelly is right, I've become fascinated by women's health during perimenopause and menopause. Of course, I can't just listen and learn. Me being me, I need to take this further; I need to know everything.

6

"How are we going to get bookings?" I say out loud, playing with the handle of my favourite mug over breakfast with Ronan.

"Are you asking the tea leaves or me?"

Since our Tranquilla Room discussion, we're mulling over the idea of inviting strangers into our home. It is Ronan's second cup of coffee and my fourth cup of tea.

"I suppose booking engines like AirBnB?" He suggests.

"I don't think I want to put the house on anything like that. I'd want to know who is coming to stay in the house."

"We don't have that many friends, Rosie."

"We don't have to know them, but I would like them to know of the house and us and it is our home and what to expect."

"Are you sure you want to do this?"

"Yes, of course! But I'd like bookings to come by word of mouth."

"How do we get customers by word of mouth when there are no mouths to spread the word?" Ronan asks.

"I don't know."

"What about your friend Lisa? She knows marketing. Maybe ask her."

I've known Lisa for years. We both did the same online business course about fifteen years ago about how to make money from creating online courses before it was a thing. I created online courses teaching people things I knew; how to set up and run a successful wedding planning business and another course on how to create an online magazine. From the sales income, I saved enough to move our family to Italy.

This was before everyone-and-their-mother started producing online courses. And I mean everyone and their mother. I met someone whose cleaner has a 'Clean like an Italian Housewife' course and her 87-year-old neighbour is a pasta granny who goes viral every week on Youtube.

My online courses eventually became dated. All my wedding planning marketing secrets I taught, such as creating YouTube shorts about venues, became mainstream and there was no way I could, or wanted to, keep up with social media marketing techniques.

While I made my side income creating online courses in an early wave, Lisa created a successful business helping course creators, like me, market their courses. Her business and marketing skills grew with the rise and popularity of social media.

"You need to make people drip with envy wanting to be you," Lisa says during our brainstorming Zoom call about how I should market our house, Casa Anam Cara, for retreats and as a BnB.

"The way my life has gone in the last couple of years, no one would want to be me. And I don't want to be envied. Can I not just be likeable?"

"Likeable? No. Is that even a word? You want people to come to your villa and you want people to buy your books, don't you? You need to market yourself, make people curious, dying to come to stay. You need brand colours and fonts and a message you are going to embed into every picture you post. You have nearly four thousand followers on Facebook, that's a good start," Lisa says, scanning my presence on social media.

I'm already groaning. Facebook is the way I chat with my readers. Whenever I need a lift or encouragement, I post something on there and I get a flood of love in the comments. I don't want it polluted with sales stuff.

"You need to make your Instagram more personal," Lisa says, continuing to scroll at high speed. "Get a gallery of shots of yourself in typical Italian situations. Walking through a field of sunflowers for example, with a sun hat on."

"Have you ever walked through a field of sunflowers?" I say with an element of disgust. "The stems on those things are like sandpaper and the amount of grasshoppers and snakes and, oh god, other creepy crawlies that jump around and up your skirt. And getting into one of those fields is usually across a wide ditch. You could probably get shot for trespassing."

I know what I am talking about. I took photos like this of brides during the years of our wedding planning and photography business. Lots of brides wanted the idyllic shot amongst fields of sunflowers but would settle for photos standing in front of the fields when they saw the amount of clambering they would have to do over a ditch or fence and the size of the bugs they would encounter. Sunflowers are crops after all. They are not just planted as a tourist amusement or to make the idyllic Italian scenery even more pretty than it already is.

"Okay, then photos amongst olive groves."

"The light is too dappled." Again, my years of wedding photography experience in Italy steps in.

"Then vineyards picking grapes."

"That only happens in September."

"Rosie, I feel you are putting obstacles in my way to helping you."

"I can't make grapes grow faster."

"Buy a bunch in the supermarket and pretend for goodness' sake. Use your imagination, like all the other influencers."

"Influencers? I am not an influencer. Their lives are not real life. I'm tired of influencers portraying these idyllic lives they manifest. Ugh no, I'd be crap at that. I don't like being in front of the camera. I prefer just taking photos of Italy."

"Okay then, gather a gallery of before and after shots of the house renovation."

"I have a folder of before shots, but after shots–that would mean furnishing each room and styling it." I'm groaning again.

"And?"

"It's a lot of bloody effort for one friggin' Instagram post."

"You need photos to advertise the house for retreats."

Lisa's right. I need to get some photos together. I can do photos but pressure is building in my head again.

"How should I style them?"

"Well, what are people expecting from retreats?" Lisa is back in marketing mode.

I think back to the one retreat I had been to: up the mountain in the sacred forest. At the two-star hotel with the colony of cats sitting on top of the rusting vintage motorbike collection, while lightning bounced off the trees around me to the crack and boil of thunder.

It was far from what I was expecting, but once I got over my first impression, it was the exact thing I needed at that moment in my life.

"I really don't know what they want or would expect."

"Well, you need to do some research, decide what you like and don't like, and create an image and brand of the retreats you want to offer."

"They all look similar on websites."

"That's why Rosie, you need to go to a few and experience them firsthand. Get booking."

I really do need to experience a few retreats to see what people expect.

Later that evening, with a glass of wine in hand, I google retreats in Italy. From the pictures on its website, a spiritual retreat centre in the north of Italy looks amazing; built specifically as a retreat centre with an outdoor jacuzzi overlooking

Lake Orta being one of the main attractions to me. Two Dutch guys, who made their millions running raves in Europe, bought an old hotel and built this amazing place after they spent time in India.

Listed on their range of retreats on offer is a retreat for energy. That is definitely something I could do with having more of.

For months we have done nothing to the house. It is like our bodies have gone into hibernation. I still wake and start writing by seven, but trying to do anything in the house is like a weighted body suit has been thrown over me. My writing is also lacking lustre. After the two years of continuous grief from losing my dad and my brother, I've lost my funny bone, which is not a good thing when I make my living from writing humour. I needed a break from writing to find it again.

Since I first did the Qi Gong retreat in the Sacred Forest, I have become obsessed with it. So much so, I signed up to train as a Qi Gong instructor. I am practicing Qi Gong daily, and while I feel good, my enthusiasm for progressing the house stops dead. I start with good intentions, but then I just feel incapable of doing anything. During the odd warm winter day between the rain, we get outside in the garden and our energy is somewhat improved. But not inside the house.

The description has a lot about chi flow and clearing blocked energy. It sounds exactly what I need.

A Qi Gong energy retreat would be perfect to help me correct my technique and the location is mouth watering. It is why retreats at this retreat centre get booked up fast. However, the energy retreat has 'late availability due to cancellation' written beside it.

There is another retreat with a guru the week following the energy one with a space available to. I go back and forth, trying to choose between the two.

I should have learnt from experience, booking trips online should not be done with wine in hand. Especially when the contents of half a bottle are already working their way through your digestive system. I book both. Two retreats back-to-back. Both very different. I didn't realise how different.

wo weeks later I'm on a train to Florence, then Florence to Bologna and Bologna to Milan, and then Milan to Malpensa where I will meet the private transfer to the mountain high retreat centre.

Train is my favourite way to travel, and the trains are good in Italy. They are clean, comfortable and the stations tend to be in the centre of a city. However, today I hate them. I am due to get a train at 7.10AM in the morning, with a series of connections that would get me to Malpensa at 12.10, in time for the retreat centre's final transfer. I should have followed my instinct and got the earlier train, but getting to the station for 6.00AM would have been more challenging. Today I learnt to always leave time for delays if catching a sequence of trains. Because today I did not do that.

Arriving at the station, I check *Trenit*—my go-to app for figuring out train journeys in Italy. The app tells me the train is running forty-one minutes late. I check the screen and it says it is running twenty-five minutes late. I'll still make my first connection. The announcement says in Italian and then in English that the train is running twenty minutes late. I have a coffee.

With five minutes to go, they announce the train is running thirty minutes late. The app is still letting me in on the inside knowledge that it's arriving forty-one minutes late. Thirty minutes after the scheduled arrival time, the announcer informs us the train will be forty-five minutes late. At forty minutes, they announce it will now be seventy-five minutes late. I am not sure if I heard that correctly. I check my app and it says in red it is now running ninety minutes late.

Some people on the platform are leaving and taking the two flights of stairs to the waiting room. I follow. In the waiting room there is an announcement every ten minutes and gradually the announcer breaks it to the Italians that the train will be eighty minutes late, before telling them the truth ten minutes later, that it will actually be ninety minutes late.

The ninety-minute late train is going to Milan. However, the train app has helped me find a route to get there quicker. So I am doing it the Italian creative way. I am getting out at Bologna and taking the fast train to Milan, rather than stay on this one which arrives two hours later as it stops at each station.

Ronan and I learnt about Italy's fast and slow trains the hard way a few years ago going to a wedding job. There were two trains leaving the same time going to the same place. We had bought tickets for the fast train but we got on the wrong one. It stopped at every station while the other was direct. It took us two and a half hours longer. There are never any train staff on the stations to ask. We learnt we need to know the train number, not to just go by destination on the information board.

Idyllic Italy whizzing past, soaked in early winter sunshine, triggers the feeling of guilt I always feel when I hear another storm is brewing in Ireland; as if I am responsible for the crap weather in my home country.

I haven't taken a long train journey in ages. I love watching for the unexpected and beautiful things. Like the faded red slide from a water park blotched with mould, taking up the whole of someone's back garden in a terraced house backing to the train track. I imagine the story of them erecting it and the fun the whole family must have had that initial summer, but now they don't know what to do with the moulding eyesore.

The land around Bologna is flat. I think it's the first time I've seen an Italian landscape without a backdrop of mountains or an ancient town perched precariously on top of a hill.

But my joy is interrupted by one noise jarring to another, and to another and another, in quick succession as the guy sitting at the opposite window mindlessly scrolls through his phone and another guy watches a football match. When did people start thinking it is acceptable to listen to their phone without headphones? I become that older lady who gives the evil glare across the carriage. My long, grey hair gives the bonus witch affect. Luckily, I had paid extra for a seat in the quiet carriages of the next train for the longer leg of the journey.

Away from flatlands of Bologna, we come back into mountain territory. Bits of cloud are stuck onto the hills like cotton wool on a kindergartener's Christmas decoration.

Eventually, I arrive at the pick-up point just in time for the final transfer. I'm sharing a transfer with another participant, Mavis. She reminds me of a doll I made as a kid out of a wooden spoon, with a perfect in line fringe and black shoulder length straight hair, rosy cheeks with speckled freckle dots all over her face. When I ask her where she's from, she immediately launches into telling me everything about herself. Her grandparents were from Italy and Germany, her parents were from Belgium and France.

"I am not from Switzerland, but I live up a mountain in Switzerland with my girlfriend-lover and her parents, two donkeys and a gaggle of geese. This is the eleventh time I have been to this retreat centre. We will have an hour before dinner and the introduction, so the first place I am going is to the spa."

"It looks amazing from the photos."

"It is. It is the place to go first and also book a massage as soon as check-ins are finished. They get booked up quickly too."

Mentally I am searching my bag for where I packed my swimsuit and note to grab it and go to the spa before unpacking.

"My girlfriend went to Goa for two weeks to recover from the grief of the death of her husband—a renowned violin maker and thirty-five years her senior. She didn't feel she had grieved properly when he died three years ago, so the two weeks on yoga retreats in Goa was a medicinal experience. She has gone from retreat to retreat and her trip has now lasted two months."

I am wondering is that going to happen to me since I have booked two retreats back-to-back. Will I become a retreat addicted bunny, bouncing from retreat to retreat, trying to find the missing piece of myself?

"She'll be home when I get back and she says she has news. I can't wait to see her."

Mavis seems excited by the prospect of news; whereas I'm thinking the news might not be going in a positive direction for her, since her partner extended her travels by nearly two months. By the end of her thirty-minute monologue, I still don't know where she is from.

The chatty driver takes over as soon as Mavis stops to take a breath. "We are three hundred meters above sea level and the retreat centre is nine hundred meters above sea level. I am from here. This area is famous for its water-tap factory," he says proudly.

Soon the vista unfolds in front of us, a long, narrow, black glass lake, protected on all sides by mountains. "This is beautiful Lake Orta, sixteen kilometres long and one-hundred and forty-three meters deep, a glacier lake carved out in the ice age."

"I've never heard of this lake. I am familiar with Lake Garda, Lake Como and of course Trasimeno, but not this one."

He laughs when I tell him Lake Trasimeno is only six metres at its deepest. "That is like a puddle in compared to Orta. There are more than a thousand lakes in Italy. Some are natural–dug out by glaciers or volcanoes–and others are man made, created by dams often to generate electricity."

"Is that an island?" I ask noticing a band of water cutting off a clump of land from the lake shore. The sun catches the facades dominated by a basilica and what looks like a monastery.

"Yes, the little island of San Giulio. It is home to a cloister of silent order nuns. They live permanently on the island in the Benedictine Abbey. You can only reach it by a short boat ride."

The friendly driver continues, "Legend says the island, which lies not more than four-hundred metres from the lakefront of Orta, was once a bare rock inhabited by snakes and terrible monsters, until the day in 390AD when San Giulio landed, crossing the lake on his cloak and guided in the storm by his staff. There is a narrow street that goes around the island for silent, meditative walking. There is not much else on the island other than the basilica, abbey and bishop's palace."

The word 'palace' jars the serene image of spiritual beauty being built until then. Escaping from the world to a cloistered order, on an island in the centre of a beautiful lake, sounds very attractive.

"Can the convent be visited?"

"It is a closed order, but once a year they open at Christmas and sing hymns. Ever since I was a child, we would go. It is so beautiful and spiritual. It is a very special experience."

"I wonder what do they do all day. Surely they can't just sit around praying in silence?"

"They pray, study and they restore old church books and vestments. They also make communion wafers and 'pane di San Giulio', which is famous in the area."

With that, a small Fiat, with five nuns squashed into it drives past us from the opposite direction, the oldest one in the driving seat.

"And do you see that building there above the ring of cloud on the mountain?" the driver asks. I can just about make out the building on top of the world, by the glint of sun's glare reflecting in glass.

"That is the retreat centre."

"How are we getting up there?"

"Like this," he says, turning onto an uphill road that does a hairpin bend onto another. Bracken, like ginger haired monsters, is the only thing growing on the sheer rock face of each of the twenty-one switchbacks to the top of the mountain.

We drive through one of those villages which is only suitable for a certain type of person to live in–a cross between a hermit and mountain goat–who like to eat a lot of cheese and brew their own beer. The type of people who live until they are at least one hundred because of the clean air, and strong hearts and bones from all the hiking.

Up a winding road and finally through electric gates, where Mavis and I get out with our luggage and follow a path to the amethyst encrusted entrance of what will be my own spiritual cloister for the next ten days.

8

M y Scandinavian style room has its own private terrace with a view worthy enough to be a movie backdrop. The mountain, behind the silhouetted bell in the stone church's campanile, is white with the odd rock jutting out. Is it marble, like the mountains in Carrara, or is it snow? It's snow. The first snow I have seen this year.

Illuminated by golden up-lighting, the bell tones Ave Maria. The same tune as the church on the hill near Casa Anam Cara. I wonder if there is a salesman setting up auto-tune systems in bell towers, where priests can choose different tunes like ring-tones on a phone can be chosen.

But I have no time to lose. I grab my swimsuit and head to the spa.

There is no one at the spa other than one woman in the hot tub. She looks like a curly haired version of Harry Potter. Me being me, I start to chat.

She comes here three times per year. Mostly silent retreats. She works in the Humanitarian sector, and she comes because she wants to feel something—she needs to believe in goodness again. "I have to book early. The silent retreats fill up really quickly. They are the most popular ones."

So many people in the world seeking permission to turn off all their devices and step into their own silence.

I'm sitting in an outdoor hot tub high above the lake and valley below, with snow topped mountains surrounding the retreat centre. Steam rising from the bubbling cauldron. A white streak falls from the top of one of the mountain to the bottom. I can hear its distant thunder.

"I just finished a silent retreat today and booked this one. But I will remain in silence as much as possible. I have a silent pin on my clothes, but not my swimsuit."

"No problem," I say, taking the hint. Although for me, it is a problem. I find silence with another human in my space awkward. I try to relax into it, but I notice the time. It's only thirty minutes before the evening intro session and I want to see what else the spa has to offer.

"Okay, see you later," I say, getting out of the tub. The woman nods in my direction back to her silent self.

I walk into the sauna. The door closes behind me before my eyes become accustomed to the dim light and I notice the only other person in there is a guy lying on the lowest bench, completely naked. It would be rude to walk back out, so I sit on the seat furthest away from him and feel myself getting hotter. His eyes are closed, making him appear indifferent.

I'm not sure where to look. I'm getting hotter, not because there is a naked man lying opposite me in a very small space, but because I'm now having a hot flush in a sauna. I want to get up and leave, but I worry he'd think I'm leaving because of him, and I don't want him to feel awkward with all his nakedness. I sweat it out for another minute. Saunas and steam rooms are like baths to me—the idea sounds nice, but the actual partaking in them is just a hot, sweaty, uncomfortable, claustrophobic experience.

I'm trying to look everywhere but at his genitals.

I glance towards him; I can't help but stare for a moment. It's not that I want to see his genitals, it's just the amount of hair he has makes it look like he has an afro wig caught between his legs. I can't see anything else, so he might as well be wearing Speedos. Of course, just as I glance, someone else comes in. It's Mavis the Goose Girl. She doesn't look twice at him, but instead, stares at me looking in the direction of his willy. She climbs up to the top shelf and lies down on her towel. She's just showing off, I can barely stand the heat on the lower seat. With someone else in the sauna, I feel it's safe for me to leave without making the guy feel embarrassed. It has been a common occurrence all my life; to save someone else from possible embarrassment, I embarrass myself.

Just as I'm about to stand up, Mavis suddenly says, "An 'omm' is good in a sauna. Can we 'omm' together?"

"Sure," says the passed out guy with the genitals, his eyes still closed. He starts us off, and the loudness of his 'omm' surprises me so much that I automatically look towards him again, just as another woman walks in and notices my line of vision.

The second woman takes no notice of him, sits on the second highest platform and automatically starts omm-ing.

My 'omm' is more of a gentle hum as I assess the situation and again feel it would be rude to leave the sweat bath midst omm-ing. The woman who has just joined is giving it her full lung capacity. She's even louder than hairy, naked guy. Mavis ramps up her vocals; it was her idea after all.

The sound is deafening, the heat intense and there's nowhere for me to look other than the nakedness in front of me. This is one of the most un-relaxing, uncomfortable experiences of my life. It reminds me of my bath. I need to get out before I pass out.

Bursting out the door, I slap on the shower outside and gasp in so much air I feel my lungs might explode.

A screechy squeak escapes my mouth, but it's drowned out by the ongoing omm-ing. I was not expecting it to be ice cold. 'Spring water from the mountain for your enjoyment' states the sign beside the faucet.

————

At the intro session there's a mix mash of people. This workshop will be conducted in English even though the participants are mostly Dutch, with a smattering from Belgium, Poland and Germany. I think I'm one of two native English speakers. I am embarrassed how everyone can speak such good English as a second language when I struggle with Italian.

Rex, the retreat leader, hands out the itinerary for the week:

Morning meditation. Breakfast. Class 1. Thirty-minute break.

*Class 2. Lunch. Class 3. Thirty-minute break. Class 4. Dinner.
Meditation. Bed.*

Where is the time for the jacuzzi? And what are all these classes
about?

"In the coming week, we are going to be looking at energy in
buildings—the flow of chi and in the ground," Rex opens his
intro talk with as we all settle onto chairs and not onto yoga
mats. "Have you ever entered a place, and it feels heavy, it sucks
your energy?"

Yes, that's my house, I think to myself. Perhaps he's going to tell
me how to Feng Shui my sitting room for better Qi Gong
practice.

"This energy clearing workshop will teach you to clean
houses."

Clean houses? This retreat is not sounding fun. I check the list
of classes and try to find Qi Gong.

Still confused, I nudge Mavis, who's sitting beside me. "I think
I'm in the wrong room. I signed up for a Qi Gong energy
retreat."

"The Chi (Energy) Clearing Retreat?" she says, pointing at the
name at the top of the itinerary sheet.

Then I notice there is no 'gong'. Not physically or in words.

Rex continues, "It will teach you to find metaphysical disturbances in houses and clear them.

I am talking like a robot again.

"Metaphysical disturbances?" I repeat the words to Mavis. "By that, does he mean ghosts?"

"Yes. My lover's farm is riddled with ghosts. I can't wait to dissolve them."

"Hang on... We are at a ghostbuster workshop?"

"I know. I'm so excited too."

9

"In The Netherlands we call them wiggle rods," Rex says handing me an L-shaped copper coloured rod. Rex seems like a very sane, reasonable person, nothing woo-woo about him.

He's also got piercing blue eyes and a nice face to look at, so I decide to play along and not say anything about getting the completely wrong end of the stick regarding the workshop description. "They are simply non-magnetic welding rods bent into an L-shape. Nothing special. And you need your pendant."

Everyone pulls crystals hanging from chains out of their bag or pocket. Except me. I must have missed a memo. I feel like a kid forgetting one of my school books. "I forgot mine." I lie.

Rex gives me one from a wholesale box of pendants. "Hold it over your hand and ask a question, like: 'Is today Saturday?'. And note which way it spins for 'Yes'. If you flip your hand over, you will see it spins the other way."

It's not working for me. No matter what question I ask it, it's not moving. I try another pendant from the box. It's not working either.

"There's a lot of resistance," Rex observes.

You don't say. I remind myself to be open-minded. I am here and living in the now, so I'll give it my all. "Maybe I need to be connected to it. Can I use something else?"

"Sure. Anything can be used as a pendant."

I take the pocket watch on a chain Dad gave me for my twenty-first birthday. I never use it, but brought it with me when I read it was preferable to leave your phone in your room and disconnect from the internet while at the retreat centre, to help stay fully present and relaxed. To the surprise of my cynical mind, the pocket watch works like a charm; spinning right for 'yes' and left for 'no'.

"The Yin Yang ration of a building should be forty percent to sixty percent. If there is too much Yin, it means too much passive energy, which indicates metaphysical disturbances. If there is too much Yang, there is too much active energy, which is a sign of geopathic and or electro stress energy. Later, we will go outside and you will ask your wiggle rod to find the direction of magnetic fields."

We are sent off with our wiggle rods and pendants to follow the chi in our bedrooms. I follow what I have been instructed to do: holding the rod lightly balanced in my hand, it waves smoothly from side to side in a snake pattern. When I come to a disturbance, the rod turns abruptly on itself. I then use my pendant to figure out, by a process of elimination, which type of disturbance it is by asking a series of questions that have 'yes' or 'no' answers.

"Energy vortexes can be caused by traumatic death to emotions such as fear and anger left from people in that space. Sudden violent death can leave a metaphysical disturbance. As can suicide or contemplated suicide." Rex had explained. "Negative thoughts and emotions such as anger, fear, trauma, etc. of current or previous occupants can be left behind. Beds and pillows are good places for these to build."

My rod weaves smoothly with the energy of my room and I don't find any antique dolls with spinning heads under the bed. My room is as clean as a whistle.

When we return from using our wiggle rods in our room and me finding nothing thankfully, Mavis proclaims with joy that she discovered something; the person who built her bed had suicidal thoughts. I suppress the urge to burst out laughing.

Be still my cynical mind.

"When clearing the energy of a house, there may be a principal cause of disturbance or there may be many. It could take weeks to clear a building. Energy can attach to old antiques, jewellery, statues, masks, especially wooden furniture," Rex explains.

I think of all the old stuff in our house. And the garage full of old wood worm infested beds. Maybe it's that which is sucking our energy.

"Experienced energy workers don't need the pendant to tell them what form of energy blockage it is as they feel the difference in their bodies. Perhaps a metaphysical disturbance gives a tingling sensation, or earth radiation gives a warm feeling in their neck. Each individual feels different energies differently. By acknowledging it and being with it for a few moments, the trapped energy is released and the blockage is cleared."

It takes me a couple of days before I admit to Ronan I booked onto a completely wrong retreat and I am actually being trained as a ghostbuster, rather than participating in training which would complement the Qi Gong instructor course I am doing.

"Maybe there's a hidden vortex sucking us of our life force?" Ronan says enthusiastically.

"If there is a vortex, it's definitely in the garage full of all that crap. You need to clear it."

Ronan groans.

Over the following days, there is very little time for spa visits or massages. Instead, I learn about energy disturbances in buildings and land; How they can build up from intensely positively or negatively charged magnetic fields. And how naturally occurring underground water can cause gamma or microwave radiation flowing through a narrowing in the earth, fault lines and radials from fault lines.

Rex teaches us how a building can be affected by disturbed emotional energy in the land or other surrounding constructions such as a cell tower, castle, prison, power cables, a train line.

"When approaching a clearing job, you need to pay attention to historical places such as places of battle, cemeteries, sacrificial sites. Or places of occult worship." He loses me when he mentions astral energies from other dimensions.

However, I can't help but be aware the area around Lake Trasimeno was the place where Hannibal with his last elephant and hordes of Celts killed thirty-thousand Romans and spent seven years following the battle burying the dead so they wouldn't come back to haunt them. I am also aware we have a train line just beyond our back garden.

"You can clear and reset some energies but they can build again overtime," Rex explains as we are trained to check each room of a house to see if residents are negatively affected by electro stress and how far this emits. We can set a shield against gamma and microwave radiation. I feel like I'm training to be a Marvel superhero.

"What did you learn today?" Ronan asks that evening.

"I learnt it might be a heap of dead romans or trains sucking our energy source." It's not a sentence I ever expected to say.

On the second last day, a local who works at the retreat centre, tells of a house nearby that has been resold four times in a short space of time because it is supposedly haunted. He knows the estate agent; he gives him a call, and we are given access.

Rex learns the history of the haunted house from the estate agent, but he will not tell us yet. First, we are to experience it.

10

The following morning, those who want to participate take the mountain walk led by the local guy to the haunted house.

Some of the people in the workshop have decided not to take part because they feel they are too sensitive to that type of energy. My cynical mind is hard to quieten when I see them walking towards the spa with their rolled-up towels as we trudge out the gate with our wiggle rods.

But I'd rather be here, experiencing something new. Even if it is a haunted house in the Italian mountains with a team of Dutch ghostbusters.

On the way, I text Lucia: Thought I was going on a Qi Gong energy retreat, but instead, it is a ghostbusting training workshop.

The walk itself is worth the effort. In the distance, a curved line of sharp conical trees sits silhouetted like a dragon's back, against the delicate blue and translucent pink sky. The dragon sleeps, restfully breathing mist, lying below the small hilltop town where the haunted house stands.

At the house, we spread out in different directions with our rods in hand. We are not to clear the energies, but to sense how they feel in our bodies. I'm not sold on this.

Although, I can't help but feel the house has strange energy. Walking up the ornate stairs that turn halfway, a coldness comes from the corner. I ignore it. On the top floor of the house, there's a staircase to the attic.

"Does anyone want to come up to the attic?" Rex asks. It sounds like a line from a horror movie, but like the movie characters who go into the basement when there is no electricity and a serial killer on the loose, I find myself saying "I'll go!" and practically jogging after Rex up the attic stairs.

On the far wall of the attic, there is a small door. A door that could easily be hidden behind the large wardrobe pushed to the side. Rex opens the door. Inside, there is a bedroom and a small stove. Our rods are going crazy. It feels uncomfortable. Too uncomfortable for me. I step back down the stairs and follow my rod down a dead end hallway. My body goes cold, sending a shiver up my spine. Stagnant fear. I don't feel afraid, but I am sensing fear. For a beautiful house, it has a lot of issues.

Picking up spirits is not something I really want on my resume, so I head down the stairs to wait outside. But on the way down I feel it again, the sharp coldness in the corner.

"What are you feeling?" Rex asks, seeing me pause as he comes down from the attic.

"Coldness. Frozen with fear. Perhaps it is a child or woman

afraid of what they know will happen when they go downstairs? But it is fear in the extreme...I'm going outside."

The house has beautiful terraces on the first floor overlooking the mountains, with frescoed designs on the plastered exterior. The frescoes at the corner side are pockmarked through to the stone below. Bullet holes.

More of the participants follow onto the terrace with Rex. "Okay, now I tell you the house's history. Partisans stayed here during the Second World War. The Nazis found out where they were," he says, pointing to the facade riddled with bullet holes. He did not need to say more.

Back at the venue, we have a last exercise to do before we say our farewells. Each of the participants has brought a floor plan of their home and exchanged it with another participant. I missed the memo about this requirement too and so I had spent the previous evening sketching out my three floors and exchanged them with Ralf, who had brought architectural drawings of his apartment. I overhear Mavis doing long explanations of her floor layout, including the geese and the donkeys to her paired up partner for this task.

Using what we learnt during the week and our pendants, our assignment is to find any stagnant energy spots in the other person's home, find out what they are, and clear or shield them.

I can't imagine what Ralf is going to find in my house. I start with his, and try to take myself seriously. "I am finding radiation here, I point to a spot in the corner and I am finding stagnant energy here, I say pointing to where the dining table is, so I cleared that. There is nothing metaphysical in your home, but there is an energy drain over this side outside the house, which I have set a shield against."

Ralf is impressed by my findings. "This is where the microwave oven is," he says in response to the first thing I mentioned, "maybe we need a new one or get rid of it altogether. And the dining table, we never use for eating, it is just used for stuff. And there is a large power line over this side of the house. I will keep it shielded."

I've nearly impressed myself. "What did you find in my house?" I am hesitant to ask, even though I am skeptical, I am worried he is going to tell me there are ten ghost Nazis hanging out in our attic.

But he doesn't say that. "I found very little. A few little patches of grief, but nothing sinister. The only thing I found was a ley line running this way through this room with water in it," he says, pointing to the backroom sitting room we use as an entrance and exit rather than the front door. It shows energy escaping and draining this way. So I set up a shield around it."

I smile and remain skeptical. All the guys on the course are finding ley lines and magnetic fields, whereas the women are finding ghosts and piles of emotions stagnated in corners. One woman suggested there was an old burial ground and an occult worshipping site in someone's back garden.

The week has been interesting, and while all the participants leave, I retreat to my room, having booked two retreats back-to-back. I am not leaving for another six days. I am here to retreat but also to learn what I want to offer guests at Casa Anam Cara. I make notes of observations:

There were over fifty people on the workshop and I didn't really get to know any of them, which felt strange for me. There wasn't down time between classes, no time to chat. It was too big; even if we did have free time, we could not all have got to know each other.

Lesson learnt for my retreats: Keep groups small and intimate. Don't have the schedule too full.

Having made my notes, I get ready to go to the spa. As it is a check-in/check-out day, I will have it all to myself while I wait for the new participants to arrive in the coming hours and registration opens for the next retreat.

This is the second retreat I booked without being clear about what the actual retreat involves. I read the description again: For the tenth year we are honoured to host retreat space for Guru Manya Araina.

Evening Satsangh sessions will be an open space for questions and answers where Guru Manya Araina will offer her wisdom as encouragement, inspiring direction, and clarity. Through this experience, we may find deeper self-knowledge, and then, wisdom.

By holding Sacred Circle and meditation, she will guide us into these new and changing times by acknowledging the Sacred Within. There will be a daily Yoga practice, Magical Mystery Dance workshop. As well as exploring LaQi for healing.

This all sounded fabulously elusive and out of my comfort zone.

On the way to the spa, my phone bings with the response message from Lucia.

You are a ghost cleaner? That makes you a new level of witch! You have to come and do ghost cleaning at La Dogana. It is so ancient, you might find Hans Cristian Anderson's ghost. I will pay you! She responds, followed by a laughing face emoji.

I know she is not serious, but I also know she, like me, would be curious about this stuff. And then an idea clicks.

"Actually Lucia, could you employ me?"

"As a ghost cleaner? I don't think there is that category of employment on the tax forms."

"As anything. If you employ me, I can get my health card and get the scan I need on my water blob."

"Yes, of course. I use you for consulting advice about weddings all the time anyway."

As a foreign resident in Umbria, even though I pay taxes as a self-employed person, I cannot get a health card until I am five years resident. I am only a three-year resident, and the water blob on my liver found by my GP, Doctor Fab Chicken, needs to be dealt with by a specialist.

If I am employed by an Italian company, I will automatically get a Tessera Sanitaria (health card) for my period of employment. The health card permits people to avail themselves of the public health system.

Maybe something good will come from this experience after all.

"We got a speeding fine," Ronan says coyly when I call him after I return from the spa. "We were going twelve kilometres over the limit."

He's a very good driver, but I'm always telling him to slow down. Once we gave a monk a lift from a train station who was going to the same place as us. I thought the monk was meditating in the car, as every time I looked back at him, his eyes were closed. When we got to the venue which was up a lot of winding roads, the monk said, "You can do thirty years of meditation but fifteen minutes in the car with him driving does the same thing: you realise your life or destiny is not in your hands, you need to leave it in the hands of God."

Ronan drives like an Italian and says he just keeps up with the traffic in front of him. And like the Italians, he thinks the speed numbers are recommendations rather than a requirement. He doesn't take any notice of sell-by dates either.

"You mean YOU got a speeding fine as YOU were going twelve kilometres over the limit."

"They'll also put three points on your license, but there's a form you can fill out to say it was me driving and not you."

"You mean there's a form YOU need to fill out when you pay the fine."

"We can pay it by scanning the QR code."

"You mean YOU can pay it by scanning the QR Code."

At last, he grasps what I am saying. I am not taking responsibility for this. We have an unspoken rule all things car related are his responsibility.

"I don't trust QR codes. I'm going to buy cigarettes, I'll see if I can pay it at the tobacco shop."

An hour later, he calls and tells me the blow by blow account:

He found a parking spot outside the tobacco shop. There was a traffic warden on the prowl, but the spot he'd found is a white parking space—meaning you can park in it for an hour or two for free.

"Can I pay this here?" Ronan asked, handing the fine with the QR code across the counter of the tobacconists. She made a phone call to her boss to check and smiled, "yes you can."

He paid the sixty euro fine. It would go up to one-hundred and twenty euro if he didn't pay it within a week. And if not paid, then it would just keep increasing.

I have read online horror stories of speeding fines in Italy. One guy got forty-two speeding fines delivered over three days coming to six-thousand-five-hundred euros. All the fines were for the same stretch of road over one year.

Another guy's car got towed as it was parked illegally, and he got a speeding fine for later that day. The photo evidence was his car on the back of the tow truck. The tow truck was speeding, but his car's licence plate on the back of the truck got picked up.

"Tickets for driving offences never go away. Instead, with the passing of months and years, their value multiplies like Jesus' 'pani e pesci'. So just pay it online," someone with experience responded to an online cry for help. It's notoriously difficult to dispute a parking or speed fine in Italy.

"I tried, I really tried to pay the three tickets I got the last time I was in Italy online," said the respondent. "I am not driving in Italy again. Over six-hundred euro by the time I got the ticket."

A fine should arrive within ninety days from the date of the violation. For those abroad, the period increases to a year. The notification limit is for them to send it, not for you to receive it, so if a fine gets lost on the way, you'll still have to pay it, no matter if it reached your mailbox or not.

If the offence is detected in a rented car, the time can be even longer (ninety days plus three-hundred and sixty days).

Ronan's receipt of payment is stapled to the sheet, and Ronan felt accomplished having achieved an admin thing in Italy in the space of five minutes.

He walked out of the tobacco shop, and the traffic warden was walking away from our car with a parking fine under our window wiper.

"Hey!" Ronan shouted after her. "It's a white parking space."

"Ah, I am sorry, but you do not have the clock."

"The what?"

"You can only park here for two hours."

"I was only here for two minutes in the tobacco shop."

"I am sorry, but you have not the clock."

"But you walked past here when I was arriving five minutes ago, and the spot was empty, so you know I haven't been here for an hour."

An Italian woman who was parked behind Ronan arrived and was equally furious with her ticket. She spoke good English.

"You need a cardboard clock in your window when you park in a white spot and put the time you arrived," she explained.

"I am sorry, but my commander says I must do it." The traffic warden smiled apologetically.

"Can't you tear it up?"

"No. I am sorrys," she said.

Ronan snapped the ticket from the windshield.

"I am going in to pay it. So don't put another one on my car while I am in there for five minutes."

He stormed into the tobacco shop. "Now I need to pay this. Unbelievable," he said to the counter assistant.

"Maybe I should open an account for you!" she laughed. "I will add this to the bill?" she said, holding up a cardboard parking clock.

———

With time to spare, I take a walk around the grounds of the retreat venue. The grounds keeper is raking the leaves into the shape of love hearts, leaving them on the ground to return the love into the earth, as the trees gently shakes off more to top up the supply.

The air is so clean and fresh it feels sharp to breathe. Maybe I could live in the mountains. It would be cooler in summer for sure. But on second thought, I am not a snow lover. Sweet chestnut cases lie scattered like a carpet of mini hedgehogs. Hedgehogs remind me of Dad.

Without my phone attached to me and with time to myself, thoughts start to filter in. I think about the last year and how I have felt at times life has cheated me. I have lost three of my close family who I turned to when things didn't go right for me and first about anything; from how to fix a plug to what my cat's temperature should be. My sister Eileen, my dad, and my brother Jamsie. Three of the few people who had loved me since the day I was born were gone forever. Pangs of guilt have pricked me in the last few months during moments of lightness and laughter. They are gone, how could I feel a moment of happiness?

When the other participants arrive, I need to go to register for the retreat at the check-in desk, like everyone else. Three women are ahead of me in the line. They all know of the guru. One is from the UK and has been at the guru's ashram in India and has followed her to several places. Everyone seems to know the guru and have stories of previous encounters in India, France, and the USA.

There is a new box of 'I am in Silence' badges on the counter. "I am tempted to buy these as Christmas presents for my family. It might shut them up," I say to the woman and guy waiting separately to register beside me. I don't mean it, but I know it might get a laugh and break the ice.

I'm right, it does. She laughs easily, throwing her head back, her mouth wide open showing her tonsils, pressed down tongue and perfectly lined up flaw free, pearly teeth. Her 'hahaha' laugh makes me laugh and the guy notices her.

"I'm Katya, I'm from Finland." She looks like snow. The guy introduces himself to both of us as Francesco. He says he is Italian, but with the thickest London accent I have heard in a long time. His parents are Italian and he moved to the UK when he was a toddler.

At registration, Katya gives her date of birth. I calculate she's forty, but she doesn't look over twenty-six. Perfect skin on perfectly toned facial muscles, not a line in sight. Elf like eyes and nose slightly pointed upwards and white blonde Scandinavian hair. She's beautiful. Francesco is beautiful too. Her snow whiteness contrasts with his dark skin, like the shadows where he would need to sit under to hide from the strong Mediterranean sun.

It makes me think we are all made to blend into the background of the place on earth we are from, not dominate it. That's very philosophical of me, the retreat space must be soaking into me.

I'm also thinking they would make a great couple—snow and shadow.

12

B right yellow treetops stick out of a cloud stuck in the valley below, being woken by the golden light of the sunrise. A cream ruin with its roof caved like an art instillation. Even ruins look artistically done in Italy. It's 6AM and I am on my way to morning meditation in the temple.

We are to remain in silence until breakfast this morning. In the custom-built, round temple room, I join about thirty other people on yoga mats. Wrapped in blankets, we sit in silence as the sun creeps up over the surrounding mountain peaks. When the gong is sounded, the group slowly leaves the temple and disperses in different directions.

I go back to my room before breakfast and lie on my terrace sun lounger, enjoying the warmth of the early sun. A vibration going through the ground from a helicopter approaching travels up through my sun lounger and into my body. As it passes, the air pulsates in my ears like the way it is vacuumed out of your hearing canals when you enter a tunnel in a fast train. It lands in a field not too far away and I see a riot of colour spilling out of it accompanied by a dog's yap.

The vegetarian breakfast food buffet is as spectacular as it has been every day. I am going all out on a health binge while here; I mix Spirulina in with porridge and yogurt and add chia seeds. It looks like a swamp with frog spawn, so I add some berries to make it look more palatable.

I sit with Katya and a woman who introduces herself as Sara. She is from Amsterdam but speaks fluent Italian, as her grandfather was from Calabria. It is where she spent her childhood summers, hanging out with her aunts. Her grandfather sold flavoured ice in The Netherlands and had a monkey and music box he used to busk with. "He grew an ice lolly business and made a lot of money." She used to be a catwalk model and had lived in Milan.

Together, the three of us read the cute notes attached to each tea bag. 'Trust in the question.' 'Love is the solution.' 'Love knows no boundaries.'

Katya tells us how she has started a commune in the woods of Finland. She tells me of her ex-husband, whom she still loves but no longer likes. He lives in the commune house too with his new partner.

Another woman sits further up the long bench table. She is wearing layers of clothes with the sole purpose of covering her body and keeping warm. The dominant piece is a long velveteen skirt patterned with large cabbages on a silvery grey background with the elasticated waist band half way above her boobs. On her feet are old mountain boots tied with mismatched laces. Her hair is wiry and dry, fluffed by the mist. Her ruddy red cheeks, eyelids and chin contrast with her wide mouth full of unruly yellowing teeth.

Cabbage Patch's friend leans down and says to Sara, "I am electric-magnetic sensitive. Could you please switch off your phone," pointing to Sara's phone on the table.

"I have it on silent mode," Sara responds, tucking into her sour dough toast and avocado.

"Aeroplane mode instead of silent mode is better for me, because I am electric-magnetic sensitive," she repeats.

"Of course you are," Sara says, switching off her phone.

"She's my assigned roommate," Sara whispers. "A bag of laughs." Her eyes roll. "I can't have my phone in our room because of her and I am waiting to hear from my daughter about her exam she was worried about. Has she not noticed there is a tower of satellite dishes just fifty metres away? And we are surrounded by electrics?" A microwave in the catering area lets out a perfectly timed bing.

Sara's roommate is thin and dressed like a puritan. Her clothes are made from organic materials that she has probably bought individually over time and washed regularly with her own laundry soap made of nuts and lavender.

I imagine only vinegar and baking soda are under her kitchen sink with the waste leading to a wastewater tank she waters her vegetable patch with. I used to strive to live that sort of life, but I found it smelled of damp and mould.

I am thinking of offering my new superpower of shielding rooms from electro-magnetic energy to Sara and her roomie, but decide not to. I am glad I paid the extra to have a room to myself. After my experiences so far, everyone will get a room to themselves on my retreats.

"I went to the spa this morning," Katya says.

"Was there any naked men in the sauna?" I ask.

"No, why?"

"The first day I went there was a naked man there."

"Which guy?" Sara asks looking around the room full of people.

"I don't know. I didn't look at his face, I'd only recognise him by his pubic hair."

This makes Katya laugh so hard she throws her hair head back and cackles. Francesco is just leaving the buffet, having filled his tray and comes over to join us.

"This sounds like the table to be at."

"What are you talking about that is so funny?" Cabbage Patch Woman asks.

"Naked men in saunas," Sara says.

"In the mountains where I am from, saunas are popular but without clothes. But it's changing now, my children's generation, they go into saunas with clothes. I do not know why," Cabbage Patch says.

"I would never go into a sauna," Electro Sensitive Woman says. "It would be too much heat for my head."

"What's on our schedule today?" Sara asks, "I can't see it as it's on my phone." Her eyes roll in her roommate's direction, just as two guys with long beards whoosh in the front door and are greeted with a gaggle of greetings and hugging from the people behind the reception desk.

I have never seen such a striking couple. The Indian guy, with a long black bushy beard which has grown way beyond his youthful facial features and short sculptured hair, is wearing layers of vivid pinks, including his crocs. He wears a thick silver loop in his ear, which I will notice his husband wearing later.

His husband is older, bald and taller, with a longer, less thick beard dyed ginger. He's wearing pink trousers, a pale moss coloured knit sweater and a lime green, mohair fitted coat with army boots custom made in blotched blue leather. Black Beard has the same coat but in a darker shade of vivid green. These were the bundles of colour I saw tumble from the helicopter. Their miniature Pomeranian on a cerise pink lead yaps around their ankles at all the fuss.

Katya hasn't noticed. "It's yoga now, then La Qi," she says, checking the timetable on her phone. "Freetime after lunch," she continues reading, "and then this evening we have Satsang with Guru Araina. Tomorrow we have sacred dance, circle breathing, that is always interesting to do, and La Qi and a sound bath."

We head off to the only thing on the activity list I am familiar with: yoga.

The class is gentle, with the focus on breathing. It prepares us for La Qi. Something I am looking forward to experiencing since my experience of Qi Gong.

We start with an exercise to show the power of the mind. Lining up our wrists and pressing our hands together, we observe how both hands are the same size. As we relax our hands and sit with our eyes closed. Durla, our instructor, walks us through steps of imagining our right hand growing and growing and becoming like a giant's hand. At the end we open our eyes and told to line up our wrists again and put our hands together.

"Any difference?"

My right hand is noticeably bigger, with my fingers nearly half a joint longer. Lots of other people experience the same.

"Any questions?" she asks.

"Yes," I say. "How do I get it back to normal?"

Chuckles go round the room and the instructor moves on. I don't want to say, "I am serious, I want my hand back to the size it was."

Instead, I decide to wait it out and guess it will go back to normal.

"La Qi is about experiencing chi. The energy source." Sitting in a circle, we rub our hands together fast until they are warm, then move our hands apart.

"What do you feel?"

Warmth, tingling, magnetic pull.

"Keep your hands in that position and try moving them in little circles. Try opening and closing them a little. Try different movements. Play with the energy you feel between your hands." Durla is the personification of peace, sitting cross-legged in her tangerine, linen, Indian two piece.

"Now let's try the eastern way of pulling in energy, which we can use for healing and expanding energy to spread healing. Turn your palms inwards and imagine a ball of that energy between your palms and slowly pull it open. Lead the pulling with your elbows," she says as we imitate her movements.

"The Qi energy ball expands bigger and bigger, then push it together and the Qi ball condenses as it gets smaller and smaller. Keep doing this expansion and condensing small and slow movements. Now include your breath exhale and expand, inhale close and condense."

We follow as Durla continues, "If you know of someone who could do with some healing or strength sent their way, you can think of them as you expand and send the healing energy their way. And you can pull it into yourself."

The feeling of calmness in my body and the room is so beautiful. Calm, relaxing and I can't help but breathe the deepest I have ever drawn breath.

This is what I imagined a retreat to be.

13

L unch is another feast of delicious vegetarian food. Homemade soups, beans, salads.

"Normally I would love a glass of wine with lunch when on holiday," Sara says as we sit on the terrace with our plates piled high, "but who would need alcohol when you have surroundings like this to make you feel ecstatic? I don't want to dull a moment of it."

I hadn't noticed there is no alcohol at the place until now. We look out towards the distant peaks glowing ice white and observe how the mountain ridges nearby look like the backs of curled up, giant, furry animals you could reach out and stroke with the giant hands we created in La Qi.

After lunch, lying on a bean bag heated by the sun, overlooking the vista of the glass lake, we amuse ourselves by using our tea bag words of wisdom to advise each other on our life paths like a bad fortune teller. "If you add them all together, you could make a book of belief systems and start a cult," Katya says. We develop the idea of the imaginary cult we will start while living between Katya's commune in Finland and my Casa Anam Cara. Our howls of laughter attract Francesco again like a mating call. Sara and I head to the hot tub and leave Francesco and Katya huddled in deep conversation.

I do not know what to expect from the evening guru session. I have never partaken in something like this before, but Sara has and all she can say is "it's very special".

When I get to the temple, the room is already full of eager followers sitting cross-legged, joining in the chanting of repeated mantras led by a girl with the voice of an angel playing a zither.

"Soham soham soham shivoham."

I am that I am.

"Ishq Allah Mah Bud Allah Ishq Alle Mah Bud Allah."

God is Love, Lover and Beloved simultaneously.

After a few rounds of listening, I join in the chanting and feel the calm vibration hum go through my body.

In walks a serious looking grey-haired, white woman. She takes her seat at the front and joins in the chanting. She is tailed by two assistants who sit on either side and attend to every instruction she says in their direction. Gradually the chanting fades and silence hangs, waiting on her words.

"I am not a guru. I am not Christian, I am not Hindu, I don't know what I am. I am a preserver of joy and a spreader of happiness. My aim is to be in the world, but not of it."

There is silence as these words penetrate. I pretend to understand the last line, but it has gone over my head.

She waves towards the statuette on the table beside her. "This is a depiction of the Goddess Durga. Befitting her role as mother protector, Durga is multi-limbed so she may always be ready to battle evil from any direction. A multi-tasker like a lot of the women in this room. In most depictions, she has between eight and eighteen arms and holds a symbolic object in each hand."

She settles into her seat. "I was brought up in a strict Christian religion. At one point in my life, I asked god, Why am I so afraid to believe in female gods? It was the fear from how I was raised, to believe in the Ten Commandments. You shall not have false gods before me. But who decided that these beautiful female gods that stood for all that was right and pure were the false ones?"

My mind wanders back to a recent Qi Gong class I had as part of my instruction course and was introduced to Guanyin, the goddess of mercy, and considered to be the physical embodiment of compassion. In Chinese mythology, she is an all-seeing, all-hearing being who is called upon by worshipers in times of uncertainty, despair, and fear. She holds the symbol of the lotus. A thing of beauty that rises from mud.

And I think of the goddess Tara, who is referred to as the Wisdom Goddess, the Embodiment of Perfected Wisdom, the Goddess of Universal Compassion, and the Mother of all Buddhas. And the Celtic Goddess Danu–she is a symbol of creation, wisdom, and the nurturing forces of nature and maternal energy.

"I was taught to fear God and that all those who do not believe in just him were wrong and doomed. True love cannot have any fear. I wondered why the love and care of the world was just placed on one domineering male god's shoulders? So I went to India and there I found love and meaning."

After her ad lib talk full of wise words, which I try to absorb but I am a little too distracted watching how the crowd hang on her words, the room is opened for questions.

Her followers have come armed with questions.

Someone asks how to still the mind.

"Sit quietly and ask yourself 'what is my next thought?' That will quiet your mind."

Red Beard says, "I can't pray or meditate. What can I do?"

Without pause, she answers, "I know you dance, and dance is a form of meditation. It's what many tribes around the world do to communicate with God. Such as the rain dance. So dance."

His husband also has a question. "With a world so in turmoil, I feel helpless. It feels wrong to have moments of happiness when there is so much suffering. What should we be doing?"

"You need to preserve joy, especially now in these difficult times. It is our responsibility to keep joy alive."

I am not the only one that loves this answer. I am in a room of bobbing heads.

"How do I live without my job? Without it, I feel I have no purpose," Sara asks. I wondered why she was here. She hadn't volunteered the information, but now that she is fifty-five and graded too old to be a catwalk model, she is feeling the effects of invisibility in the world as she ages.

"Change is inevitable and is never easy. Anchor your identity not to what you do, but why you do it."

"Listening to the news, I feel so hopeless for humanity. What can I do?" The woman from the UK asks.

"I have good news for you. We are all blessed, as there are people all over the world praying for humanity. That is you. So many people. From Tibet to the Navajo, peoples in India to China, Christian, Muslim, Hindu: they are all praying to ease the suffering of the world. They are all praying to ease your suffering. They are all for you. There is a shift happening in the world. I don't know if I will live to see it, but our role is to preserve joy."

"How do I become enlightened?"

"You can't become enlightened. The spark of perfection and enlightenment is inside you—you just have to find it and nurture it."

"I always seem to be getting sick with stress. How do I start to improve my life?"

"You don't need chaos going on inside your body. Simplify your food. Simplify what you drink. Nurture your body, it is your temple. Remove noise and chaos."

There is a pause and an assistant asks, "Are there any other questions for Manya Araina?"

I have nothing to ask. Others seem to be still too star struck from being in her presence to speak. And then the Guru turns and looks directly at me.

"Grief makes you look at yourself and life differently."

Her piercing blue eyes are seeing into me. "We are inherently built for this. Integrate pain and loss into your life. Your heart is still beating, life is going on."

As if reading my mind, she says, "We need to have been loved and to have loved so much to feel strong grief. Part of us was lost with them, but part of them lives on in us. Guilt is often a companion of grief. Sometimes, if we live fully again, we feel it is disrespectful. But it's the opposite. Let go of the guilt."

She gives me a small nod.

She has given me permission to be happy again without guilt.

14

There is more singing of mantras as Manya Araina leaves the gathering, but the warmth stays in the circular room.

We take a short tea break and return to the temple room, now lit only by the soft amber glow of tea lights in the multiple wall nooks and the scent of sandalwood incense curling in the air.

With a gesture from Jane, a woman with dreadlocks and genie-in-the-bottle style pants, we quietly take a place on a yoga mat and lie down, covering ourselves with a blanket. Jane, who exudes calm, sits cross-legged in the centre, surrounded by dull brass hued bowls of different sizes and some more candles and a range of mallets wrapped in soft leather and cushion topped drumsticks.

It takes me a little while to get comfortable, both on the mat and with the idea of just lying doing nothing other than listening to the sound of bowls gently struck.

The murmur of recorded chanting is faded out and the room quietens in the stillness of anticipation as the door is closed and the last participants take a place. Jane chimes a bell and begins.

The first strike of the mallet against the biggest bowl resonated like a ripple in still water, filling the room with a humming vibration. Strike two and three intertwine before a deep hum grows steadily in the background. I glance towards Jane, to see what's making the sound and watched as she circles a bowl's edge with the mallet; the continuous drone tangles with the ripples that were not just heard but felt through my body and into my chest. Not like the helicopter—this is different. It's in my veins.

With concentration and her eyes lowered, Jane draws sound from the range of bowls—each releasing a unique tone, some high and clear, others deep and resonant, forming a symphony of dancing frequencies. The sounds are a balm to the frayed edges of my grief, like someone re-tuning me, as they would a piano or guitar; plucking at the strings, adjusting them until they are right again. The vibrations start to soothe and carry me away to a level of relaxation where deep sighs are required.

Jane weaves a delicate chime and the soft rattle of a rain stick into the tapestry of sound as the tones gradually soften.

In a state of deep relaxation, Jane's soft voice guides us:

"Imagine you are sitting in a favourite chair at home and picture that which represents the divine to you, god; a goddess, the higher self, whatever, as an energy ahead of you and off to your right, of swirling golden light radiating out lots of love. Imagine this energy getting closer and closer to you, the feeling of love getting stronger and stronger. Closer and closer, stronger and stronger.

"Next, imagine you are stepping into this vortex of love, surrounded by pure unconditional love. Feel yourself enveloped in love and warmth. Now imagine this energy entering you through the rear of your heart chakra, filling every cell in your body with love. From the bottom of your feet to the top of your head. Filling every cell with love, clearing all negativity out of your system.

"When your body is full of love, imagine the energy bursting out through the front of your heart chakra, filling your auric field with divine love. When the aura is full, expand this energy outwards to fill the room you are sitting in. Gradually work through the process of filling the entire house with this loving, golden energy. When the house is full, picture this energy bursting through the doors and windows to fill a great bubble that surrounds the house, wrapping your house in divine, unconditional love...

"Slowly come back into body conscious awareness by becoming aware of your breathing...then take a deep breath, maybe another, and open your eyes."

But I don't want to open my eyes, the feeling is too beautiful.

The bell chime heard at the beginning draws the session to conclusion. I open my eyes, my body heavy with relaxation but somehow lighter, as if coming out of a beautiful dream.

My first sound bath and I am hooked.

"That was kinda witchy! I love witch stuff," Sara says as we sit for dinner. "Have you ever been to the town of Benevento in Southern Italy? A friend of mine bought me a bottle of Strega Liquor from there."

"Strega? As in witch?"

"Yeah, it's the town famous for a magical walnut tree where witches used to gather from all over Europe a thousand years ago. Then some duke who converted to Christianity had it cut down. It was on the banks of the river Sabato. The association of the word Sabbath with witch gatherings came from there. The witches replanted the walnut tree from a nut, and it still stands in Benevento."

I always loved the idea of witches and being a witch 'someday' and felt flattered when people would refer to me as a witch of some sort. However, since I started researching a book idea I want to develop, I now have a love-hate relationship with the word witch—it's a cute word, but it was also a derogatory label put on women to disempower their wisdom of not only healing, herbs, natural cures but also any woman who spoke sense about life, politics and the wrongs of society.

"Witch gatherings. Sabbaths," I tut. "It was probably a place where wise women gathered to exchange knowledge about herbs and enjoy each other's company."

"I once went to a Sabbath," Katya says. "A coven of witches near where I live invited me along. It was pretty lame, no sacrifices or devil worshipping, just some petal throwing and dancing. Have you ever been to one?"

"You know there is no archaeological, written or historical evidence of Sabbaths ever happening?" I say. "It was a myth made up in medieval times to demonise women and give men an excuse to torture and burn women. A way of mass fear mongering against any woman who didn't conform."

"No history of magic or devil worshipping?" says Sara.

"All made up to kill off women like us. They particularly

targeted women past childbearing age." I surprise myself at how fired up I feel about this all of a sudden.

Francesco joins us, and the conversation switches to how walnuts are the oldest tree food known to man, and how they are shaped like a brain and good for your brain.

But I'm still thinking about the word witch. It's like the sound bath has woken a need in me to defend the women who suffered because of the lies made up about them and labelled as witches. I feel a book brewing.

15

Today, Black Beard is wearing a blend of greens; vivid green cashmere sweater, sap green cloak, emerald green pants. While Red Beard's ensemble is wine and tangerine focused, topped with a matching raspberry cloak.

Yoga is different today, it's laughter yoga. I catch Sara's face. She isn't laughing. Actually, she looks like she is going to kill someone.

"Today I want you to think about this," the instructor points to a whiteboard on an easel "What do I need to give myself permission to do this year?"

Other than giving myself permission to whack the brambles in the front garden, my mind is blank.

The next session is circle breathing, guided by Marino.

"We are going to send our body into various stages of crisis," he explains as we all lie on the floor in a circle, resting our right hand on the person's left hand beside us. The cozy room is quiet, with only the sound of Marino's slippered feet and his assistant slowly padding around the room. I wiggle to get comfortable on my yoga mat and connect with the warm hands of the women on both sides of me.

"This is done, through a guided way of breathing. I want you to k-no, I am very k-nowledged about this technique and 'ave trained to supervise and guide this. So do not do this on your own at 'ome and do not panic with the experiences you feel or the crisis you go through. I am here with my assistant to watch over you."

I don't laugh at his pronunciation of silent Ks. I know I slaughter the Italian language when I try to speak it.

The breathing sequence method is intense. Soon changes start to happen. My body goes cold, so cold I am trembling, shaking. I continue on the guided breathing. This is horrible, but I am going through the first crisis and then into the second.

In the second crisis, I stop feeling how stone cold my body is. The woman's hand on my left is cold. Ten minutes later my mind goes to her again. She's still ice cold and hasn't moved. Maybe she's dead. Can you die during this? It feels like you can.

I can hear Sara laughing. Laughing so hard, it sounds like she could be hysterical and about to puke. In the same direction as Sara's laughing, I can hear someone else sobbing hard.

I don't know what my mind is doing.

I continue following Marino's breathing instructions as he calls them out. I don't notice whether I am hot or cold anymore; my body is numb. My mouth has fallen into an ugly D shape like I am a corpse, and one of my eyes is twitching like crazy.

Through the next crisis and my body is still and comfortable, it has no sensation. I can hear the guides walking around the room as they continuously instruct on breathing. Are they shining lights on us? White light in my stomach and then a golden light comes in from the side.

I can hear the guides' voices on the other side of the room. I realise I am not seeing the light in my eyes or with my eyes, the light is in my body. Around my body. My eyes are closed, but I can see it. My right hand floats up from the floor. Marino gently pushes it back down but it won't stay, then both hands lift and float in the golden light. Dreams I have had come back to me about Dad, James, Eileen.

White balls of light are in the palms of my hand. I am confused; I try to think of who died first and when: Eileen, Dad, James. They are all one. They are the white light in the palms of my hands, through my arms and around the back of my body.

Darkness. I'm sobbing.

Scream, they are telling me. Release, let yourself go. I can't. I have never screamed.

My hands feel they are being held in theirs, but it is more than just holding my hands. They feel part of me. An extra skeleton across my arms and shoulders.

The white light feels strong on my back, supporting me, going through me. I can't make out which one of my passed family it is, but I am not trying. It is them and me. We are all the one white light together now, in the past and in the future. Our spirit is one. We are all part of the same spirit with no past, present or future. Between my eyes, purple and then orange light, a beautiful blue, yellow and red.

Marino guides our breathing back to normal. Stepping back into reality, we quietly retire to our rooms to comprehend what we have just experienced.

Lunch is quieter, murmurings of experiences in the circle. Everyone has had something unique; a stress release, calmness and stillness like they never experienced before, or a rush of energy. I keep mine to myself. I can still feel the white light support and want to savour it. And while I sip chamomile tea flavoured with Manuka honey, the answer to the question posed to us at yoga comes easily.

"I give myself permission to be free. To say yes to experiences. To have an easy year. To let myself go."

We have a blessings dance session led by Red Beard. This is what he does in his hometown of Verona; dance therapy.

"I can't pray or meditate, but I can dance." He bellows, before his unusual music starts; it has a mix of indigenous chanting and rhythm that gives you no option but to move.

"Let your body move towards where your eyes go. Now imagine your right hand has an eye on the palm and it can see the invisible. A second eye has grown on the back of that hand. Now there are eyes all over your hand. Then two hands. Follow what the eyes are looking at."

We move around the room. It's obvious by the giggles and pink faces others are feeling as awkward as I am, but some are really into it, with manic eyes wide open. There's a woman rolling on the floor. Black Beard follows her example. They are both on the floor rolling around, following imaginary eyes on their hands. Eyes following hands, hands getting away from eyes.

At first, my inhibited body can't make eye contact with anyone. Even when we are told to find each other's eyes, I find it difficult to hold the gaze.

I could watch Red Beard dance all day. His hips and feet move in smooth jerks in time with his undulating shoulders. Passion with each move. His intense eyes staring back at me. Some would find them demonic, but in them, I find love.

"Pinch the energy with your fingers, feel it go through your arms and down your spine. Be loose like a jellyfish. Let yourself go," he instructs.

I'm being loose like a jellyfish and getting into the sounds. At last, I am dancing.

"Don't dance," he shouts. "Remember your hands."

Fuuug, that was directed at me.

Don't dance. Be a jellyfish.

"How is going?" Sara whispers as we pass each other, following the eyes on our hands.

"I just got told off for being a dancing jellyfish. But otherwise, I'm starting to get into it."

At the end of the session, we are told to pair up with whoever is beside us.

"Put your right hand on your heart and look into each other's eyes... See all of humanity there. Reach out and touch each other's hearts. Make the connection." I'm beside Francesco. He has kind eyes and I try not to feel awkward gazing into a man's eyes who isn't Ronan. Although I don't think I have ever stared into Ronan's eyes this long in one session. It stops feeling awkward.

It's too much for some and they snivel and gasp, as tears of emotion flood their cheeks.

By day three, Sara and I are experts at following the eyes on our hands and I am joining in the chanting with ease. Didn't something like this happen in Eat Pray Love? Am I having an Eat Pray Love moment?

That evening I go online to book my train sequence back home, but because it will be on Sunday there are fewer trains. It's adding up to nearly three-hundred euros, whereas on Monday it will cost me seventy-one euros.

"Come stay in Milan for the night. I am going on a nostalgic tour of my old haunts. I haven't been there since my catwalk days," Sara suggests.

I immediately go to say no, but then I remember I no longer have kids at home in need of me. I no longer have clients waiting on responses about their wedding plans. I have no one to worry about. For the first time in my adult life, I am free. And I have given myself permission to be free and to say yes to experiences.

"Good idea. I haven't explored Milan, so why not?"

I look up hotels and book one in the city centre. It's the cheapest I could find, but the photos don't look too bad. How bad can a cheap hotel be in the city of style and fashion?

16

The bearded couple cross the courtyard in a wave of turquoise matching outfits. Katya and Francesco are ahead of them and walk into the breakfast room together. They were just friends until yesterday afternoon. I saw them from a distance after lunch, both throwing back their heads, laughing, chatting, and then they skipped up to his room. My prediction was right, they make a great couple.

At dinner, the change in both of them was glaring. They sat quietly together, swapping tea bag messages. She said they were her religion. He didn't understand, because it was our joke, but he didn't laugh either, because he can't laugh at her now, he might offend her. Previous to the change from friend to lover, she was a shrub you could fall on, and it would bounce back and even get one up on you with a thorn. Now she has turned into his delicate flower.

As soon as he leaves the table with a squeeze to her hand, myself and Sara swoop in.

"So we are going to Milan, you should come with us," Sara says before laughing her way through the description of the dance class where we had to do a sequence together and change position every time he clapped without losing physical contact with each other. We ended up knotted on the floor, crying from laughing." Katya and Francesco had missed the dance class because they were together in his room. They missed it because one could not leave the other. Katya was sorry she missed it.

"That's what happens with lovers," Sara says when Katya leaves to find Francesco to see if he wants to do the dance class later. "They compensate what they want to do for something more bland to meet the other person's wants and needs. With friends, you don't have to. One friend can say 'Fug you I'm going' and you could still be friends. Say that to a lover and it scars forever."

Later, when they came back from their second shag or cigarette, there were no seats left together. They have had to sit separately and pretend this does not bother them. Francesco is with me and Sara. Katya is sitting with Cabbage Patch.

When Katya passes, looking like a cloud of snow, Francesco pauses his laughter and conversation with me and reaches out to touch Katya, to give her reassurance that he is here—in case she trips and falls and skewers herself with a fork, presumably.

She glances down, holds his eyes with hers for a moment and gives a soft smile—a different one to the previous wide, spectacular friendship ones. This was a gentle flower smile that said; "thank you for being here and reassuring me I am not alone amongst all these friends. I feel more confident now walking with my cutlery and finished plate to the kitchen."

Her walk is now different around other people; More forward, as if walking in wellies two sizes too big and against a strong breeze whereas before, she walked upright like a ballerina. She has found a mate and doesn't want to be noticed or chosen by anyone else. She doesn't want anyone else to speak with her. She is on her way to him.

When this retreat is over, they will remember the heartbreak of leaving each other, instead of the bounty of love and new friendships and joyous experiences that have filled my heart.

I feel relieved I no longer have that feeling of needing to be desired I had years ago. I want to have the laughs, the friendship. It's so much more fun.

Our final session with the guru involves an option to have our feet anointed with oil infused with gold by her. Her followers are excited before it and pious after it.

Sara and I share a taxi back to the train station with Electro Woman.

As soon as we are in the taxi and driving down the mountain, Electro Woman says to the taxi man, "Can you lower the radio please, so I can sing you a song I made up?"

I can see Sara visibly twitch. She has reached emotional saturation point with her assigned roommate. Electro Woman does not seem aware of it, she launches into bellowing out her lyrical:

"No is nooooo, Yes is Yesssss. I love you, you love me, this we can agree."

And that is it. She is finished. I nod and smile towards her waiting face.

"How far is it to the train station?" Sara quickly says before she can start again.

Unfortunately, Electro Woman is going to Milan too and clings to us. She seems to have no problem with the surrounding people on their phones, just Sara's.

"Would you mind not using it near me?" She reminds Sara.

"You can't be serious? We are in a train station full of electricity and surrounded by people on phones and you want me to turn my phone off?"

She hadn't noticed when I used my phone to text Ronan "I don't know if I've indigestion or if I'm clearing peoples' negative energies and ghosts from the train. It's running twenty minutes late but I am hoping it can pick up time and we get to Milan in time for me to visit the Duomo." Ronan texts me back and tells me to use my newfound powers to speed up the train.

"My favourite part of the weekend was the anointing," Electro Woman says, sitting away from us phone wielding enemies across the carriage against the other window. "I feel so pure of soul after it."

"How did you feel after the anointing with oil?" Sara asks me.

I think for a moment the best way to describe it and decide on the perfect word. "Greasy."

———

I haven't had phone contact with the outside world other than Ronan, so while Sara and Electro Woman doze, I walk down the carriage and give Mam a video call.

Mam is sitting on her armchair, in her yellow room throwing seed out for the flock of birds on her balcony. She has her easel set up and a half-finished painting on it, with eight other oil paintings drying for the exhibition the nursing home is hosting for her. It's such a relief to see her happy and doing what she loves, having been through so much.

"Do you like my new bag for the bird seed? I won it in Bingo." She holds up a pretty fabric clutch with a velvet wristlet.

"I'm so glad we found that home for you."

"Sure where else would I be? I'm grand here. Just the food isn't as good as my own."

"Oh. What do you have for breakfast?"

"Oh, breakfast is lovely. I get tea and toast and then a bowl of fresh fruit and yogurt."

"And lunch—lunch is the main dinner—yesterday I ordered the turkey dinner from the menu, it was nice but it was the sliced turkey you buy in the supermarket. Disgraceful."

"Sliced turkey from a deli? Like you used to buy?"

"Yes."

"I don't understand. What was the problem?"

"It was just one slice."

"But you usually only eat one slice. I am sure they will give you more if you ask."

"I didn't want more. It was enough. Then yesterday, I asked for sausages and mash, and what did they come out with?"

"Sausages and mash?"

"Mash with three sausages! You should have seen it. I said take that back."

"Why? What was wrong with it?"

"Three sausages? It was too much, I couldn't eat all that."

"Mam just eat the amount you want and leave the rest."

"I ate it all. I don't like wasting food. Then last week they had pastries at five o'clock."

"You love pastries. What was wrong with them?"

"Nothing, they were gorgeous. But I felt sick after it because I can't eat anything in the evening."

"Then why did you eat them?"

"Because they were nice! Anyway, I need to go. We are having a party, I hear the music starting. Bye."

17

The exit of the massive and beautiful Milan Central train station smells like candy floss, whereas my hotel room smells stale and stuffy. The walls are scuffed and chipped and the air-con unit's only function is to make some noise. The cheap veneer furniture is dated and cracked, it hasn't held its age well. I open the window to the whiff of gas.

There's a bed, wardrobe and a deep purple sink and bidet, all in the one room. The sheets on the bed and towels are crisp and clean.

I go back down to the reception. "This may be a stupid question, but where is the toilet and shower in my room?"

"It is down the hall. You booked a room with a shared bathroom."

"I did? Can I upgrade to an ensuite?"

"Not unless you book a new room and pay full price." The man at reception smiles.

"No need." It's only one night and a clean bed is the most important thing. Back upstairs at the end of a dark wood panelled hallway with old pile carpet on the floor, I find the bathroom.

The door of the bathroom is grubby. The toilet is clean but missing a seat. And I will not be using the shower with the precariously hanging, yellowing perspex door. I should have guessed not to expect five-star luxury from the cheapest, central hotel.

I have a couple of hours to spare before I meet Sara for dinner. I can't wait to explore Milan. First up: the cathedral.

I have been to Milan previously on a wedding discovery trip and stayed in a very nice hotel decorated with rabbits and wonderful detail like a complimentary dual language story book left on my pillow. I got to see the opera rehearsal at La Scala and had a tour of the halls of the Braidense Library; a magical realm with a large globe dominating one end of the hall and a spectacular chandelier in the centre of its ornately plastered curved ceiling. An archivist showed us, with gloved hands, the original hand painted costume ideas for Puccini's operas. We dined in a restaurant overlooking some of the cathedral's one hundred and thirty-five roof spires, each topped with a statue of a biblical figure guarded by the same amount of gargoyles. A gold statue of Mary standing on the highest spire.

Huge, rectangular, white and cream is how I describe Milan– the city named after a legendary sow half covered with wool (Medio-lanum or half-wool).

On my previous visit, I hadn't time to go into the massive cathedral. I find it inspiring that people in the old days started things they knew would not be finished in their lifetime, such as this cathedral. Its construction started over six hundred years ago and was only finished about one hundred and fifty years ago. There were canals built specifically to bring the marble needed from the mountains to Milan.

The cathedral is the centre point of the city, the rest of the city was built round it. It's one of the largest cathedrals in the world and can hold forty-thousand people. With three-thousand-four-hundred statues inside, it's said to have more statues than any other building in the world. One of them definitely stands out from the crowd. It's of Saint Bartholomew, who was skinned alive. The marble statue is of him, standing post skinning, with his own skin draped around his shoulders like an elegant toga.

Each small individual panel of the three huge stain glass windows depicts a story from the Old Testament, New Testament and Book of Revelations.

Near the main entrance there is a sundial on the floor. A ray of sunlight from a hole in the opposite wall strikes the clock, on twenty-first June, the summer solstice, and on the winter solstice, twenty-first December. This was done in the 1700s. It doesn't impress me. I come from Ireland after all, where we have Newgrange–a stone chamber, older than the pyramids. It has a small window above its entrance where the sun beams through to the back of the chamber on the Winter Solstice.

Near the Duomo di Milano, there is a much smaller church with a very different interior design; San Bernadino alle Ossa. Its interior walls are decorated with countless human skulls and bones, reportedly the victims of the plague. Bones seemed to have been a trend with Catholic Church interior designers for a time, as I've seen churches like this in Puglia and Rome. I hope the trend, like shoulder pads and mullets in the 80s, never comes back into fashion. Neither the cathedral nor the boney church inspire me to fall on my knees and pray. Something simpler, like the temple at the retreat centre, is much more my type of spiritual connection space.

I meet up with Sara and we wander through an old district she used to live in.

"There is a coffee bar we used to go to. It has the best coffees. I want to see if it is still here," she says, turning the corner. "Yes! There it is."

A small, beaten up looking bar, near the corner of a square. On the opposite side of the square, women in long evening dresses and men in tuxedos are waiting for a wedding to begin at the church. Sara is very attractive. She is divorced, but still living in the same house as her husband as neither want to leave it. They divided it in two, but it's not really working out for her.

"I miss living in Italy. It is not like anywhere else I have lived in the world. In Italy, they don't care if they are living in debt; they have nice cars. Designer clothes. Great food. They stroll into work at ten and then have a three-hour lunch starting at twelve and take extensive time off in the summer and Christmas. That is living."

Sara orders a ristretto.

"What is that?" I ask.

"It means restricted in English. It is a smaller version of an espresso; uses less water."

"Is that possible? It sounds like you will be just chewing the coffee beans."

"Most coffee bars will only do double ristretto shots but this place does single. It's where we'd come before a fashion show–a quick shot of energy. Do you want to try one?"

"Oh no, I love the smell of coffee, but I don't really drink it."

"You better start. It's the only thing they serve here," she waves towards an extensive menu of coffees on the wall.

"I'm coffee ignorant. I only know espresso and cappuccinos. And I am aware it would be criminal to ask for a cappuccino at this time of day."

"Then how about a caffe macchiato? It is an espresso with a small amount of foamed milk. Macchiato means stained or spotted, so it literally means stained coffee. It is more intense than a cappuccino."

"Oh no. Cappuccinos are strong enough for me. Maybe a latte?"

"If you want a latte like you get in other countries, don't just ask for latte as you will only get milk. You need to ask for a latte macchiato." Without further ado, Sara orders me a latte macchiato. "I used to work as a barista. When you come to visit me, I will show you how to make the perfect cappuccino. Actually, you probably will never come to visit me so I will tell you how to do it. You need one third espresso, one third steamed milk and one third milk foam. The layering is important as the experience becomes more intense as you drink it. They are perfect for the morning, as they have enough espresso to wake you up and enough milk to keep you from being frazzled. The macchiato is better as a mid-day pick me up."

Two men in their late thirties and dressed for the wedding come in and stand at the bar next to us.

"Are you living here?" one asks Sara.

"No, just visiting. I lived here in the 80s."

"Are you in your fifties?" He asks, shocked.

"I've heard some great chat up lines in my life," Sara says to me, "But that tops them all."

"No, you look great." He tries to correct himself.

"I don't need your approval," Sara states before taking her coffee outside. The two guys down their espressos and jog back over to the church just as the groom arrives in a Ferrari.

The groom is young, very young. In his mid-twenties at most.

He pulls up at the church, gets out and walks around to the passenger side of the car and opens the door.

"Wow, this is a new way for a bride to arrive," I say, sipping my very enjoyable latte macchiato while watching the antics of the wedding. A woman's legs in high heels swing out of the car, her green silk evening dress falls to the side of the above knee slit. Taking her hand, the young groom bows and kisses her hand as the crowd of guests clap and cheer. With her hand still in his, she rises out of the car. But it is not his bride. It's his glamorous mother.

Two nonnas lean their elbows on their balconies watching the spectacle, a regular occurrence for them. They are the ones to go to if you want to know who was wearing what at all the weddings, so you can outdo everyone else at your own son's wedding.

The mother lines up with her son at the entrance, her hat perfectly angled, his suit perfectly pressed, posing for well-rehearsed photos. The guests file in before the music starts and the mother makes her grand entrance with her son linked at her side, before the bride arrives.

As everyone is already in the church, there is less of a fuss about the bride's arrival. The driver helps her out of the car, but not out of performance, like the mother of the groom. It's pure need so that she can get out with the big skirt and heels. She looks about twenty-two—that's with makeup.

We don't wait around. We already know the bride's fate is going to be competing with her mother-in-law for the groom's attention, and him running to his mother every time they have an argument. Perhaps they're all going to live in the same house, as that's still common in Italy. Parents in Italy, after all, are legally responsible for supporting their children until they are financially independent, which could be into their thirties or forties.

"I finished my modelling career when I got pregnant. I had spent years staying at home, taking care of our three sons. I never went out." Sara shares her life with me over dinner in a little restaurant she knows along one canal. The area is buzzing. It seems to be a popular spot for restaurants and nightlife. "I lost touch with so many friends, while my husband went to launches and parties and travelled with his job. I once seriously considered becoming a hooker so I could just get out in the evenings."

We both ordered the ravioli with sage butter and parmesan, a dish so melt-in-your-mouth delicious I find it hard to concentrate on what Sara is saying.

"The last straw with my husband was when I came home from work and I asked my husband and my three teenage sons if they'd eaten or if the dinner I had left prepared that morning was cooking. All they had to do was switch on the oven."

Sara takes a bite, but unlike me, she can still find words. I'm happy to just savour every mouthful of the buttery sage and pine nut combo, enhanced by sips of a crisp, delicate white wine, and listen.

"And they looked at me as if I had told them I had cooked the cat. 'Dinner?' they said, as if they had never heard the word before. At that moment, I snapped. I realised they were following in their father's footsteps, doing nothing all day on the weekends other than playing sports or watching sports and waiting for me to feed them. They did the same with laundry piles of washing and ironing, never done. Waiting and presuming I would do it."

We talk about the topic I seem to end up talking about with all women I meet of a similar age to me: peri-menopause. Sara switches back to the subject of her husband.

"My husband took early retirement when I started working as an estate agent so he could play golf all day. He said he needed a break like I had had staying at home and not working! The difference was my 'break' from work involved fifteen years of looking after our three boys when they were babies and toddlers and little kids. Not like his break when the same boys are practically grown men.

"So the day they all looked at me with their stomachs grumbling, waiting for me to cook after working all day, I went in and packed a bag and left. I texted my husband and told him I wanted a divorce. Like Katya, I love my husband, but I don't like him. I need to look after myself to survive and age with dignity."

We also talk about the weddings we had. She had two weddings.

"I was briefly married to a baby seal."

"A baby seal?"

"A navy seal." She exclaims laughing, before describing her big fancy wedding to husband number two which featured in fashion magazines.

My wedding with Ronan was very different.

18

W e didn't want a big wedding. In fact, my plan was to elope to Saint Lucia, get married on a beach, come back and have a party. But being pregnant after having a miscarriage, I decided it was best not to fly. We'd wait until after the baby was born and then go to Saint Lucia. But my Catholic parents wanted me to be married before having the baby and I gave in, but there was no way we were having it in a Catholic church.

We kept the wedding in Ireland as simple as possible. I booked a community hall near where my sister lived for sixty pounds. It had a bar, a stage for a band, and tables and chairs. All it needed was decoration. It was the 90s and balloon decor was the trend as bottled helium had arrived in Ireland. I don't think I saw a helium balloon in Ireland before the early 90s. We just had the variety pack of blow-up balloons which included the long ones, no one with normal lungs could get started. So, I blagged a deal with a decorator to provide string lights, a balloon arch at the entrance, and a helium balloon bouquet on each table. I can't remember the colours I ordered.

'Sense and Sensibility' had hit the movies and some woman's magazine had a free pull out pattern for an empire line dress. That would do nicely. I had made the evening dress for my final year of school dance, with a pattern I made up myself with a similar look to it. I liked it, so I decided I'd make my wedding dress.

My mam and I went into a fabric shop in town and bought raw taffeta silk for the bodice, and French silk chiffon for the skirt. The contrast of textures made by the same worms amused me, but they were also gorgeous to the touch. The chiffon felt like how I imagined as a child how clouds would feel. I also found a simple pattern and check fabric for my two flower girls—my sister's daughter and Ronan's eleven-year-old niece whom I had yet to meet, as she lived in The Netherlands.

Getting my sister's petite 6-year-old's measurements was easy as she lived close by, but the other flower girl's measurements were not so easy. They use centimetres in The Netherlands and I was used to inches. Her mother gave me the measurements by phone and I politely asked for them two more times before giving up. The family were arriving the week before the wedding, so I decided to wait until she arrived before making her dress as there was something off with the measurements.

Well, I thought the measurements were wrong—until Hanna arrived and indeed the excessive measurements were not off. Hanna was already eight inches taller than I was and was excited to be wearing her first pair of wedge heals for the wedding. So one flower girl was up to my elbow and I was up to the elbow of the other. My bridesmaid, Denise, arrived home from back-packing around India a few days before the wedding with a shaved head, so that saved me money on hairdressing. Let's say I don't have the classic bride-with-her-bridesmaids photos.

We had a low-key hen's night at my house the week before the wedding. I can't really remember it other than my aunt asking to see my dress, which was still in several pieces not yet sewn together. I was a very laid back bride-to-be. "Give it to me" she said. She was a dressmaker and had it finished in time for the wedding. She included pearl buttons she had from her youth, kept aside for a special occasion.

Mam, being the crafty woman she is, did the flowers. She had done a flower arranging course, so she could do the flowers for my sister's wedding. And like some women look forward to the first dance with their father, a highlight marker I looked forward to for my wedding, since I was a girl, was to go to the flower market on Mary Street, the day before my wedding with Mam to buy my wedding flowers. I had gone there with her for the flowers for the wedding of my sister and many times after that, for the flowers for cousins and neighbours' weddings.

We needed to be there at dawn to get the freshest and best choices. To me, the Mary Street Market is the scent of Dublin. An old cobbled maze of stalls undercover, bursting with the sweet scent of sweet pea, roses and carnations mingling with the cold sea water air scent wafting from the fresh fish market running alongside it. We bought blue poppies for my crown, irises, daisies and grasses for my sheaf. And a couple of pounds of fresh cod on the way out.

Mam also made the wedding cake. A two-tier Dundee fruit cake covered in smooth sugar icing and decorated with a garland of wild flowers and grasses, wheat and barley. It was another thing I dreamed about for my wedding day since she had made my sister's wedding and learnt from a black and white book how to do the piped icing decoration and make the seventy-two delicate royal icing, pink roses needed using glycerine.

Glycerine was not available in Ireland at the time, so Mam had to wait until she heard a relative or neighbour was going to be travelling to the UK and get them to go to a bakers supplier to buy it and bring it back to Ireland along with the mini plaster columns needed to balance the tiers on top of each other. Eileen's wedding cake was three tiers of fruit cake, made months in advance so the alcohol matured the fruit to the richest taste. I still automatically make a petalled rose when any pliable material is left in front of me, just like Mam, Eileen and I did together on the run up to her wedding.

On the morning of my wedding, I went to the hairdresser, got my hair blow dried and a manicure. Because I was told that is what you have to do for your wedding. It was the first and last manicure I ever had. Why would anyone torture their cuticles regularly?

"Where's John?" I asked as the time to leave for the registry office got closer. "He was to be here an hour ago." John was our friend with a good camera and a keen amateur photographer who'd volunteered to photograph the wedding for free pints of beer all night.

With that, John turned up at the front door, holding a polaroid in his shaking hand of a newborn tiny baby in an incubator. His wife had gone into labour and given birth twelve weeks early. Talk about stealing the show.

"What should I do?" He asked, trembling.

"Get back to the hospital to your wife and baby," I said without hesitation.

"I'll leave my camera gear here. Maybe you could get someone to take the photos?"

"I'll take the photos," piped up my brother Tony, who never took a good photo in his life. This was before digital photography.

Thirty minutes later, when I was due to leave for the registry office, I had another question. "Where's Tony?"

"He's gone to the registry office to find a good spot for photos." With his new profession, Tony forgot his previous assignment as wedding car driver.

The only people left in the house were my dad, my bridesmaid and my elderly Aunt Rita, who was the only one left in the house with a car.

At the time, the only place you could get married at in Ireland, other than a church, was a government registry office. These were often just a room in a health centre where it was possible to have the public dentist in the next room, and your nuptials could be done to the background sounds of someone having a tooth extracted. Luckily, we had booked the registry office on Molesworth Street, a Victorian building in the centre of town.

It was a small room, only big enough room for direct family. That's what we wanted.

I was forty minutes late, as my aunt didn't believe in driving above third gear, and we got stuck on a roundabout for several circuits as she was afraid of roundabouts, and then got stuck in rush hour traffic. My dad and I sat in the back trying to avoid being seen in her rear-view mirror so she wouldn't see how much we were laughing.

I wanted the tradition of my dad walking me to my beloved, waiting for me at the top of the aisle. The last person I was expecting to see standing outside waiting for me was Ronan.

"Ronan what are you doing here? Get inside. You are not supposed to see me." He was ruining my romantic notions.

"Guess what? I have already been a witness at a wedding today. I arrived early and the couple before us hadn't got witnesses, so I stood in and—"

"Ronan get inside, I do not want to hear about someone else's wedding right now."

I took a deep breath and gave him a moment to get into position in the room, while I linked my dad's arm.

I hadn't thought of having music. And the first person I saw when I walked through the door of the small, crowded registry room was Mick. A random person from work, someone I never really had a proper conversation with, standing there along with our families. He wasn't even smiling. It completely knocked my focus off.

The registrar was disgusted that I was so late. He sped through the words. We didn't have time for readings or romantic words. At one point, he scowled at Tony and told him to get down when he climbed on furniture to get a shot, grappling with the long lens attached to John's camera. The only shots we have of the ceremony are very close-up shots of my face. We exchanged rings, I reminded Ronan he needed to kiss me, and we were done. I was already planning our renewal of vows for our tenth anniversary on the beach in the Caribbean.

After the registry office, we went back to the house where we were going to have a quiet puja in the garden by ourselves.

Ronan had been practicing Transcendental Meditation since the Beatles made it known when he was fifteen. I had learnt the technique the year previous. And while we were not Hindu, we thought a puja style blessing in a quiet corner of the garden with just the two of us would make the wedding day special.

My TM teacher obliged by doing the honours. He had set up a table with a white tablecloth. A framed photo of a long-haired, bearded Indian chap called Guru Dev in saffron orange, stood in the middle of scattered flowers and burning incense.

As it was a beautiful sunny July day, everyone from the ceremony came back to the house and piled into the garden. Soon they were all standing around with their shoes off. As the TM teacher chanted the ceremony, I glanced at my dad. He was holding back tears. I found that touching. Years later, I was told he was crying because he thought I had joined some cult.

By the time Ronan and I drove to the community hall and made our grand entrance for the party, the caterer had arrived supplying the paper tablecloths and napkins and the bar was open. But the decorator had not turned up. No one knew there was to be a decorator, so no one was the point of contact. Luckily, the DJ arrived and set up lights, so at least we didn't have to have the glaring tube lights. We had an Irish céilí band called Anam. They had never played at a wedding before. Everyone had fun, the food was great, and we forgot to cut the wedding cake.

We left at the end of the night and went to stay at a local hotel, the same one my sister stayed at on her wedding night and the same one my brother stayed at on his wedding night. One side of the bed was held up by a brick and Ronan's drunk brother and equally drunk girlfriend gate crashed our honeymoon suite with curried chips. They only left when I started to cry out of frustration. I was five months pregnant after all, and a couple of drunks surrounded by the stink of curried chips in our room was not how I had imagined my wedding night.

Our afterparty BBQ the following day was cancelled as I had a bit of scare and thought I was miscarrying. So I spent the day after our wedding in hospital, with the nurses telling me I might need to stay in hospital for the rest of my pregnancy. After about five hours, I was given the all clear and let go home. Again I self soothed, dreaming about how our renewal of vows would be in ten years' time, on a beach with this little one who was clinging to life inside of me, playing in the sand.

We hired a boat to cruise down on the River Shannon for our honeymoon. We picked up the boat in Athlone and Ronan convinced me the first evening to climb into the rowboat attached to the motorboat and go for a row. He played rebel songs on the tin whistle while I knitted booties.

There was not enough room for Ronan and my pregnant belly on the cabin bed, so he slept on the floor of the galley.

The boat had just been repaired, and we discovered the following day they had put the bilge pump on backwards, as the boat began to pump in water in the middle of Lough Ree, which is a large lake in the centre of Ireland...with notoriously choppy waters. As the boat's hull filled with water, Ronan took out the emergency flag and waved it in desperation, but distant passersby thought we were Norwegian and just waved back. "We should have gone to fugging Saint Lucia," is all I remember shouting, while Ronan bucketed out water as I steered the boat to a marina in time for it to be rescued and the boat company gave us a replacement boat.

We came back from honeymoon and remembered we had not cut our wedding cake. It had been stored on a top shelf of the kitchen. We took it down and noticed the grasses and barley decoration had become the eco system for lots of tiny bugs. At least something got to enjoy it.

Four years later, I thought how it would have helped our wedding to be memorable in better ways had we had someone to suggest hiring music for the ceremony and do some readings, to suggest hiring a photographer rather than a friend with a good camera, to ensure I had a car to get to the registry office and keep a check on time. To ensure the decorator arrived, and remind us to cut the cake.

And that was one of the reasons why I started a wedding planning business. The business that brought us to Italy. We never did go to Saint Lucia to renew our vows, and I am okay with that. Some dreams burn out and get replaced by new ones. Moving to Italy became our new dream.

19

That night, the shudder of the badly fitted hotel door seeps into my dreams, showing up as two men trying to get in and I'm trying to get help. Waking from the dream, I can't get back to sleep—instead I lie thinking about the two retreats I had just been on. They were interesting and enjoyable, but running ghost busting training workshops or guru retreats with demonic dancing is not something I want to do. I need to fine tune what I can offer.

When I get home, my contract of employment from Lucia is in the mailbox, along with a note from the post office saying that a delivery was unsuccessful and will need to be collected. We are waiting on a replacement part for our strimmer and as the front garden brambles are now sneaking through the fence and snagging passersby; the need is becoming urgent, so I go to the post office, queue for half an hour and hand over the note.

After the woman behind the counter, who we affectionately know as SauerKraut, tells me to come back tomorrow as my package is still in the postal worker's van, I take my 'contract of employment' to the clinic so I can get my Tessera Sanitaria (TS) card and make the hospital appointment I need. But the clinic is closed.

The sign on the door says it's open three days a week for TS renewals and applications. Monday 2.15PM to 4PM, Wednesday 3–5PM and Friday 11 to 1PM.

By the time I am in the car, brain fog has kicked in and I can't remember any of the days the sign said it was open, never mind the times. I should have taken a photo.

After a wonderful night's sleep in my own bed and several cups of strong Irish tea, I feel ready to face SauerKraut again. I queue again and hand in the note to the same woman. She checks the number on the notice against her list.

"Yes, it is here. But I cannot give it to you until tomorrow."

"Why?" I am quite pleased with myself for understanding what she has said, but I am miffed by her logic.

"I am sorry," she says, with a glimmer of emotion in her eyes, like she is sympathising for the loss of a favourite pet. "But it is not available for collection until tomorrow. "

"But it is here?" My basic Italian is making me sound like a robot.

"Yes, but you cannot have it until tomorrow."

"Why?"

"Because it says so on my computer."

The woman behind me in the queue wearing a turban and dramatic square framed, Audrey Hepburn style sunglasses says in English, "It does not make sense, but this is the post office in Italy, nothing makes sense."

The following day the strimmer part arrives, so the package waiting the post office is now a mystery.

I persevere and return to the post office for the third time, loins girded.

I again hand in the note. SauerKraut smiles a bitter smile that makes her nose scrunch and her lips tight and small. She gets me the registered envelope and I open it in front of her. It's a water bill we have missed that needs to be paid.

"While I am here, I will pay this." I try to say in my best effort of Italian except I can't remember the word for 'while' so I just say; "I am here. I will pay this." I am talking like a robot again.

SauerKraut looks at me blankly. As if she doesn't understand Robot.

"I can pay this bill here, right?" I know for a fact that bills can be paid at the post office; the are smiling people on poster are doing it, they make paying your utility bills at the post office look like a fun day out for all the family. But by the look on Sauerkraut's face, it seems news to her.

"Emm." She hesitates. It's like she needs to go and change her head to the one that deals with bill paying and it might take a while for her to do it. "This window is for parcels. You need to join the line for bills." I look around at the line she is pointing to snaking out the door. She seems pleased about it, I can tell because she is doing that thing with her mouth again to try to make it smile but failing.

"Never mind," I sigh. "I'll pay it at the supermarket."

The supermarket is closed for a three-hour lunch. I stop by the clinic, but I've got the open days and times wrong and it's closed. At this rate, I should get my health card by the time I'm seventy.

At least I got one thing done today: I collected the bill. Rosie the Bill Collector. Sounds a bit like a mafioso hit woman. Tomorrow I will make another effort to pay the bill and become Rosie the Bill Payer. That has much less of a sexy ring to it.

But having been away, something else is on my priority to do list for tomorrow. I need to clean the house...of ghosts.

————

I'm not rushing into doing it. Ronan is dying to know what I will find, but while I was cynical at first, I want to give the house energy the respect it deserves. If I am going to bust ghosts, I am going to bust them, with respect.

With my wiggle rod out and my lapis lazuli pendant, I start at the front door and follow the flow of energy through the house. The rod weaves from side to side beautifully without even a hint of a metaphysical disturbance or me being sucked into any energy vortexes.

Upstairs, all I find are little pockets of emotion here and there, which I gently clear; standing and acknowledging it, the way Rex taught us to do. To my relief, and Ronan's disappointment, our house is not riddled with ghosts like Mavis's farm. I check the furniture and paintings the previous owners left behind. No bad energy. My wiggle rod is as limp as a month old stick of celery.

Back downstairs, the last room I check is the entrance lounge, which was the kitchen originally. Beside the big, old, open fireplace, the rod spins like a windmill caught in a cyclone. A large blob of sadness and grief sits in the spot where a fireside chair would have been. There is more sadness where the kitchen table was—where the family would have gathered and listened to the news reports during the Second World War, from the Art Nouveau radio cabinet we found in the attic.

I do not find ice cold patches of fear like I did on the staircase of the mountain partisan house, so perhaps the family who previously lived here were in their residence in Rome on the twentieth of May 1944 when allied forces dropped bombs on the town aimed at the railway line to stop the German retreat from Casino, killing forty-four civilians and destroying parts of the town.

I still have yet to discover the detailed history of our house, but I guess it was one of the few left standing on the road after the attack, since the houses around us are not built of old stone. The keystone above our front door reads '1923' and from some of the items I found in the house, I am guessing at least one of the previous family members was involved in the air factory in town as an engineer. The factory was initially established during World War I, and produced aircraft and aviation equipment for the Italian military.

In the 1920s and 1930s, it became a major center of aviation research and development in Italy. The factory's engineers and technicians developed new types of engines, propellers, and other equipment, and they also conducted extensive research on aerodynamics and other aspects of flight making significant contributions to the development of aviation during the early twentieth century, and I've been told their work helped pave the way for many of the technological advances in the world of aviation.

However, the factory was heavily damaged during World War II, and eventually closed in the 1960s.

With the help of my pendant, I relieve the room and fireplace of its sadness and set up a shield against the radial from the ley line deep in the earth below that Ralf identified and I have found too. Thankfully, my wiggle rod shows no signs our garden was the burial ground of any Romans or Celts—though I'm still keeping an eye on a suspiciously lumpy patch near the outhouses at the end of the garden.

Within days, Ronan feels his energy returning. Were we just recovering from renovation burnout or were the balls of stagnant sadness in the entrance lounge draining our energy every time we passed through it? Co-incidence or not, I am just glad that we might now be able to tackle the jobs that need to be done. I've done my job clearing the stagnant energy clutter. It's now Ronan's job to clear the garage clutter.

20

I call by Lucia's the following day with my wiggle rod ready to go. Just as I arrive, Lucia texts to say she got delayed and will be with me in half an hour and please wait. It's not a problem. I sit on the low wall of the arched entrance, spinning my rod, not thinking of anything in particular.

Lucia's neighbour, Signora Greco, comes around to the door looking for Lucia. We have never met, but Lucia has pointed her out to me before, a short stocky woman that waves from side to side as she walks like her legs are welded in place at her hips. "I am glad to meet you. Lucia has told me about you." She says slowly in broken English. "Lucia told me you will, eh, clean her home," she hesitates and wraps her arms tightly around herself, looking at Lucia's place uneasily. "Will you come and do mine? I need help." A deep crease borrows into her brow, and her lips tremble as though she's holding back words.

"I can try. I am only learning. How big is your house?" I ask in my broken Italian. I need to tell Lucia to not be spreading the word about my ghost busting. It's difficult enough to be accepted in a new town without the addition of being considered a weirdo. It's not like ghost busting was a career move decision or something on my bucket list. But everything happens for a reason, and maybe the reason for me doing the accidental ghost busting workshop was to ease Signora Greco's nerves.

"Not big. Two bedrooms, a sitting room, kitchen and bathroom. Seventeenth century. I'm selling it but no one will buy it. Because–" She hesitates, "Because of the way it is."

"If you like, I can have a look for you now," I say, holding back the urge to reach out with a comforting hand to ease her inner struggle.

"Now? Great!" Her eyes suddenly wide and distress free.

I text Lucia back—someone should know where I am, in case I get sucked into an energy vortex. Going to Signora Greco's house to try out my ghost busting skills there.

We take a shortcut to her house by walking across a field strewn with olive trees, and she manages the little dips and hills surprisingly well with her stiff gait. I, on the other hand, am struggling to keep up, without twisting an ankle on the lumpy roots or losing an eye to a low branch. The lake in the distance twinkles, reflecting an inviting shade of green. Signora Greco is talking too fast for me to understand her Italian. But in the few words I'm able to interpret, I gather she thinks I will see things Italians won't. What the hell has Lucia said about me?

"I don't actually see things, to be clear." I piece this sentence together in Italian without effort, surprising myself.

"Sì, sì," she says, avoiding a root hole.

Like a lot of houses for sale in Italy, there is no obvious for sale sign outside. Just a small Vendesi sign that no one passing could read from a bicycle, let alone a car going at a slow speed. Houses for sale tend to be spread between different agents, so that might explain the lack of branded for sale signs in a lot of Italy. Maybe there is a gap in the market for sign printers. That might be easier than ghost busting.

There is definitely a gap in the Italian market for house stagers for houses for sale. One quick look online will show photos of Italian houses and apartments crowded with furniture or their clothes drying in the living room beside their bicycle. When I first step foot in her house, it's clear Signora Greco could definitely do with advice on this. The only thing she doesn't have for the typical photo is the bicycle.

After a quick tour, she hesitantly opens the door to the bathroom. It's the size of a hamster's bathroom, clad in ugly, garish orange tiles which are not unlike the Austin power style we banished from one of our bathrooms during renovation.

She can't go into this bathroom, she says. She is afraid. Of ghosts, orange tiles, or getting stuck in the corner, I'm unsure. I think Signora Greco expects too much from me, but I would be afraid too, if I had tiles like that on the wall.

I have been twirling the rod in my hand all the time since we met on Lucia's porch, like it is a fidget spinner.

"Can you give me ten minutes?" I ask in Italian, slowly but surely.

"Only ten minutes?" she asks, appearing in disbelief that I can clear such negative energy in such a small amount of time.

"It's a small house," I say with a smile. I don't know how to explain that I don't really know what the hell I am doing here and I am not even sure if I believe in it, so I definitely don't want an audience.

"I will wait outside," she says, probably expecting a phantasma to appear as soon as I wiggle my rod.

Starting at the front door, I follow the rod's movements to the kitchen and sitting room. There are a few small pockets of depression and grief to be cleared, but nothing major...until I get to the second bedroom.

This is not good.

There are disturbances all over the place in the bedroom—grief, sudden death, anger. A lot of anger. I do the clearing practice like I've been taught using my pendant and then test again. There's more to be done. Especially on the bed. What have I got myself into? The silence in the room is eerie and then I hear ... "Il bagno?"

Signora Greco standing in the doorway behind me makes me near leap out of my skin. "Il bagno in un minuto," I say, flustered. "Leave me to clean here first. Five minutes." I manage to say in broken Italian with my heart still pounding.

She hesitantly leaves.

My arms are too short to follow the flow of energy across the bed where the rod is pointing to. I slip off my shoes and step up on the bed, then dutifully follow the rod's direction.

Standing on the bed, wobbling on the squishy mattress, I see Signora Greco outside through the large window, talking on her phone by her car. She spots me, and we give each other a small wave. Hers is more of a slow hand lift. Within a few minutes, I have the response I want from my pendulum. It at last answers yes the disturbances have been cleared. I'm quite surprised at myself.

I'm straightening the quilt back on the bed when Signora Greco comes to the door. I hear a car pull up outside. The screech of a loose fan belt tells me it is Lucia. I keep telling her to get it fixed.

"Okay, I think I am all done here. I cleaned your problem," I say in English, forgetting myself.

Signora Greco's eyes narrow slightly, scanning the room as if searching for something while wringing her hands.

"Il bagno?" she asks cautiously.

"Okay. I'll check your bagno," I say, trying not to feel irritated by her lack of appreciation of the invisible act I have just performed for her.

I go into the bathroom and ask the question, "Is there a disturbance in this room?"

"No," my pendulum indicates. Thank goodness. It's just the orange tiles making her feel possessed.

"Your bathroom is fine," I call, happy to report good news. "All good."

"Permesso? Lucia calls the polite Italian arrival greeting from the front door asking permission to enter like they are vampires. However, the amount of garlic they eat proves they are not.

"Sì." Signora Greco shouts in return before talking really fast and loud at Lucia, while she follows our voices to the hallway outside the bathroom.

"She wants to know why you stood on her dead sister's bed and when will you clean the bathroom. Rosie, what are you doing here?" Lucia is looking like she is on the verge of laughing but also trying to gauge the seriousness of the situation.

"There is nothing in the bathroom to be cleaned. It could do with a good decluttering for sure," I say, looking at the hoard of shampoo bottles and creams filling the small shelf unit, "but it's not my place to say. And there was a lot of negative resistance in that bedroom. I was waiting outside your place and she said you told her about me and asked me to do her place. I can see why, that negative energy would stop anyone buying this place."

Signora Greco is still talking in high-speed Italian at Lucia while I am talking. The ability of Italians to listen to two people talking at them at once still fascinates me. Or maybe it is the ability of Italians to ignore that someone is speaking at them while they are talking to someone else is what I find fascinating.

Lucia turns to Signora Greco and says in Italian, "This is not Laura, this is Rosie. Rosie is Irish, not Albanian."

Then she turns back to me. "Rosie, she thinks you are here to clean her bathroom, because she cannot get into it because she had knee surgery. I had told her about Laura, the cleaning woman who is also coming to my house today."

"Oh god. Don't tell her what I was doing. She might freak out."

Lucia talks rapidly in Italian to Signora Greco. The woman looks relieved, and then laughs and gabbles at me in Italian while Lucia and I walk out the door and Signora Greco kisses us both and waves us goodbye as we pull away in Lucia's car with its screeching fan belt.

"She has been trying to sell that house for two years. I told her you were an interior designer, and you were measuring the walls with a new device. Her sister was a very grumpy, old person. She did not want to sell the house. She made life very difficult for Signora Greco."

When Ronan hears Signora Greco's house is sold two weeks later, he gets very excited. I am sure he doesn't believe my energy clearing helped, but while eating his porridge, he talks about printing ghost busting leaflets and a possible whole new career which sounds like it is based on exploiting people. I know he wouldn't do it if it was him, but supporting me doing it, if I believe in it, seems okay. He's just short of selling me off to a circus. Though part of me feels like I'm owed a small commission from the sale.

"I've had enough of ghost busting. It's not for me. I am retiring my wiggle rod." I say, much to Ronan's disappointment. "You're always welcome to learn to clean."

21

I call Mam while I'm unpacking my case from the retreats. She answers the video call and I immediately hear a background voice say, "Two fat ladies, eighty-eight."

Angela, Mam's friend who is sitting beside her, shouts back at the Bingo caller: "We're over here!"

Mam sniggers and says in a hushed voice, "I'll call you back. We are playing Bingo and I think I might win this round."

"Okay," I say, distracted by the sight of a smartly dressed man in a navy polo shirt and belted pants trying to communicate with Ronan over the gate. He's holding what looks like a square drink carton out to Ronan. Ronan spots me at the window and calls me to come down.

When I reach the front gate, I immediately spot a man with the word 'Polizia' embroidered on where a breast pocket would be. "Not again. What now?" Is what I want to say, but then I notice he's wearing see through plastic gloves. He is indeed holding out a carton, but it's not a drink. It's the small, mouldy carton of cream that had been left in the fridge when I was away and Ronan forgot about.

I make out what he is saying with a cheery smile on his face, "this can be recycled in the paper recycling." I take it from him with a look of dismay.

"Has he gone through our rubbish bag we left out?" Ronan asks me as the man moves on to our neighbour's house and starts going through their bin. "Is he going through everyone's bins to check if there is anything we could have recycled?"

"Apparently so," I say as we watch him. "He must be going through awful stuff. But he looks thrilled with his job, doesn't he?"

We watch him rifling through the next neighbour's bin. It clearly states on the garbage collection company's laminated leaflet explaining recycling, that cardboard and paper need to be clean and dry. 'Don't put soiled, dirty paper or card in the recycling'.

That carton was definitely dirty and soggy and not fit for recycling.

Recycling is the law in Italy (and Europe for that matter) so it's not only required—it's mandated.

Each community has different recycling requirements, and each town has specific guidelines for recycling. We have trash bins for plastics, paper and cardboard, compostable waste and general waste, with communal bins for glass and clothes nearby.

If you don't sort waste properly, the operator leaves a notice of non-conforming waste and invites you to correct the violation. If it happens a second time, the operator will inform the recycling office and the problem will be referred to the local authorities, leading to a possible fine of several thousand euros. Also, burning your waste is a violation of the law.

Italian authorities have always been creative with their rubbish disposal. In Rome there is a hill made entirely of fifty-three million old olive oil jugs-Monte Testaccio. The world's classiest rubbish dump.

However, in more recent times, they lost this classiness. Trash became a huge issue in Italy.

In 1960, Rome handed management of the city's trash disposal to four small private companies, including Cecchini & Co, owned by Manlio Cerroni. Cerroni eventually took over all four companies.

In 1984, the city of Rome decided to make the dumping site called Malagrotta, Rome's main garbage dump. Cerroni owned it.

Rome and Naples produce two thousand and seven hundred tonnes of non-recyclable trash every day. While garbage may seem unglamorous, one man's trash is another man's treasure. Cerroni soon owned a volleyball team, a local television station, and a villa in a leafy neighbourhood of Rome.

Other organised crime families saw trash as a lucrative business and began taking over waste management contracts, which involved illegal waste trafficking. One mafia family took charge of collecting and disposing of hazardous waste, mostly from Northern Italy and dumping it in caves, quarries, fields of Campagna and the sea. The operation grew and began to ship in waste from other European countries for a fraction of the cost of legit toxic waste disposal facilities.

With bribery and political corruption running amok, the garbage trade became more lucrative than the drug trade.

After sixty years of making a personal fortune on rubbish 86-year-old Manlio Cerroni faced trial on a string of pollution charges.

The European Commission found that one hundred trash disposal sites in the south of Italy were illegal, because they did not pre-treat waste with chemicals that reduce their volume and toxicity. It ruled that Malagrotta—Romes main landfill disposal site and Europes largest at the time—was the worst offender among the illegal sites. It was shut down in 2013.

Though garbage no longer arrives in Malagrotta, the site is still brimming with mountains of trash up to eighty meters high. The city of Rome plans to transform it into a park, with three hundred and forty thousand trees within thirty years.

Campagna has five thousand dump sites—most concentrated in what is called the Triangle of Death—an area just fifteen miles Northeast of Naples city. The National Health Institute reported that Campagnia's history of illegal waste dumping increased cancer, birth defects and lower life expectancy rates.

Thankfully, there is solution on the way out of this problem—a state-of-the-art waste processing facility and incinerator is being built and will open in 2026. It will process six hundred thousand tons of waste and convert it into energy to power Italy's towns and contribute to heating thirty thousand homes. It will also decrease the rubbish collection charges Rome citizens pay, which ironically, are the highest refuse collection taxes in the world.

Until then, Rome will continue to ship nine hundred tonnes of trash weekly to Amsterdam by train, where it is turned into clean energy.

After the rubbish policeman leaves, I call Mam back.

"Well, did you win at Bingo?"

"I did! I won an extra water bottle. You get to pick the prize and a second water bottle will be handy to have on the other side of the room."

In the shade, I can see her face clearer on my phone screen. "Your left eyelid is looking red. It looks like a sty starting?"

"Yeah, I noticed that yesterday, so I did what I always do, bless it with a wedding ring."

"You did what?"

"Bless it with a wedding ring. It's what you do when you have a sore eye," Mam says, as if I have lost my mind.

"Maybe ask the nurse for some ointment?"

"I will if the ring doesn't work, but it usually does. Never mind about that. Did you know you now have to fill out a load of forms in the bank to get coppers out?" At first, I think she means policemen, but of course she's talking about coins of low denomination.

"No. Why were you in the bank getting coppers?"

"Oh, it wasn't me. Angela sent her daughter in to get them for us because I'm teaching Angela how to play poker, and it's more fun when you're betting. So her daughter is bringing each of us in five euros worth of coppers when she comes in on Friday for Angela's birthday."

"Oh, that's nice. How's Angela's poker skills?"

"Not bad, but she gets too excited when she gets a good hand. She needs to work on her poker face."

"How old will Angela be on Friday?"

"Ninety," Mam says. "I've bought her a bottle of Baileys. We'll have our Baileys and whiskey and a game of poker to celebrate."

22

The Menopause Coach training is quite a long course. No one is credited with contributing or writing it, so it makes me suspicious that it is AI generated. The images are definitely AI generated. One image is of a woman with a stray third hand on her own shoulder, giving comfort and reassurance.

Other images range from women with grey hair and superhero style abs, down to a woman with a grey bun holding a therapy session for... a man? It's not a good image to use in a menopause course when rage hormones are soaring through my body.

When I was happily lost in London during a recent visit to Izzy and Luca, I happened to pass through Smithfield Market. It's striking Victorian arched roof, and ornamental facades made me want to know what the structure's purpose was. The vibrant hues of its painted columns give it an almost theatrical charm. But there is nothing charming about its history I found out from the tourist information board at one of its entrances.

Besides hangings and burnings, the wife sale became popular there in the early nineteenth century. 'Divorce was exceedingly difficult and men brought their unwanted wives, along with their normal goods, to the meat market to sell them.'

With my current midlife hormonal rage and lack of energy, I would definitely have been a contender for the meat market. Something needs to change in case I happen across a time portal and end up back in early nineteenth century London.

Having listened to knowledgeable female doctors who are doing great work educating women like me about HRT research and dispelling misinformation, I was shocked to learn doctors, even gynos, to date, got little or no training in western medical schools about menopause health. Their women's health training focused only on reproduction health.

Apparently, once done having babies, women don't have any health issues to contend with worth talking about, other than checking our boobs for breast cancer and our Pap test for cervical cancer. "It's bizarre that even though one hundred percent of women everywhere in the world who reach the age of fifty will go through peri-menopause and yet there has been no research done on hormone health and menopause to date," I rage about this to Izzy and my nieces, who are far from menopause age but I still feel the need to tell them, warn their future selves.

"GPs are resistant to prescribing HRT but give anti-depressants instead, because to date, doctors in the western world do not get any medical training about the effects of menopause; all women's medical health training is focused on reproduction. And doctors are so overworked, they don't have time to update themselves with current research."

I believe knowledge is power and at fifty and a bit, I know my own body and its needs. I realise I have to educate myself and tell my doctor exactly what I need, backed up by the research I have found.

Now that I have my Tessera Sanitaria, I go see Doctor Chicken about arranging a bone scan to check for osteoporosis and the specialist appointment I need regards my internal water blob that is the size of a small rabbit. I hate the word cyst. So I prefer to refer to it as my water baby or water blob. While there, I approach the other issue playing on my mind.

"I want to ask you about going on HRT."

"It is dangerous to take. It increases your chances of getting ovarian and breast cancer a lot."

I have heard HRT is not a 'thing' in Italy and I had a feeling this outdated belief was going to be his response. Based on the only research done twenty years ago that has since been discredited and incorrect, but the textbooks haven't caught up.

"I have done my research and want to go on HRT," I say to him.

"For what?"

"For ongoing health. If I was diabetic, I would take insulin. If I had a thyroid problem, I would take a replacement hormone to fix that. It's the same thing. HRT helps protect our heart health, brain and bones. I know you enjoy going to conferences. If one about menopause and HRT comes to Italy, go to it. You never know you could become a leading doctor in Italy about it."

He smiles. "Did you get the autograph?" He's referring to a movie Izzy has worked on with his favourite actor.

"I will try harder if you give me HRT." It sounds like a fair tradeoff.

"I cannot give you HRT. I will need to refer you to a gynaecologist who will do a blood test and assess your need for it."

"Why do they need to do a blood test?"

"To see if you are in peri-menopause."

"I am fifty-two. Of course I am in perimenopause. It would be very unusual for a woman my age not to be. I am having lots of symptoms—aching joints, brain fog, night sweats, anger. I could go on."

Dr Chicken hands me the prescription for the bone scan and a gyno appointment.

I now need to take this to the pharmacy where there is a CUP desk and they will make the appointment with the gynaecologist, who will do the unnecessary blood test.

"You'd be better off going back to Ireland and talking to your doctor there," an expat friend advises when hearing of my dilemma. "I was on HRT but then the Italian pharma company stopped producing it and there's none available now."

"Can't your doctor give you a prescription for another type?" I ask her.

"No. when I asked my gyno what I should do, she shrugged and said to buy some HRT online."

That does not sound safe.

"Even though every woman will definitely go through menopause—we still need to make doctor appointments and get blood tests and explain why we feel we need something that will stop the effect of our plummeting hormones from affecting our heart health, stop dementia, stop our bones getting brittle and all the other wonderful things our hormones do for us, it's bloody ridiculous." My rage is rising again.

I want to be in the best health and shape I can be during my second spring. I am no longer interested in being thin, I just want strong bones. Although being round in figure is not practical in Italy—you need to be able to plaster yourself against the walls on narrow streets when cars pass. And with all the wonky pavements, ancient steps and cobbled roads, you need to be agile and have strong bones so you don't break when you fall over.

I don't bother making the appointment with the Italian gynaecologist, instead I contact a female doctor I know in Ireland, she talks me through HRT and how to use it and prescribes me six months worth of it without the need of a blood test.

I take the prescription she gives me to my local pharmacy in Italy. I feel like I am doing something edgy—like when Ronan and I tried to get condoms in Ireland when we were first going out together and they were still a controversial thing to sell. It was illegal for shops in Ireland to sell condoms in the early 1990s because of the catholic influence. The fact the IRA often used condoms to make bombs, perhaps had an influence on the decision too.

The Italian pharmacist looks alarmed at my HRT prescription. "No, we cannot get this for you. We could perhaps give you an alternative, but it would be very dangerous," he says grimly.

I decide to skip the alternative that sounds as dangerous as the explosive Irish condoms in the 90s.

152 | ROSIE MELEADY

Instead, I get a friend to collect the prescription in Ireland to post it to me in Italy, and I hope for the best that the contraband makes it through customs.

I work my way through the menopause coaching course. It has good information at the start but by the time it gets to the coaching stage, it focuses on how women are dealing with empty nest syndrome, aging parents, possibly divorce, grief, pressures at work, loss of libido-which can happen all around the age of menopause.

The coaching sessions are about how to deal with this stuff by taking up yoga, breathing and talking to their partner. Their partner—who can get a pill to keep him hard while his wife's vagina lining is disintegrating, causing perhaps a litany of symptoms that makes sex the furthest thing from her mind. But according to this menopause coaching course, some breathing, journaling and yoga will get you through it. Thankfully, I have no issue with my vagina lining and intend to stop it possibly happening with the help of HRT if I can get my hands on it.

I write an email to the course organisers in a rage:

Menopause has nothing to do with these issues, yes there are life issues we have to deal with—but we have been dealing with stuff like this all our adult lives because that is what women do. We deal with all the shit and get on with life. By the time we hit menopause, women have been through a lot. We know how to deal with stuff and we don't give a shit about what other people think about us anymore. And not all women turn into fragile messes when their kids grow up and become independent.

Some of them breathe a huge sense of relief and book a trip to Peru. So let's keep the blame of why we women feel like we are losing our minds separate from the issues that surround us, and recognise menopause is only to do with hormone levels and the effects these hormones have on our bodies. We are feeling crap and have low energy because our hormones are plummeting—nothing else.

I don't finish the course. Instead, I get my money back and use the refund to book on to a women's empowerment retreat in Sicily.

23

"I've got tickets for a music festival in Bologna. Will you come with me?" Shelly asks.

The fire-flies are nearly gone and the cicadas have taken over for the summer. Spooky and Juno chase lizards together while the elders of our furry clan members, Paddy and Looney, watch them amused from their favourite sun spot on the terrace.

The magnolias on the giant trees out the front are blooming and people are stopping and gazing, which makes me very conscious of the brambles taking over the front garden. We keep them strimmed back but with every cut they seem to bounce back more aggressively. There is only one way to rid the garden of them, and that is pulling them up by the sprawling roots. It's a task I vow to do as soon as my HRT arrives, which I am still waiting on, but the Italian post is notoriously slow.

I phone Mam while waiting for Shelly to call by to discuss our plans for our night at a music concert in Bologna.

"Hi Mam. How are you?"

"You have wine on your mouth."

"Mam it's 10.30am, I am not drinking wine. I ate a choc-ice though."

"Then it's chocolate. Wipe your face."

She says this while I already am rubbing my lips with a tissue.

"You'll never lose your belly eating choc ices. You are very red in the face. Were you out in the sun?"

"No, that's just my face now. I'm perimenopausal. I don't go out in the sun."

"You'd want to be careful of that sun. It's very hot."

"Yes, it's thirty-seven degrees today."

"What? That's too hot, that's ridiculous."

"Well, it's the weather. That's just the way it is."

"Now Rosie, it's too much for too long. That's just ridiculous."

"It's not my fault. I don't control the weather thermostat."

She ignores me.

"You'll get burnt. Look at your face."

"Mam, I don't go out in the sun."

She still ignores me.

"Oh, your brother is ringing. I've got to go."

And she hangs up.

I have never been much of a music concert fan. I went to see Prince in the 80s; a dot on a big stage in an enormous field in Cork, lost my friends, walked miles to get back to where we were staying and ended up hitching a lift with a farmer who had a sheep in the back of his car. U2 was a similar experience: massive venue, massive crowds, more dots on the stage. Walked miles to public transport and waited hours to get home.

My Bob Dylan concert experience was worse; sat in a muddy field to see him with his hood up on stage for max half an hour. It took us days to get home from that one. We had tents.

And as for Lord of the Dance; we got free tickets and were so far away from the stage and high up, my fear of heights kicked in. We left before the second dance was finished.

Shelly is a big fan of concerts—she was the one who bought the Tom Jones tickets during the Perugia Jazz Festival and then couldn't go. I went and was pleasantly surprised.

I was going through my 'say yes to new experiences' phase when she asked me to go to the music festival with her in Bologna. July seemed a million days away when I agreed. I had never been to Bologna, so it seemed a good opportunity to visit.

The main band playing at the concert is Take That.

I was about twenty when the boy band phenomena started to grip the minds and hearts of teenage girls. So I was never a fan of boy bands, although I would find myself singing along to one of their songs on the radio and then cursing it when it was still stuck in my head three days later.

As the date got closer, a slow dread began to build of the huge crowds, the high stands of uncomfortable plastic seats, the screaming teenagers, everyone merry on too much alcohol. And the long walk out of the stadium and effort of trying to get home.

But Shelly was excited about it, and I wasn't going to desert her.

We take the high-speed train from Florence to Bologna, which only takes forty minutes. Check in to our reasonably priced accommodation—Campus Bologna, a student accommodation at the university, and then catch a bus into the centre. It doesn't take us long to get lost, walking around two blocks back to our starting point before finding the central square, where a massive screen is set up at one end. A film festival is on. People are having drinks before the film for tonight's outdoor show.

We find a shaded osteria down a side street and order what everyone has to have on their first visit to Bologna; pasta with ragu sauce. Or what anyone not from Bologna calls it: Spaghetti Bolognese. It was everything and more than what I expected. The velvety texture of the thick sauce clinging to the pasta has subtle sweetness while the freshly grated Parmigiano adds a nutty, salty richness. The tastes linger on my palate for most of the taxi ride to the concert venue.

First shock arriving at the concert: there is a mountain of water bottles of every description at the entrance, as security guards search bags and take people's drinks and water bottles.

It's hot and Shelly and I have just bought a fresh bottle of water each at an exorbitant price from an official concert stall, and we are not going in without it. I stick my bottle of water in the waistband of my trousers under my loose top and Shelly braces hers in her armpit under her top and we each hand in our other near empty bottles.

Second shock: The size of the concert venue. "The last time I went to see this band was in a massive stadium in the UK with thirty thousand people and a massive stage production," Shelly says. This was nothing like that. This is the size of Signora Greco's bathroom in comparison. There is no stadium like I expected. It's more of a hockey field and there are no chairs. There is no major stage set up.

Third shock: the fans are not teenagers. Well, they were when I was twenty, but not now. Those teens, which are the majority of the crowd, are now in their forties. Some have their kids with them.

Fourth shock: not many people are drinking. There are drink stands around the field perimeter selling alcohol and water, at even higher prices than outside, but there are no queues or people drinking alcohol. This would not be the case in Ireland or the UK. The need to get full of alcohol to enjoy a concert is not a need in Italy.

Fifth shock: the main sponsor is a brand of Italian washing powder. I find this oddly offensive.

We find a spot to sit near the Red Cross, where other groups of women are also sitting. A few of us start pulling some yoga moves between slurps of our illegally smuggled-in water. There are perhaps one and a half thousand people in the hockey field at most. I'm enjoying sitting on the grass with no mud in thirty-one degrees evening light, sipping my stash.

I think I hear Take That revving their Harley Davisons to make an entrance. But it turns out to be a heavy metal band playing on a stage in another field in the distance. Take That's entrance is much more muted.

Thirty-four years after getting together and going through split ups and attempted solo careers, three of the lads are back together and this is their sixtieth show on their tour.

It is like an expat karaoke session on a cruise ship, but they seem to be enjoying it, getting through it but still giving the crowd a good show. I sing and dance and wave my arms in the air in the warm night under the orange sickle moon.

As they reach the last lines of their last song—Never forget where you're coming from, Never pretend that it's all real, Someday soon this will all be someone else's dream—Shelly and I leave the field along with the rest wanting to get home at a reasonable hour.

We catch the bus and are back in our student accommodation, brushing our teeth before bed within thirty minutes of Gary Barlow singing his last note. The whole experience was very civilised. Nothing like my previous experiences of concerts.

The next morning, with clear, well rested heads, we meet at eight for breakfast in the uni canteen. The scrambled egg, yogurts, fruit and croissants, makes it one of the best non hotel breakfasts I have had in Italy. Both of us have work to get back to, so we plan to catch the early train and be home by lunchtime.

Mam calls me, just as we are boarding the train; "We're having an Indian culture day today and a beautiful woman dressed in the most gorgeous sari came in to me this morning and said' I'll be dressing you today for the celebrations'. She offered to do my makeup too, but I'm doing my own. Are my eyebrows okay? I haven't used an eyebrow pencil in about twenty years."

I can see Mam's excited by the idea of the party. She always loved dressing up and going out to dances and parties with my Dad.

There is a huge shortage of care workers in Ireland, so a lot of care workers for nursing homes are now recruited from India and African countries. Without these people, the care of the elderly in Ireland would suffer greatly. There is a minority in Ireland who scare monger about immigrants coming to Ireland 'and taking our jobs', but they are doing jobs that few Irish people want to do anymore. Sometimes I have to remind people I am an immigrant in Italy from Ireland but because I am white and of western nationality, I get to be called an ex-pat.

Mam had no opportunity to interact with other nationalities throughout her life in Ireland. Ireland was not a diverse country. Interacting with the lovely care workers has opened her eyes to other cultures.

"You look fantastic Mam. And I can't wait to see you in your sari. I've always wanted to try one on. Send me a photo later when you have it on!"

When I get the photo of her wearing her sari, looking so beautiful and happy and standing taller than she has in years looking confident in her beauty, it fills my heart with love and joy.

"We had Indian food and played party games from India and some of the staff did traditional Brolly Wood dancing. The food was so delicious, you should try it sometime."

"Mam, Indian food was Jamsie's speciality but you would never touch it. He had to make you and Dad a separate dinner of spuds and chicken whenever he was having us over for Indian food."

"Well then, I am sure he is very happy looking down on me today."

"He definitely is Mam."

I love that my mother is having opportunities to discover new things and grow as a person in her later years.

Lucia calls by to show me her new olive oil labels and to ask how the concert was.

"It was a very painless and surprisingly more enjoyable than I expected. My only niggle was the washing powder sponsor. I thought that was very unprogressive considering the audience was ninety-five percent female forty somethings."

"Really? I am surprised too. What was the name of the brand?"

"Lavoro Più."

"Rosie, you are confusing words. It was not washing powder. Lavaro means 'I am washing'. Lavoro means 'I am working.' Lavoro Più is the name of a recruitment agent for creative people."

Now the ad makes more sense. The women were celebrating together because their friend got the job she wanted, not because she got the strain out of her favourite blouse.

24

The women's retreat near Taormina Sicily is one of the most expensive I have booked and that's with a shared room. The retreat leader looks radiant in her photo. "Women who are at a crossroads of change, come to revive a forgotten part of themselves."

That's me. This is what I need, it is just not what my bank account needs. It's all in the name of research, though.

I miss the main transfer since my delayed short flight had a knock on effect, so while waiting for the car and driver to return, I take a walk through the plaza of checkerboard pale and dark grey slabs in Taormina. I am surrounded by a different beauty of Italy. Tree blobs covered in blossom of startling pinks against a backdrop of low rugged mini mountains dotted with scrub.

Pale peach tones accentuate the angles of the chalk white church looking like an elaborate wedding cake with the spire as the topper. A woman in a red, sun dress caught in the breeze perfectly photo bombs the setting. A rooftop oozes with over-flowing greenery, making my mouth water at the idea of what the tropical terrace garden must look like, a respite from all the beauty an eye can hold for only so long. The bell bongs a light bong from the campanile.

I give Mam a call while I am waiting as I intend to go phone free for the week of the retreat.

"Hi Mam, just giving you a quick call before the retreat starts and I switch off my phone."

"Are you Buddhist?"

"Are you asking me this because I am going on retreats, or because I said I would not deal with the mouse traps Tony set in the house before I left after my last visit?"

"I saw a documentary about Buddhists, believing they come back as different things. And they had a temple, and the rats were running across their feet and all over the place because they thought they were their ancestors."

"It is because of the mouse traps, then."

"I'm telling you now, I am not going to come back as a rat to run around your feet at a temple... Someone is after giving me a present of savvy non blah."

"What's that?"

"A bottle of savvy non blah. It's wine. Do you want it?"

"Do you mean Sauvignon Blanc?"

"Whatever. Will I keep it for you to drink it when you come back?"

"When I come back as a rat?"

"Well whatever you choose to come back to Ireland as. A rat or Buddhist or whatever."

"No Mam, re-gift it to someone else. I don't drink alcohol much anymore."

"Why? What's wrong with you?"

"Nothing!"

"Are you pregnant?"

"No!"

———

The retreat farmhouse is up a narrow winding road where someone in a hired car would definitely scrape the sides against the dry stone walls on some of the tight angled bends.

My room is pretty and has two single beds. An ample and thoughtful goodie bag awaits me holding a lightweight beach towel, period pants, body oil, a beach kaftan, sunglasses, notebook, moisturiser, lip balm. Ear plugs and an eye mask. I'm impressed.

"There are spare bags for the wastepaper basket on the shelf. All toilet paper needs to be thrown in the bag in the wastepaper basket, not in the toilet. The bags can be deposited in the dumpster at the side of the building, I'll show you where." Zara, the PA of the woman running the retreat, says when showing me around. She does not seem to notice the alarm on my face. I have spent over two grand to come to a place where I am sharing a room with single beds and a bathroom with someone I don't know, where we have to put our used toilet paper in a communal bag? I suddenly wish I'd booked a single room even if it was five-hundred euros more.

I can hear a woman with a Scottish accent outside my window chatting to at least three other voices: "She said; Seriously? For my dry vagina, I need to go in and ask for Vagifem from the village pharmacist's son? It sounds like I am sticking Marmite up my hooter." There are howls of laughter. I'm laughing myself. "Then she said; Men get to ask for Viagra. That's a powerful name. It's not like he has to ask for Floppy-male." More howls of laughter. Then she adds, "I think she's Irish."

Are they talking about me? I need to get out there before they start discussing me, and it gets awkward.

I don't have time to unpack or check the mirror. I scramble out the door and swing around the corner before anyone else can say something, I interrupt without hesitation or greeting, "I have never talked about Marmite nor my hooter in my books... have I? I never remember what I have written until readers remind me. "

The conversation stops.

"Och, you must be the Irish lass!" says the Scot. Her strong cheekbones makes her twinkly eyes seem more sunken when she beams a wide smile. Her short auburn hair loosely bounces around her ears as she stands and outstretches her hand for a shake. "I saw on your profile you are a writer. I haven't read your books yet but now I am intrigued that you might talk about Marmite and your hooter and then forget about it."

The five women sitting closest to where I am standing burst out laughing.

"I was just talking about another Irish woman, an Irish comedian. I'd go see her again. Actually, that is what we should do for our reunion, go to one of her shows. Come join us."

It's soothing that she is already talking about having a reunion and discussing vaginas before we have been introduced.

"I'm Sue, this is my mate Alice. We've been friends forever, so if you hear us bickering, pay no heed. And this is, sorry, I can't remember your names—"

The other women introduce themselves. An eclectic mix of nationalities and personalities. All but one are in their fifties. Felicity is the youngest at thirty-six.

We sit in the courtyard of the low rise villa. It's beautifully finished in stark white walls, blue shutters and blue and grey accents and accessories from the deep outdoor sofas to the ceramic fish on the walls strung together with brown string and drift wood. Central to the courtyard, shadowed by palm trees, is a long fish pond with walled sides high enough to sit on. It's hitting twilight and the frogs hanging out on the lily pads are so loud it is deafening.

"Oh, here's Yvonne, have you met her yet?" Scotty Sue directs the question at me as the woman who is running the retreat whooshes out into the courtyard to a Disney like soundtrack about empowerment. She's wearing a silk Kaftan with geometric shapes in bold colours and flanked by two kitchen staff with trays of Prosecco and orange juice. "As you know, this will be the last alcohol we'll have until the last night. And I would like to use this moment to raise your glass to yourself— for giving yourself permission to come here and do something for you. I have read all your applications to be here and you are all women who have gone through deep challenges, giving so much love to others and forgetting about yourselves. We're often doing for others, but do not do for ourselves. This week will be a time to rest and restore. Reconnect with yourself. So congratulations on making time for you." We follow her lead in raising a glass and clinking a toast.

"And remember, the slower you go, the faster things repair."

I have no idea of their stories, of what they have gone through, but I can see I am going to love these women.

25

I t's early. Some of the group have already been to the infinity pool that is fed by a natural spring for a dawn chorus swim, before the sumptuous buffet breakfast and yoga class on the forest platform, led by the bendiest woman I have ever seen. She happens to be sixty-five.

We gather in the Dojo, a one roomed building with solid roof and accordion glass window doors on all sides.

"Before we start this morning's session, I would like to say a few words to keep in mind throughout the coming week," Yvonne says, sitting cross-legged on the floor in yoga pants and an open silk robe revealing her gorgeous purple lace bra and silver streaked belly folds. She looks beautiful, although you would never see this version of beauty in a magazine.

"When we talk, we need to practice neutral compassion. We extend to each other in a neutral way, not feeling sorry for each other. We acknowledge whatever is said as something that happened and then we can move on together. Listen. Offer guidance rather than solutions. Are we ready to begin to work on ourselves?" Her radiant smile warms up the room of wonderful women I already feel camaraderie with.

"Today we are going to workshop motherhood. This could be your relationship with your mother or a matriarchal figure in your life. It could be your own experience of being a mother or not being a mother. It could be a funny story about a mother-hood experience. Who wants to start?"

"I am not a mother," Felicity volunteers. "I think I want to be a mother, but I think it is only because it is what is expected from me. But I don't even have a boyfriend. My mother and sister sat me down recently and told me I need to lower my expectations. And end up like them? No thanks, I would rather stay single. "

"I'm fifty and single," Alice adds naturally to the conversation. "Deciding to be a mother is a big decision."

"Being a mother is difficult," Sue, who is a GP, says. "You first have the worry about if you will get pregnant. Then the pressure to carry the baby safely to full term and you can be judged about everything you do, eat, drink and whether to have drugs at the birth or do it 'naturally'."

"After giving birth you are their life line 24/7 for the first five years getting them through the fearless stage; don't eat that piece of glass, don't run out in front of the car, don't fall into that river. Then they go to school and you try to make all the right decisions so they have the best future possible and be their genius selves."

Those of us who are mothers, nod. We all have stressful stories we could share about our kids when they were young.

"Then they are teens and they possibly hate or resent you. I was lucky. My kids liked me for the most part. You stand by and try to guide them through their challenges and mistakes," Sue continues to talk sense. "When they finish school, they leave to go travelling, or college or work; they might move hundreds of miles away. They make friends, fall in and out of love, and you slip gradually into their outer circle while they remain in your core. They don't need to call you often. They have the deep conversations they used to have with you with their friends or partner now. "

"We probably did it to all to our own parents, so why do we expect our kids to do different?" Alicia says.

"As a GP," Sue says, "I hear stories of despair from mothers in my clinic all the time. The actions of their kids have everlasting effects on the mother's mental health. Being a mother brings great joy, but it can also be very difficult."

"I didn't like my son when he was born. He was so yellow from jaundice he looked like Bart Simpson," Mathilda, the American lady says, lightening the mood. But then she is somber again. "I am here because I feel my kids stole my life. I love my kids, but I don't like being a mother. I had a career. I married an ass. I didn't want children, but he did. I had twins. Premature. I feel I never bonded. They wouldn't stop crying."

The circle breathes and gives her the safe space she needs. "My husband was jealous of them. He had always been possessive of me and friends stopped calling. I remember a cousin gifted me an inspirational calendar for mothers. I remember crying when I opened it. I didn't need the gift of inspirational words. What I needed was a day off and a full night of sleep. The twins were only four months old when he stopped coming home and then filed for a divorce. Having kids was a mistake, he said. They are now ten and he is remarried. He sees them twice a year."

Yvonne hands out boxes of tissues at appropriate times, not in a 'dry your eyes and shut up way' but to help with the snot so the speaker could continue talking when they felt ready.

"My mother is very demanding; she expects me to be at her beck and call," Ana, the Asian American woman, chips in. "She pushed it too far recently, and I told her, I have a husband and children to look after. And she replied, I don't want to hear about them. You had a mother and brother before they came along."

"Mother is an aspirational word," wise Scotty Sue says. "It's impossible to achieve the standard of perfection that the title demands. It helped me when I accepted my own mother was just a woman trying to find her way through life, just like I was. I stopped condemning her for all the wrongs in my life."

Near the end of the session, we are each given a bookmark with a poem by Elizabeth Gracely:

Before I am your,

Daughter,

Your sister,

Your aunt, niece, or cousin,

I am my own person,

And I will not set fire to

Myself

To keep you warm.

· · ·

As Yvonne hands them out she asks, "How was your childhood Rosie?" I haven't shared, just listened. There is a book idea forming in my head.

"Magical." I answer. "I feel awkward sharing happy memories when so many don't have good motherly memories."

"Good memories are as valid as negative. They bring joy. What are your motherly memories?"

There is that word again: Joy.

"My main memories are parties and my mother painting to make extra money for Christmas and always singing. And her dancing with my dad in the sitting room to Perry Como and Mario Lanza. Although I do have a negative memory that pops up now and then: My mam went through a stage of unplugging the home phone and taking it with her when she went to the supermarket, so we wouldn't run up the bill."

After some laughs and explanations to Felicity of what unplugging a home phone meant, Yvonne asks me, "Do your family still have parties?"

I think for a moment before answering.

"We used to. But not anymore." Parties are something I have become cynical about and as I speak, I figure out why. "They feel forced, as if we're trying to recreate times that have gone without the main people involved. It is like trying to make a jigsaw with half the pieces missing."

"Sometimes we need to do something completely different," Yvonne says. "Not to try to recreate, but to create something new."

It is at that moment I realise I could not do what Yvonne is doing. I can't do retreats like this. It is not my talent to heal women's hearts or make them feel empowered enough to know what they need less of in life to have more. Or that grumpy, sad and frustrated are as valid feelings as happy and excited.

But instead of a sense of panic rising in my stomach, a strong feeling of knowing what is to be will come to me. In the meantime, I am going to just enjoy what the week brings.

After lunch and more bonding as strong as superglue, we meet again in the courtyard. As usual, I haven't checked the schedule of what we are going to be doing.

"We are going to create self-portraits through photography. Rosie, you are first."

I haven't put on makeup and I'm just wearing an old, but favourite, t-shirt. At one point in my variety of careers, I did photography professionally, but I never took a self-portrait. And nearly every photo taken of me I hate, even though Ronan was a photographer. I am not expecting any miracles. I could do this at home if I gave myself the time, so I just go along with the exercise.

I have ten minutes with the handheld clicker to control the shutter in a shut off room on my own with a chair in front of a camera on a tripod and fill-light. "No one will see these except you. Take portraits of yourself. Have fun with it."

At first, I do the usual poses with fake smiles, getting used to the room and the shutter click on my thumbs command. I know time is ticking by. My hair is long and silver, so I use it as my main prop. Throwing my head around, I try to capture my hair mid-flight. I silently scream, pulling my face in different directions, dragging my eyes down, contorting my face under a veil of hair. Clicking the self-timer until I run out of crazies, the fun shots.

I still have five minutes left in the room with just the camera staring at me. My eyes connect with the lens and I let it see into my soul, telling my story of the last year. *Click.* How I got through it. *Click.* The person I have become because of it. *Click. Click.* This is me now. *Click. Click.*

While the next person has their turn, I view the images I took on Yvonne's laptop. I have taken eighty photos. Most are of me looking possessed. But the last five or six show a strength I have never seen in myself before. There are no smiles, but there is a woman there who I now respect and love.

26

T he week is filled with workshops run by fabulous women. We dance, sing, chant, act, play, explore, walk, eat gelato in the pool and have a wonderful back massage each. We explore topics such as shame, archetypes, trauma, boundaries, self-image.

Sue gives a workshop on the effects of peri-menopause and menopause. It is so much more informative than the menopause coaching course I did. She rounds off her talk saying, "With a small HRT patch, that can sometimes feel like a bit of a crisp bag stuck to our leg, we can get back these hormones and feel as good as we felt in our thirties, but this time, with more wisdom and self-confidence to know the strength and needs of our female spirit."

There are two workshops near the end of the week which we are all 'curious' about: Sensual Senses and Vulva Hugging Meditation.

"I don't care how much I've got to know and love you girls, I'm not hugging anyone's vulva," Alice says over breakfast.

"As long as we are just hugging our own vulvas, I'm in," Sue answers.

For the Sensual Senses, we meet in the candle-lit Dojo spread with yoga mats and a kit of items beside each mat. The room is warm enough to lie fully clothed without a blanket. I choose my mat because it has a white ostrich feather that looks particularly fluffy. It's next to a jar of pot-pourri, a small jar of body oil, a foil wrapped chocolate and a blindfold.

"As women with vision, we leave a lot of our observation to sight and neglect our other four senses. This is why there are blindfolds."

Once we are all lying comfortably, we put on the blindfolds; warm acoustic tones of uplifting harmonies and rhythmic percussion fill the room.

"We will start with the feather. Run it over your face, arms, stomach. Feel its softness and the contact with your skin."

I'm quietly smug about my preempted choice of feather. The tickle of the soft plume feels delicious.

"Or if you prefer, use your body oil on your arm. Leg. Wherever you have exposed skin."

I am greedy. I am going to do both. Blindfolded, I pick up the small jar of oil and pour it onto my hand.

A strong smell of bergamot erupts. Much stronger than when I smelled it before I had put on the blindfold. I am so distracted by the surprise of how removing sight has made my sense of smell stronger that it takes me a moment to realise I am not feeling oil on the hand I am pouring into. Instead, I hear the dribble and momentarily later; I feel the warmth of oil seeping through my t-shirt onto my chest. Bloody hell, I have missed my hand completely. Never mind, it's an old cheap t-shirt.

I put the jar down, wiggle my shoulders back into a comfortable position and go back to my feather, soothing myself with its tickling softness to the music of Yaima-A new music artist this retreat has introduced me to.

"Fully soothed and relaxed, we will move onto the sense of taste with a nibble of the chocolate." I feel around and unwrap the chocolate kiss from its wrapper and pop the whole chocolate into my mouth. Chocolate was not invented to be nibbled.

I haven't eaten chocolate in quite a while. Its creaminess increases as the heat of my mouth melts the outer layer. "Next, take up the pot-pourri and take a deep inhalation. See how strong the scent is, compared to when you smelled it without the blindfold."

I lift the glass jar. The tempo of the music has risen. Lying flat, I tilt the small open jar of pot-pourri and stick my nose into it but can't smell much. It's probably because I still am moving the chocolate lump around my mouth.

I tilt the jar too much and the pot-pourri is suddenly on my nose, cheeks and mouth, immediately going under my mask and into my eye. The unexpected heap of dried bits of leaves and small flower buds on my face, makes me inhale quickly and with the air up goes a piece of dried leaf, mouth opens. In goes the pot-pourri as the chocolate lump in my mouth makes way by moving to the back of my throat. I'm gasping.

The music reaches fever pitch as I try to sit upright but just manage to get onto one elbow while choking as quietly as possible. Yvonne is over and with a clap on my back, the chocolate dislodges and is back in my mouth before I swallow it down the right pipe. I pull off the blindfold, and fish what feels like a whole tree out of my eye, while my brain tells me pot-pourri flavoured chocolate is not a good flavour and chocolate should be nibbled.

Yvonne continues as if nothing has happened. "Now if you wish and if you feel comfortable," she says guiding the group in her warm voice, "you can place your hand above your clothes between your legs and leave it resting there, giving your vulva a hug. Or you can just send warm wishes of gratitude to your vulva."

I'm not participating in the vulva hugging, and I'm too busy still rubbing my stinging, watering eye, to send any part of my body gratitude.

The session ends and everyone else sits up looking blissful and rested, while I am sitting with a large blob on my t-shirt that looks like I am lactating, a streaming red eye and me snorting and coughing trying to control the snot and spit trying to escape from my face.

"The vulva hugging was a bit of an anti-climax wasn't it, excuse the pun!" Sue whispers. "But I like what you have done with your feather."

Looking around where I am sitting, I can't see my feather, so I don't know what she is talking about, but then I catch my reflection in the glass. The ostrich feather is stuck in my hair, sticking straight up in the air from the top of my head. I look like a drunk coming home from a burlesque party.

That evening by the pool I watch the light of the village on the hill glow orangey red through the gaps of the trees, like a huge cracked glowing furnace. I scribble notes about what our house and I can offer, if not women's retreats.

I note the house has a magical quality. It has allowed me to write. It is quiet enough without being isolated. I can walk down to the lakefront and have a meal or drink. I can walk to the train station and get a train to Florence, Assisi or Perugia or a connection to Rome. It would be an excellent base for someone looking for somewhere to base themselves in Italy for a week or a month with no need for a car.

However, it is our home and we can't handle having a lot of people in the house. We like our quiet time and non interference with our space. Also, my one hundred percent focus is needed when I run group retreats, so I can't be dealing with blocked toilets or worrying about the caterer turning up while giving a workshop.

Scribbling brings clarity. My passion is writing and helping women tell their stories. I will run group writing retreats but not at the house. And instead of being a place for group retreats, the house will be a friendly bed and breakfast (BnB); a safe place for women to come to stay when they are travelling alone and a retreat space for individual writers who want a beautiful place to come to work on their writing projects without disturbance while having a gorgeous place to walk and quaint towns to visit during their time off.

The decision is made. The house will be for individual creatives and women travelling alone, and I will find alternative beautiful venues for my group writing retreats.

I now need to find what I need to do to set up a BnB in Italy. Setting up a business in Italy can only mean one thing. More Italian bureaucracy headaches. Mamma mia!

27

I t was tough saying goodbye to such a wonderful group of women, but we know we have made friends for life. The retreat has reminded me of the power, creativity and strength that grows when a group of women come together. And it all comes from a place of love. It is good for the individual, good for the group, and good for the world.

It also reminded me I definitely need to get on HRT. And as if by magic, when I get home, I find the package with my prescription has arrived. From the sticker attached, it has been opened and inspected, but luckily my friend included a copy of the prescription to prove it is for a potentially explosive woman in need of hormones.

I am so desperate to feel more energy and have a clear head, I tear open the package like a kid at Christmas and slap on the HRT patch.

Ecstatic, I gallop around the house, which is an appropriate comparison as they used to get estrogen from the urine from pregnant mares. Not anymore, thankfully.

But it is not the only mail that has arrived. While I unpack, I tune into a podcast for writers I enjoy, and listen to an interview of a well-known author. She mentions the name of her publishing company. It sounds familiar. Something she says makes me check back on my emails.

Bloody hell! I thought it was a spam mail when I saw it before the retreat and ignored it. But reading it now, I see it is genuine; I've gotten an email from one of the biggest publishers in the United States. They want to talk to me about book one of A Rosie Life In Italy—A mainstream publisher is interested in getting my books onto bookshelves everywhere. This is the dream I've had forever and now it's finally coming true. I can hardly breathe while I double check to ensure they haven't confused me with someone else. If they have, I will not be the one to correct them.

I notice the date the email arrived—my sister Eileen's anniversary and our anniversary of signing for the Sighing House. Dates have become more significant as I get older. The more of them I repeat and experience, the more I have to associate and cross reference, and justify there are no such things as just coincidences.

I email the editor, apologising for the delay in response and wondering if they were still interested. A Zoom call is arranged.

"We recommend you get an agent to negotiate the terms of contract," advises Erin, the wonderful editor who had discovered my book. The advance offered is low, but after three years of it being out as a self-published book, having the first in the series with a mainstream publisher may help it get a wider audience.

Within a week, a second dream from my teen years comes true. I get an agent, one of the first I contacted in a major agency in New York. Having a deal in hand helped get my foot in the door of course, but she likes my humour and during our second Zoom meeting she says, "I'd love to see a women's fiction novel in your style of writing. Do you have anything?"

"I'm working on something," I say immediately.

I wasn't. Unless panicking counts as a genre.

"What is it about?"

"It's a story about..." Think fast Rosie. "Some perimenopausal women starting a retreat centre in Italy. A story of friendship amongst women and its importance as we get older."

There was a silence.

"It's a comedy." I'm grasping at straws.

"Hmm, yes, I'd give it a go. When could you have it to me?"

"Three months?" I say feeling I might lose her interest, but three months is the fastest I can write a novel.

"Oh, you are that far into it already?"

Crap, I should have said longer.

"Yes," I lie.

"Great, I look forward to reading it. I really think you could be on to something with this."

I get off the call, stunned. A literary agent wants to see my work and believes in my idea. What was the idea again? Bloody hell, I need to write it down before my brain fog gobbles it up.

Just as I start to write the notes, Mam calls and it comes through on the bigger screen of my laptop rather than my phone.

"Did your top shrink? It looks very tight on you."

Ronan gives Mam a wave as he passes in the background to the coffee machine.

"Look at him!" she shouts, "Ronan, you look great!"

Ronan has put on a clean un-ironed shirt, whereas my top is brand new.

"Why do you always wear dark colours?" I can hear Mam's friend Angela shuffling playing cards. Mam turns to her as if I am not on the call and says, "She always wears black."

"I rarely wear black!" I can't help but respond. "This top isn't black, it's green. I just don't wear florals or patterns. I wear solid colours: blues, greys, greens."

"Why are you getting all dressed up anyways?"

"I have friends coming over," I lie. My head is still swimming from the call with the agent. I want to process it before I share it with mam and she asks a hundred questions I don't yet know the answer to.

"Oh, a party! Well for you. Angela, my daughter in Italy is having a party."

"It's not a party, it's just—" I start.

"I hope you have everything ready and have Prosti- what's it called?" Mam says, thinking out loud.

Angela tries to help Mam find the missing word, "Prostitutes?"

"No, the drink." Mam says. "Pros-"

"Prosecco?" I guess.

"That's it."

By the time our call is finished, I have forgotten the outline of the story I told the agent about. I want to write fiction, but I need to figure out what genre I want to write, where my passion is. So I make a cup of tea and take it out into the garden. It always helps ideas to flow.

"Aw no, it must be dying," I say out loud, noticing for the first time that the green fruits on the elegant silvery tree have turned black. I hadn't been paying any attention to it since I stripped it of its heavy cloak of ivy.

As I reach the tree, I hear the sound of the wind picking up, but I feel no breeze, just the warm sun and the tree's leaves are motionless. I look down and the ground below the tree is dotted with the blackened fruit. I pick one up. The blackness is soft in my hand, but I am distracted by the eerie gust building and getting closer from behind. Looking up the leaves are still motionless. The source of the sound is above me and close.

A murmuration of thousands of starlings rip across the blank space above the garden. The hushed and primal sound reverberating in my chest rather than my ears, like the sound bowls, makes me grasp for a deeper breath. Spiralling upward and condensing into a tight ball, before, folding in on themselves, forming dense, rippling shapes that twist and scatter into an undulating wave like the air itself has become liquid. The flock pulses and shifts, stretching into a thin ribbon caught in the wind, towards the lake like a Spirograph design, before disappearing from sight.

My hand has clenched involuntarily on the blackened fruit. Its softness falls away and reveals its solid core. A walnut. I have a walnut tree — like the magical witch tree in Benevento! And it is facing the entrance gate of Casa Anam Cara; A place where wise women can gather to exchange knowledge and enjoy each other's company-just like the old gatherings.

28

The following morning Ronan comes in very excited. "This was in the letterbox," he says, holding out a business card to me to read. "Alessandro. Painting, plasterboard, garden maintenance."

"I suppose a good contact to have now that Alex is so busy."

"But look at the back." Ronan says, still way too excited. "It says he does rubbish removal. We could ask him to clear out the shed." I've never heard Ronan squeak before.

"You could!" I say, matching his enthusiasm. I've become good at deflecting tasks back onto Ronan that I would have in the past immediately taken control of. My control freak nature has disappeared into the ether like all our builders pre this new guy, Alessandro. My deflections have stopped Ronan using me like an AI robot for any question that comes into his head; "What date is Sunday?... How long is the train to the next stop?... What age am I?"

"I will." Ronan says enthusiastically, bouncing down the stairs to get his phone.

The following day Alessandro—a stocky, strong looking guy in his thirties and dressed too well to be clearing out a filthy garage —arrives. I compliment him on his English.

"I have lived in Italy since I was born, but my parents are Romanian. They escaped before the revolution," he responds with a sense of pride.

That explains it. I can't imagine an Italian setting up a business clearing rubbish unless they were going all-in like Cerroni and getting someone else to do the dirty work.

"So, this is the garage we need cleared out," Ronan says cheerily. The garage is not a big garage, just big enough for a Fiat 500 to fit neatly in.

Alessandro looks at it uneasily. "There are probably snakes in there." His idea of rubbish removal is definitely different to ours.

"Yes, there are probably snakes, but at least if there are snakes there are no rats," I say with Huckleberry Finn style cheerfulness about the task ahead. Alessandro does not look comforted.

"I would need to charge eight-hundred euros."

I balk. My world is a little shattered, thinking how I am going to have to continue feeling the heaviness of the clutter every time I drive through the gate.

"It's okay. Thanks anyway for coming. We will call you for other work in the future. We'll clear this and take it to the local dump ourselves," I say, nodding at Ronan.

"I paint shutters," Alessandro says, pointing at the eight I have painted already.

"Thanks, but I have already painted those ones. We need help doing stuff we can't do."

"Hmmm." He's not moving. I have editing to get back to, so I begin to walk away. "I'll do the garage clearing for seven hundred. It's the best I can do. I would need to take on three guys to help me. We need to separate all the metal from wood. If there is a nail in the wood, we have to remove it. We have to separate everything for the recycling plant. And they won't take a lot of this stuff at the local dump. We will need to take it to another one that deals with general waste."

There is no way I'm paying seven hundred, but then I look at Ronan. "Are you ever going to clear it?"

"No."

At least he is being honest.

I stare at the eyesore. It has to be dealt with. If I was in Ireland, two skips would cost me about seven hundred euro. And there is at least two skips of rubbish in the shed.

"You'll take everything?"

"Yes, but I can only do it Saturday. Then I go on holiday for a month, and when I come back, I am completely booked up." He holds out his phone calendar and does a quick scroll of all the green tabs until Christmas. "On Saturday, we would start by nine and clear everything by one."

I imagine how good it would feel having the front garden as a pleasant welcoming sight. How different I would feel every time I arrive back to the house. How this might be the only opportunity we will get to clear the eyesore. It is like the last remains of the stagnant heaviness of the past that is holding us back from moving forward.

"Okay, then."

I can't believe it is costing us so much.

Having shaken on it with Alessandro and waving him off, Ronan is straight into future planning mode.

"What will we do with the garage space? We could make an entrance in the back and keep the lawn mower in it. We could make it into an office or we could make it into an outdoor kitchen with a BBQ?"

"Let's just get rid of the rubbish first and swear never to buy anything ever again without thinking it through. Anything we buy from now has to have a twenty-year plan."

If we avoid shopping online, this won't be difficult to do. There are few places to waste money in Italy. Unlike Ireland. When I go to visit, I often find myself wandering into shops along the main street of town, full of reasonably priced ornamental trinkets and household goods. You go in for a look and come out with a bag of stuff you don't need, but you feel would look great in your house and your wallet one hundred and fifty euro lighter.

I'm not saying we are saints in this department. Far from it. Only the week previous, Ronan and I went to look at furniture for the courtyard. We didn't see any furniture but walked out with a bust of Venus under my arm and Ronan with a snow shovel in his hand.

"What are you buying a snow shovel for?"

"It's only two euros." Ronan can't resist a bargain.

"But we don't get snow and it's seventeen degrees out."

"Yes, but it is only two euros!"

"But we don't have snow."

"But it's a bargain."

"Not if it is just going to take up space in the shed waiting for climate change to ramp up."

"It will be handy for gravel or sand or something."

There was no tag on the snow shovel. The till operator had to call three different departments and eventually got a nine-digit code, which she filled onto a form by hand and the price of two euro.

Sometimes buying stuff in Italy takes so long or is so problematic that it is like a cooling-off period to change your mind. Which I have done before when buying a label-less exotic looking vegetable I didn't know how to prepare to eat, and another time with a hairdryer.

I'm going to get value for my money with Alessandro, so I am up early on Saturday and moving the remains of the past I want to be rid of to the garage before they arrive. Such as the broken gold glass tabletop from the coffee table Ronan broke with his foot and I swore we would get rid of four years ago. In the shed, I reunite it with the old gold corduroy sofa—the one I wanted to throw out as soon as we bought the house but ended up being our main sofa for two years. It has been stacked in the garage for the last year, waiting patiently to be taken to its final resting place.

Alessandro arrives with a large truck and three guys. I cringe with embarrassment for having such a mess of a garage, even though the majority of the rubbish was there before we arrived or has been dumped by the builders when renovating. I have made it clear to Ronan that I will be hiding, I mean working on edits and he is to deal with them, offer them coffee and pay them at the end.

I take a sneak peek out the top window now and then. They clear and sort the big stuff first into their different categories— wood, metal, glass, other. But then give up and say they will do the sorting at the dump. I hear a retching cough and see Alexandro cover his mouth with his t-shirt and see one of them gag every time I look out. One is using the chair I had thrown out to take regular breaks sitting and having a cigarette. It must be worse than I thought. Well worth the seven hundred euros and the coffee Ronan is feeding them.

"It was not a nice job." Alessandro confirms as Ronan hands over the cash and I shout from the window. "Grazie."

"Don't forget I do other work; I can paint these shutters for you." Again, he is waving at the shutters I painted last year.

Two hours after their arrival, they are pulling out of the garden with a very full truck. I peer down at the roofless ruin of a garage and feel the energy change in the garden. The eyesore dump is gone. It is now a clear structure waiting to fulfil its next purpose. I take a deep breath and at the same time the silvery cream barked walnut tree, that was once a monster, waves its branches at me. It was like the tree sent us Alessandro's card as a thank-you card for clearing it of its ivy prison and wants us to get on with the plans.

It is now time to make the front garden beautiful.

29

Lucia calls over for tea. Well, I have tea; she has water as usual. We don't see each other as often as we'd like, even though we live close. She has been busy with her Agriturismo and creating a home with her partner. It's so good seeing her so happy and her business being successful.

"To start a BnB in Italy or to rent a room, you have to go through a process." Lucia informs me. "The process can take up to six months."

"Six months?"

"Of course. It is Italy, there is paperwork. There is always paperwork. And when you have a guest stay, there is even more paperwork you must submit to the police within 24 hours of check-in and then for the comune and government you need to submit statistics of guests regularly."

"There's so much else to think about. I am not even at the point of paperwork yet."

"I show you," Lucia says, opening my laptop and calling up the holiday accommodation regulations of Umbria.

There are fifty-three articles in the laws surrounding holiday accommodation in Umbria.

Number 1. Bed and Breakfast is the accommodation and breakfast service provided within the home where the owner has residence and habitually lives.

Yes, that is us—check.

Number 2. The activity of a Bed and Breakfast cannot in any case include the provision of food and drinks.

A Bed and Breakfast without food for breakfast?

"In Italy, breakfast is a coffee and a croissant. We don't do breakfasts like dinners with meats and sausages and eggs and tomatoes and beans like you crazy Irish. If you offer breakfast, it must be coffee and a pre-packed croissant or biscuit you buy in the supermarket in a sealed wrapper. You cannot serve any other food unless you have a food health licence."

No decent Irish person could say they run a Bed and Breakfast and not offer a full Irish or at least something cooked.

"I would rather not say I offer breakfast."

"So you will just run a B? Rather than a BnB?"

"It could be a BnC. Bed and Creative space? And let them have use of the kitchen." I like this idea I have come up with.

"You need to class it as something. There are other options to a BnB, such as Casa Vacanze; Vacation House."

We read through the regulations for a Vacation House, where guests have a bedroom, bathroom and a kitchen to use. That sounds right. But there is a problem with a vacation house: we as the owners cannot live in the house. We need to rent out the entire property.

Another option is Affitta Camere—renting out bedrooms and the bathrooms but no breakfast. And no other rooms are part of the rental agreement. Perhaps we can allow guests have access to other rooms from the goodness of our hearts, but it is not part of the rental agreement.

"I don't think I am yet at the point of dealing with this; I need to think about the practicalities first."

"Like what? You are putting things in your own way. You have a beautiful property and idea. What practicalities are stopping you other than the paperwork?"

"Practicalities like getting guest luggage up the stairs. Perhaps I need to get lockers on the ground floor and they leave the majority of their stuff there or perh—"

"You need an old wench."

"A wench?"

"Yes," says Lucia, "You see them on balconies in Italy all the time. They might be old, but they can lift the bags without a problem."

I think of all the nonnas I have seen in Italy leaning on balconies watching the world go by. I know they are known to be gossips, but I never heard anyone calling them wenches before.

"You can probably buy one online."

"Oh, you mean a winch!"

"Yes, that is what I said. A wench."

After Lucia is gone, I search online for balcony winches for sale, being careful with my use of vowels and read through the holiday accommodation laws.

I'm going to need help with this.

I message the women in Puglia who run the assistance service for expats and who helped us with our Greencards during covid and a few other admin things over the years.

"Yes, we can help. How many rooms and bathrooms have you?" They text back.

Bagno is Italian for bathroom and when I text bagno, autocorrect changes it to bango. So without my glasses on, I have written we have four bangos. I correct it and auto-correct kicks in again before I send it. This time, it has gone one step further; We have four bangs in the house. One on each floor and one halfway up the stairs.

The ladies don't acknowledge my quantity of bangos or bangs, but they send me the long list of paperwork they will need for the application, including;

- a copy of the property's deed;

- a copy of your passport and code of fiscale;

- a copy of Agibilita Certificate;

- your phone number;

- opening period.

I'll also need to use an Italian bank for payments and register every guest who stays on a complicated online system.

Later that week, I call into Blodwyn to buy some olive oil. She rents out rooms and offers to talk me through the online registration of guests with the police when the time comes.

"You are supposed to register any friends or family staying too. If they were in an accident and brought to the hospital or asked by police where are they staying, and it's with you and they have not been registered, then you can be fined thousands."

This fits in with Italy's policy that everyone needs to carry ID with them. Even if you are a passenger in a car, you should carry a copy or photo of your passport with you. Several times Ronan or I have brought people to the train station and, while waiting on the platform with them, we have been approached by police and asked for our passports, even though we are not the ones travelling.

"Do get yourself some help, don't try to do it all yourselves," Blodwyn recommends. "Get yourself a cleaner."

I think a lot of Irish people my age are embarrassed about the idea of employing cleaners. We were brought up having to clean and care for younger siblings or elderly relatives who lived with us. So we should be able to clean for ourselves.

I can't clean. Neither can Ronan.

Ronan thinks emptying the dishwasher and packing it up again, wiping around things on the counter and sweeping the middle of the floor is a day's cleaning.

Whereas I go deeper. I pull everything out of the fridge or cupboards and tut about all the out-of-date stuff; "How is there a tin of beans with a best before date of 2020 here? I only cleaned this cupboard a couple of months ago." I wipe out the dust and cobwebs and then I'm too tired to put everything back in. So Ronan does it and that explains why out-of-date stuff keeps turning up.

Or I start cleaning and then find a book I'd forgotten. Four hours later, I am on chapter fifteen and still sitting amongst the mess.

I can't reach the cobwebs in one corner of the stairwell and Ronan says he'll tackle them but never does and he hates the idea of getting a cleaner anytime I suggest it. Lucia has offered numerous times to put us in touch with Laura, who cleans her place. She would be happy with the extra work, especially as Signora Greco has sold her house and is no longer in need of a cleaner of ghosts or floors.

It's time I take a stand. With or without paying guests staying in our home, I can't take care of a twenty-two roomed house, an acre of garden, and write three books a year.

That evening Ronan is making dinner and I see his face wince when he picks up a jar. 'I hurt my little finger when trying to get the battery out of the van,' he says.

He starts wiggling it. His face winces more. "It hurts a lot if I do this."

"Then stop wiggling it. When do you have a reason to wiggle your finger like that? Rest it."

He continues to press it and wiggle it.

Later that evening, he's eating an ice cream watching TV. It's a choc-ice from the pack someone bought when visiting and left in the freezer. Not something Ronan would usually eat, he doesn't have a sweet tooth.

"How's your finger?" I ask him.

"Still sore." He holds his hand out, palm up. His little finger isn't straight like the others.

"Can you not straighten it?"

"Not really."

"Then go get it checked at the hospital in the morning."

"If it's broke, all they'll do is splint it to the other finger. I can do that myself."

There is no talking to him. I go and check the first aid box to see if there is an appropriate bandage or finger thing. By the time I return with a bandage and tape, Ronan is wincing while biting the end of the black plastic plumbers' tape that he has bound around his fingers, encasing them and the unwashed ice cream stick between them. So that is why he was eating an ice cream.

"You know I could have helped and cut the tape for you?"

"I'm used to doing these things on my own."

"We've been together for thirty years, Ronan."

The reason why he has to do these things on his own is because I refuse to stitch wounds with sewing thread or straighten bones back into place when there are trained professionals with sterile equipment willing to do it not so far away.

"I can do that myself." Is the same response I get every time I have suggested we get a cleaner.

"Tomorrow, if your hand is okay, I need you to help me clean the house."

"Why who is coming?"

A cleaner.

———

Laura, the woman who is going to help me clean the house and alleviate some of my stress, arrives. She immediately says, "Ah, you are young. You are so beautiful."

She's got the job.

She oouus and ahhhs at the house she had passed for years. "Many years ago, we were looking to buy a house and my husband said 'what about this one' but I said no because from the outside it looked terr-ee-blah. All the rubbish in the garden and the grass so high and I could see in the windows and it was terr-ee-blah. But now it is beautiful. I cannot believe it. You must be millionaires."

"Eh no." I may have elevated to beautiful and young in the last ten minutes, but I am definitely not a millionaire.

I thought she was coming just to agree terms and see if the job suited her, but instead she says, "I start now?"

No need to delay.

I'm glad we had cleaned the house before she arrived.

She asks for hot water and cloths. And then more cloths. I'm wondering if she has found an eighteenth-century ghost in labour in one of the rooms. I bring her what she needs. The stairwell already looks and feels cleaner. There's something different—the cobwebs are gone! I don't know how she has reached them as she is shorter than me.

She is busy vacuuming the outside windowsill in one of the bedrooms. I don't think I've ever opened that window.

I go quietly back to my room to work, but I find it difficult to concentrate on my writing. I am trying to control the rising guilt with the sound of the vacuum cleaner. I feel I should be out there helping her.

I call Lucia to help me through my guilt and dilemma. "It's her profession. You would be insulting her and probably in her way if you tried to help her. Take advantage of the new freed up time you have and do what you do best. Write."

She's right. And I write double the amount of words I would normally do in a day.

30

F atima, my friend from Kuwait who I met through an online writing conference during Covid and then in person at a writing conference, is travelling Italy and comes to stay for a night. We go on a day trip to Florence. I haven't been there in over a year so I'm excited to be going to my favourite city again.

The train trip from Passignano to Florence takes us past the undulating hills of silvery green olive trees and past a field of organised rows of pink, cream-vanilla and white blossoms splayed on espaliers promising an abundance of plums, pears and apricots the following autumn.

I always imagine myself living in Florence when I get older—effortlessly making friends, wandering through museums and bookshops, joining meet-ups, and diving into deep conversations about writing and life.

For some reason, I imagine I am going to turn into a social animal as I age, rather than continue my contentment living like a hermit. That's why I still can't speak Italian, I barely talk to anyone, other than Ronan, my Mam and Izzy. I think it is PTSD after doing weddings for so long. I had to talk so much I used up all the words stored in my voice box. But I'm ready to talk to people again, or at least listen to them.

"Florence is nice, but the first time I went I was disappointed with it. I was expecting more," Fatima says.

"Oh, I've heard about this. There's a name on it, Strendhal Syndrome, it's like Jerusalem Syndrome."

"Isn't Jerusalem Syndrome when visitors to the city have a psychotic religious break down and believe they are the next Messiah or some religious figure from The Bible? That is definitely not what I am experiencing. And Strendhal Syndrome is when travellers are so overcome by the beauty of all the architecture and artwork in Florence that they begin to hallucinate and get sick. I think I had the opposite," Fatima says, who is much better at facts than me.

"I know what you are talking about. It's like Paris Syndrome— when tourists are so disappointed with the reality of Paris that they get sick. It's an extreme form of culture shock. A day with me in Florence should cure your Dis-Strendhal Syndrome or maybe we should call it Strendhalitis?"

Leaving the station, we walk past the Basilica di Santa Maria Novella.

"I'll take you on one of my look up-look-down tours."

"Explain what I am getting into?"

Does Fatima know me well enough already not to trust me?

"When walking around any Italian city street," I explain, "you need to look up, as there is always an unexpected fresco or an architectural detail that makes you want to stop and stare. But then you need to look down, so you don't break your ankle on an unexpected step or wobbles in the cobbles."

"Okay, so where are you taking me to first to trigger a love of Florence?"

"The pharmacy," I announce as I start to walk.

Fatima looks perplexed, following me around the corner and down an unimpressive street.

The pharmacy I am taking her to is no ordinary pharmacy, it is the Farmaceutica di Santa Maria Novella. The waft of bergamot, rose and sandalwood strengthening with every step from the entrance, encourages her to keep moving forward into the wow-ness of the central room, with frescoed ceilings and walls brightly lit by a magnificent, massive glass chandelier.

A mouthwatering, witchy display of old style glass bottles with glass stoppers, concoctions of herbal elixirs, soaps and perfumes with smelling card sticks are lined up in polished wooden display dressers and ready for testing.

It's a delicious step back in time to an apothecary full of lotions and potions, with perfumes created to bring back memories or create new ones.

Having a kitchen dresser like this, stocked with mason jars full of homegrown herbs, teas and potions, would fill a missing part of me. My inner witch—even if I don't like the label.

"Do you know the sense of smell is the most acute awakener of memories?" I state to my friend as I sniff one sample and the explosion of lemon and bergamot in the back of my nose immediately transports me back to my grandmother's dressing table and her 4711 perfume—the timeless classic scent of all grannies in the 80s.

In a two second memory dump, I can vividly see the detailed grain in the wood of the heavy piece of furniture against the wall of my granny's room, blackened by years of polish. Its three-way mirror where my mother would check the back of her hair before going out with my dad on Monday and Friday nights and I would play with and marvel at how I could rico-chet the back of my head to infinity by tweaking the mirrors towards each other. I can physically feel the resistance of the heavy, wide drawers refusing to budge back or forth if not heaved with the same force on each side. It was these that gave me the lifelong desire for drawers with runners on the sides that glide effortlessly back into place without the need of sweat or painful nip of a finger.

I had forgotten her mirror. I wonder whatever happened to it.

"Started in the sixteenth century by Dominican friars, the Santa Maria pharmacy has an amazing range of handmade perfumes, herbal elixirs and soaps based on vinegar," I read aloud from the tourist information. My mind is immediately transported to the time and to a cozy familiarity of creating potions and remedies —something I have never done, but now I want to write about that time, dive into it through my pen. But it's the type of book that would need to be written at a roll-top desk.

"I think I'm going to write an historic fictional novel based in sixteenth century Italy," I announce out of nowhere to Fatima.

"Interesting. About what?"

"I don't know yet. But there is something about that time that I feel I need to write about. Maybe about herbalist women who are accused of being witches."

While her nostrils were tickled by wonderful scents, Fatima was not having a wow moment yet. It was time for lunch, so we skipped across the road to a discreet looking osteria where we have delicious truffle oil pasta flambéed in a giant cheese wheel.

After lunch, we walk around the side of the Duomo, faced with marble panels in various shades of green and pink, bordered by white.

"This cathedral took one hundred and forty years to build. When it was opened in 1436, it was the world's largest church, able to accommodate thirty-thousand worshippers." I inform Fatima having just read this off the internet. I'll forget it tomorrow; I would never make a good tour guide.

I take her through the leather market and to my favourite shop in Florence, Alice's Mask studio on Via Faenza. It's a cavern of colourful, feathery, gruesome and comical fantasy with the master craftsman Agostino himself, in his well worn and paint splattered apron, behind the counter working on a paper mache mask.

Fatima tries on several masks. "Oh, I think I will get this one, she says, picking up a mask with a long, bird- beaked. "Ah Dottore Peste," I say in my best Italian accent. "The Plague Doctor."

"Plague, I thought it was from the Carnival in Venice?"

"Oh no, they were invented during the Plague. The beak was filled with herbs, spices and straw to protect the so called doctors from the diseased air. You've seen the pictures, I'm sure? The guys with the waxed overcoat, the wide-brimmed hat. The mask with glass goggles and that beak."

"What were the goggles for?" Fatima asks me.

"I don't know. To look cool, perhaps?"

"They carried a scalpel for cutting open blisters," says a gritty English voice from behind us. "The goggles protected their eyes from the spatter." A man in his sixties with a bald head and pock-marked, ruddy face, bulging eyes and stinking of garlic steps forward and picks up the mask next to the one Fatima has chosen. "I collect these masks. I heard about this shop and couldn't wait to get here from the cruise I'm on. I've skipped seeing David to be here instead." He's exactly how I would imagine a plague doctor to look without a mask on.

Fatima was already hurrying to the counter to pay for her mask.

"The doctors stank of garlic, as they chewed raw garlic whenever near the plague victims. It's very good for you garlic is."

"Yes indeed," I say, trying not to choke by the overpowering stench in the small shop. "Thank you for the information. Enjoy your trip." I say, following Fatima out the door as quickly as possible, while the man continued departing knowledge on us in a more amplified voice. "They also carried a long cane to poke patients during examinations and treatments, to avoid touching them."

"I think we just met a plague doctor," Fatima says. "You could include him in your historic novel."

I'm so distracted by our conversation I get disorientated and don't recognise where we are. "I thought this road led back to the Cathedral?" I say to Fatima, looking around for some sort of landmark I recognise. A group of monks are walking with purpose and chatting with each other. They look like they would know where it is. I decide to be brave and show off my Italian skills to Fatima.

"Scusì," I say as the monks approach. "Dove il Basilico?" I ask the nearest one.

"Basilico?" He looks at me blankly. "Sì Basilico!" I say a bit more demanding. It's not that hard. "Non lo so." (I do not know). I think I see pity in his eyes. I'm frustrated, it's just three words, and he is acting as if I have lost my marbles.

"Sì il Duomo. Questa strada?" I insist.

"Ahhhh. La Basilica! Yez, straight ahead."

He walks on with his other monk friends chuckling.

I think about his correction.

"Oh, bloody hell. I said basilico rather than basilica," I say, slapping my own forehead.

"Isn't that basil?" Fatima says.

"Yes Fatima, it is. I was asking him where the basil is instead of the cathedral."

"How long did you say you have been living here?"

"I am embarrassed to tell you... nearly six years and I am hardly able to string a sentence together even though I have done a tonne of lessons. But they all focus on grammar and are not doing it for me. I must have spent at least four thousand euro on lessons so far and none have worked.

Fatima can speak three languages fluently. "Take your focus away from the grammar. In any given language, only about one thousand different words are used in everyday conversation.

And those words account for ninety-five percent of the spoken language."

Do I know one thousand Italian words? I feel I must be close.

"If you know the two and half thousand most used words of a language, then you should be able to say anything you want to say with some creativity."

Italian suddenly feels more doable.

I finish our day in Florence with a trip to the Ponte Vecchio, the oldest bridge in the city and the only one to survive the World War II bombings, followed by a stroll around a visiting exhibition of the artist Mucha. I have at least six of his prints hanging in the house. This is the second time during my time living in Italy, going to a visiting exhibition of an artist I have loved and never seen the work of. The last being Gustav Klimt in Rome. It's one of the advantages of living in a country known for art.

"I love Florence, but even though it is now outside of summer season, it is still full of tourists. I might need to find a different city to retire to when I evolve into a social animal," I say to Fatima over our last cuppa together.

"Have you been to Barcelona? It would suit you. It's a city with a beach—the best of both worlds. I have a friend there who runs writing retreats. You should go."

Before we are finished our drinks, I'm booked onto a writers retreat in Barcelona.

At the train station while I am waiting in line to buy my ticket, Fatima pops into a bookshop and returns with a bag. "This is for you. To thank you for your brilliant tour of Florence," she says, handing me an enormous book. The Italian Frequency Dictionary for Learners.

"It has the top ten-thousand Italian words listed in order of use. I want you to learn them all before I come back to Italy the next time."

On the train home, I read in the introduction that if I know the top most used five thousand words of Italian, I will understand ninety-five percent of all written text of native speakers without a higher education. That would do me.

I feel my trouble with the Italian language is my inability to recall the words needed in a timely manner; during a conversation and not two hours later when I am thinking about it again. So I'm going in a different direction with my effort to learn Italian.

My new technique is to test myself first to see how many of the top one thousand words I know. Learn any I am missing, then extend to the top two thousand and then top two and a half thousand. Once I know these, I will revise my grammar of past, present and future. And then I should have enough words and confidence to speak and read and understand Italians at slow speed.

Piano, piano (slowly, slowly).

31

After a month on HRT, not only are my energy levels, mood, joints and sleep better, but after six years of trying to learn Italian, my brain is at last retaining words and phrases.

Who knew a hidden benefit of HRT would be I will at last be able to speak the language of the country where I live? My change of attitude to the language has also helped. I am no longer focusing on getting the grammar right. I am just stringing words together without embarrassment until my message gets across.

I am more confident in day-to-day situations such as the supermarket, although I leave the grocery shopping to Ronan. I go with him now and then. Ronan doing grocery shopping is an experience I can only endure from time to time. I need to be in a particular frame of mind.

For instance, he automatically starts whistling *The Godfather* theme tune whenever he sees someone he thinks looks like they should be in a mafia movie. Today he is whistling the theme tune from *The Good, The Bad and The Ugly* to alert me to a person he passes who is wearing a cowboy hat he thinks is funny. I'm mortified.

"Ronan, you do realise whistling in English is the same as whistling in Italian? It's not like you are muttering some words in Irish to me. People won't understand."

"Oh, yeah, you're right!" He pushes on with the trolley forgetting himself and continues whistling it.

I move away from him quickly, not wanting to be in the same space as him and the man with the cowboy hat when he rounds the corner.

"Is this a courgette?" Ronan calls out, standing beside the stacks of vegetables waving the green object in the air an aisle away from me. Even from that distance, I can tell what it is.

"No, that's a cucumber," I shout back.

This is a conversation we have every time we go to the supermarket together because Ronan has a blockage. Not anything that needs hospitalisation or medical attention, he just cannot tell the difference between cucumbers and courgettes or zucchini, as Italians call them.

This leads to us regularly having roasted cucumbers or pasta with grated cucumber and parmesan. Or a cucumber salad made with sliced courgettes and no cucumber. It tastes more earthy and bland and is less crunchy and refreshing than my preferred cucumber salad, and the pasta is more of a mush mash when made with cucumber.

Sometimes he will say, "Ahh, I found the cucumbers. Do we need one?" just to test me without actually asking. And I will inevitably say, "No, what you have in your hand is a courgette."

I keep telling him that courgettes are the ones with the big knob on the end, but somehow he always seems to find knob-less courgettes when he does the grocery shopping.

As it is spring, the supermarket has packets of seeds on sale. I am determined this will be the year we start growing vegetables. Every spring I get an urge to grow stuff, something rises in me and I buy multiple packets of interesting looking seeds and then I find out I need to be a propagation master to get them to grow and then have patience as they don't flower until the second year. Those type, never get past the first year, many don't even get out of the packet.

It's while looking at the seeds a solution to our cucumber and courgette dilemma comes to me. I'll plant courgettes in the raised beds on one side and plant cucumbers in a separate bed so there is no confusion. A packet of each is added to the shopping trolley. Along with four bags of garden compost and three boxes of wildflower seeds. Since seeing lavender bushes in Shelly's garden covered in bumblebees, I'm inspired to plant a bumblebee butterfly garden.

Ronan piles nine trays of chicken livers and hearts into the shopping trolley. "They are on sale and that will be enough for three days. They are cheaper than tinned dog food and less processed," he says as I nearly dry heave.

The guy at the checkout, who sees Ronan most days and me rarely, greets me like an old friend. "You speak Italian?" He asks me.

"A little."

"I wanted to ask your husband for his recipe for these." He says, holding one of the trays of chicken bits. He buys them nearly every day. They must be very good? I need your recipe."

"No, they are the dog's dinner.".

"Ahhh," he laughs, "we all wonder why he buys so much. We stock more because of him."

This reminds me of the two rows of Jameson. The supermarkets have gone back to one row since Mam left. Although they didn't realise mam was the sole reason why their sales of Jameson had increased dramatically during the months she was here.

Back home, our dogs greet us like they are doing a drug inspection at an airport, their noses stuck in the bags to check out if Ronan has gone out hunting and brought them back chicken bits again.

"Where do you want these?" Ronan asks hauling out the bags of compost.

"Down the garden on the right."

"What are you going to use to build the raised beds?"

"I've been watching videos about raised beds and got an idea. How about we use all those big chunky cabinets as raised beds? We could build an arch in-between and trail the tomatoes and cucumbers over it."

Ronan knows the chunky cabinets I am talking about. There was a unit left in the house with shelves and deep cabinets. It was perfect in its day in the sixties and seventies for storing a big stereo unit, speakers and LPs. I thought about keeping it.

Luca wanted it for his room whenever it was done, so we took it apart without taking a photo of it beforehand, which was the first mistake, and then we promptly lost the large bag of custom sized screws and bolts that held it together. I was hoping I would find the bag again, especially when I saw a similar unit in a high-end furniture shop online selling an imitation model for over a thousand euros. I did find the screws at some point and couldn't remember what they were belonging to, so I put them somewhere safe where I could find them when I remembered what they were from. I just forgot where the safe place was every time I considered putting the unit back together.

It's now been four years since we took it apart and the big heavy cabinets have gone through many lives with various uses; makeshift coffee table, makeshift TV stand, makeshift bed for dog, storage boxes for our books until we got shelving, emergency cage for the baby bird Juno found in the garden, while two on top of each other made a temporary desk.

I did find the screws again but didn't know where all the unit parts were by then—I think some of the metal structural pieces were now holding up some of the fencing in the garden and the odd plant here and there.

Now that everything has started to find its place, and we have replaced most of the 'it-will-do-for-now-makeshift' pieces with proper furniture, the bulky cabinets sit around in odd places in the house, twiddling their thumbs and bruising my legs every time I walk into one sitting in the way of something.

"Good idea," Ronan says, and he sets about hauling the cabinets out to the garden with me shouting "Mind the wall," as he takes another chunk out of a wall's plasterwork.

The three bags of compost barely fill the base of the units. Ronan goes and buys ten more bags, plumbing pipe and fencing mesh and together we build a copy of the arch I've seen on Pinterest. It looks nothing like it, but it will do what I want it to do.

I plant the courgette and cucumber seeds along with three different types of tomatoes, aubergine and lettuce. The structure and compost cost about two hundred euros much more than I would spend buying the same vegetables all year, at the market.

32

My friend Fiona from Ireland, who I haven't seen in years, comes to stay for a week. One of the few pros of social media is that we found each other online and got back in touch.

She's considering switching to being a full-time digital nomad and wants to find somewhere with a garden away from a city but with nice towns nearby. Umbria is the perfect choice and the houses she is going to view are near to our house, so I tag along for a nose.

One house is advertised as three hundred and fifty thousand euros, and it's within walking distance of a town. The advertisement at the estate agents says it has a 'suggestive master bedroom'.

The Italians love the word 'suggestive'. I used to hear it all the time at wedding shows. "The hotel has very suggestive showers and suggestive bedrooms." I think they mix the translation up with relaxing or romantic.

We drive up a short gravel drive lined with cypress trees. The stone house, in a style similar to ours, looks idyllic on the outside. Inside, it is cluttered with stuff brought back from all their trips to Asia. It has an interesting layout and lots of potential.

However, the train line is about ten feet from the back windows. It's so close you could see what the person in the carriage of a passing train was reading if you tried. We have the train line beyond the end of our garden, but it's not that noticeable. The trains are mostly electric, and they usually go past slowly as we are close to the station.

There is also a catch to this house. There is another property sharing the courtyard belonging to the owner's sister. She too wants to sell—both houses are for sale as a package. So what they are really selling are two houses with three bedrooms each for six hundred thousand. Although they are priced and advertised individually, you have to buy both as they both share the courtyard and ownership of the gardens and entrance. It may be suitable for someone who wants to run a BnB and live on site but it's not for my friend.

The next house we go see is also divided into two separate units between two brothers. One brother has completely renovated his side of the house while the other bother and elderly cousin are living in the other half. There are faded Christmas decorations hanging on the door and in the kitchen window from the previous Christmas, or perhaps the one before it.

The brother who looks like he was just came in from rolling in a field of turnips and never learnt how to use the washing machine, takes over from the estate agent with long monologues of his Mama cooking in this kitchen and why there is a cask of wine with a tap beside the sofa in the kitchen.

A room with all its walls covered in rosettes is like a shrine to his father, who was awarded each rosette for refereeing football matches.

There is also a cabinet of dolls with china faces and broken eyes. And several mouldy corners where the roof needs repairing. The side of the house has brick patterns of different types and eras when the chimney was rebuilt and two windows bricked up. However, my friend falls in love with the olive grove of sixty mature trees and vegetable garden outback.

Having lived in an apartment for years, I understand her hunger for space and soil to grow things, but the sellers are not budging on the price of three hundred and fifty thousand. With so much work to be done to the house, it's not for her.

"I thought houses would be cheaper. How did you get yours so cheap?" Fiona asks driving back to town for lunch.

"We bought ours just before the Italian government started the bonus renovation schemes. A lot of properties in need of work were bought up when the schemes started, pushing up the prices. The renovation schemes are now finished but the house prices haven't changed."

"Did the scheme work out for you?"

"When we bought our place for one hundred and twenty thousand, we knew if we put one-hundred-thousand into it, we would get fifty-thousand back from the scheme, which we could put into it again and get twenty-five thousand back on that. And then pump that twenty-five thousand back into it again. So two hundred thousand of reno work would cost us just seventy-five thousand.

"It kind of worked, but then the government closed the scheme to banks funding the refund. And we were left short of a thirty-five thousand expected refund. But it still worked out okay for us.

"So, the house—between buying and renovating—has cost us three hundred thousand, but seventy thousand of that was refunded through the government renovation scheme, so we have a fully restored house for two hundred and forty thousand. But buying one of these houses that are now up for three hundred and fifty thousand and in need of about two hundred thousand investment and a lot of work doesn't make sense when you could buy something finished for five hundred thousand with a pool included."

"That is way out of my budget." Fiona looks disillusioned.

"You are only at the start of your search; don't lose hope yet. There are still bargains out there and the best way to find one is to go stay in the area, maybe put up wanted signs in the local bar and supermarket. Or look out for 'Vendesi' signs rather than online estate agents."

On the way to town, we swing by Helga's as I need to pick up a tool Ronan loaned them and we invite Helga to join us for lunch. Helga has a beautiful house with beautiful furniture she brought over from Scotland. Beds of latticed Rosewood, antique dressers and an enviable roll top writing desk that triggers a smile and a sigh every time I see it.

"Did you hear about that tourist in Florence who decided to have a piss when he was on the viewing point of the Duomo? He actually pissed on to the roof of the Duomo and he saw no reason not to as there was no bathroom. He was fined four hundred euro. If it was up to me I'd have handed him a scrub brush and a bar of soap and escorted him right back up those four hundred and sixty-three steps to clean up his mess," Helga says passing around the mixed board of cheeses, prosciutto and salami. The starter to another epic lunch.

"After moving to Italy, how long did it take you both to stop feeling like a tourist and feel part of Italy?" Fiona asks.

"Feeling like a tourist, stops when you have to start dealing with the bank and bureaucracy involved in becoming a resident, which is frustrating enough in any country I am sure, but doing it in a different language, adds a whole heap of new challenges and stress," Helga says taking a dollop of honey to dip her cheese into.

"I don't think I will ever feel part of Italy. I think I would have to become part of an Italian family to feel that, and I am a bit too old for adoption. But I do feel protective of Italy and I get annoyed when tourists do stupid things like that guy on the Duomo," I say.

"Venice gets riddled with them," Helga says. "Asshole tourists who think it's an amusement park rather than an historic city where people live. They are always fishing stupid tourists out of the canals there. Diving off the Academia Bridge. Did you hear about that Englishman, who swam across the Grand Canal to be like Lord Byron, who had swum the canal in the 1800s? And the Czech woman, who swam in the lagoon before posing topless for photos? They don't realise the canals are a UNESCO protected site."

"And a sewer system." I laugh.

"Drunk tourists steal water taxis and gondolas for the laugh and think nothing is wrong with it. They wouldn't do it at home."

"Well, they probably couldn't because they don't have gondolas where they are from." I am being a smartass.

"You know what I mean." Helga laughs. "One of them fell off a gondola and into the water last winter and nearly died of hypothermia by the time the police fished him out."

"I'm surprised people do stupid things like that still. Because Italy seems really strict about stuff like that," Fiona says. "I had a friend who went on holiday to Sardinia and her little boy put some stones from the beach in his bag. They were stopped going through the airport and told off. She didn't even know he had them. Supposedly tourists taking home sand, you know the pink sand they have there, and pebbles have added up to tonnes and become a threat to the environment of the Sardinian coastline. So it's now illegal. My friend was lucky. They let her off with just a warning, but they could have been fined up to three thousand euro. She was mortified."

Fiona pops out between courses to make a phone call.

"Did Shelly tell you my news?" Helga says.

"No, don't tell me you are pregnant." I say, trying to be serious even though Helga is seventy-five years young. "No, nothing as shocking. I'm doing Swedish Death Cleaning."

"Oh my god Helga, are you dying?"

"No. Well, we all are, aren't we, but no, not imminently as far as I know. Swedish Death Cleaning is when you get rid of all the clutter in your life so your kids don't have to deal with it after you have gone and it frees you up to enjoy your last decade or two without having worries."

"Oh, okay." I say, remembering half hearing about this technique at some point when I wasn't quite listening to a podcast.

"So we are selling the house. We only come here for a few weeks every season anyway, and our kids aren't interested. So if you hear of anybody looking to buy—"

"I might know just the person," I smile as Fiona rejoins us.

33

W hile opening the house to paying guests excites me, it also terrifies me at the same time. I'm concerned we will find it draining, too interfering or we'll take an entire year of bookings before realising we hate it after the first person arrives.

"Before committing to a bed and breakfast situation, I think a good way to practice is to have some random people stay." I announce to Ronan one morning as we watch as Juno run around the garden with a box of wildflower seed she has robbed off the table, scattering seed everywhere.

"Like who?"

"I don't know, that's the point. We need people we don't know to stay, so we get a feel for it. To know if it is the right thing for us." After thirty years, Ronan is used to my morning decision announcements.

"If we don't know them, how are we going to find them and get them to stay? Drag them in while they are passing?"

"I don't know. I'll find some."

I put an open invitation on my private social media page and I invite everyone in the online writers' group I am part of, to come stay at The Sighing house for free.

"I'm in!" Kayla, who is part of a late-night writing group, messages me.

"I'm working on a shoot in Egypt in a few weeks and have a week free after it. I was thinking of coming to Italy. Did you mean it when you said we could stay?" Kayla is a stunt woman from Chicago. I'd seen clips online of her car stunts, jumping off buildings on fire and sword fights.

We have a quick online chat about it and I am excited to have our first unknown guest coming.

"Is it okay if I bring my friend Lola?"

"Of course."

"She's a very interesting person, she is a holocaust survivor."

Bloody hell, I think to myself while doing the math. She must be nearly 100-years-old.

"Is she able for stairs?"

"Yes," Kayla says, hesitating.

"I look forward to meeting her. Is she okay talking about her life?"

"Yes," again Kayla sounds strangely cautious, "but she doesn't talk holocaust after 6PM, it's too heavy, it's all comic books and comedies and a couple of beers from 6PM on."

A few beers and comic books? I decide not to ask any more questions.

A woman I met at a wedding conference some years ago also sees my invite and comes to stay within two weeks.

I join her for a drink the first day before knowing she is intending to do this every day. "I'm on holiday," she reminds us while opening a bottle of Prosecco at eleven the following morning.

"Most of the hotels I have stayed offer Prosecco and strawberries in the morning as part of breakfast. You should do that." I welcome her suggestion, but daily morning drinking is not going to happen.

Her kids run riot through the house, terrorising the dogs, who are used to the quiet life and not two hyperactive kids while their mother stays semi-inebriated.

The house renovations haven't turned me into an alcoholic, but perhaps having guests in the house will.

I ask her about her wedding business, something we have in common, and it might stop her slugging more Prosecco if she is busy talking. It soon becomes apparent that she doesn't actually do any weddings. She doesn't have time between all the free trips she does to familiarise herself with venues for weddings she doesn't do.

"I have bought a bottle of good wine for lunch," she says, waving a bottle and carrying out plates. The lunch which she has taken for granted, she and her kids were going to be part of, as I lay the table for Ronan and me.

After an hour of listening to her talk about herself, and her kids sit glued to their devices without lifting their eyes or eating anything, she announces "Time for a siesta," and promptly falls asleep in the lounge chair.

She wakes in time for a walk down to the lake for an Aperol spritz before dinner, which she returns to our house just in time for. She'd offer to help, but not do anything other than open another bottle of Prosecco.

Thankfully, she only stayed five days.

After she leaves, Ronan and I agree. Neither our house nor pets are set up for kids and I'm not into people coming who want to do all day drinking in the garden. And I'm definitely not going to be hosting lunches and dinners.

The following week, I arrive at the train station to pick up Kayla and her Holocaust friend as arranged. Lola does not look one hundred, I'd say they are both barely forty.

My brain scrambles for a moment, trying to match the person to the expectations I had built.

"So, Lola, tell me about yourself."

She doesn't notice my nervous laugh as I am feeling I need to apologise to her for my mixup that she doesn't know I made.

"I'm from Illinois and I'm a holocaust scholar."

What a difference a word makes.

Kayla is a slight woman and has such a cute, soft voice she sounds like a cartoon character. I throw myself into tour guide mode, taking them to the lake for sundowners, my favourite restaurants along the lakefront and a boat out to Isola Maggiore for a hike and a picnic.

Having Kayla and Lola stay—two previous strangers who are now friends—has been a huge success, but I didn't get any writing done and I barely saw Ronan. If I am going to do this successfully and have my own life, I need to resist becoming so involved with those who stay and let them explore the area by themselves.

Fiona comes back for another look at Helga's house. She decides it is not for her. She is having second thoughts about buying in Italy and instead has another idea.

"I can work remotely for three weeks every quarter. So I think I will just continue working and stay at a co-living house in different parts of the world if I can find suitable ones. A lot of them are mixed and I don't like being hit on when I am living in the same building as the person. It gives me the ick and makes me feel unsafe."

"Do you still get hit on? That hasn't happened to me in years."

"That's because you are married. When I was married, I was never hit on either, but when I became single five years ago, it was like an invisible flashing light went off above my head, even though another relationship was the last thing I was looking for."

"And you got hit on in co-living spaces?"

"I haven't stayed at many as it's still only a relatively new accommodation option concept, but I have been to a few or at conferences in small hotels and when just having a laugh with a group some guy inevitably takes it up as a come-on and asks can he come to my room. It's happened three times to me and made me really self-conscious about being myself in group situations. I wish there were more women-only places for women travelling on their own."

That is when I tell Fiona about my vision for the house. A place for solo female travellers and writers to retreat to. "Do it! It's much needed. I'll be the first to book."

Tonya, a Dutch/Ukrainian woman I met on the ghost busting retreat, comes to stay for two weeks. It turned out she too thought the ghost busting retreat was going to be something completely different to what it was, but enjoyed it anyway.

Tonya works at her remote job on the top floor, comes down for coffee, looks after herself regards food. She takes the opportunity on her days off to go to the island and to Florence. She also has time to work on her book. Each morning when I get up for breakfast at 8am, she is coming in the gate having gone for her ten thousand steps to the top end of the marina and back, stopping for a morning coffee and meditation by the lake. "It's so beautiful to have time out to myself, time to read, do yoga and just be myself."

"By the way, I won't be here this afternoon, so bring your key if you are going out," I tell her. "I need to go for a medical exam." I have an appointment at a hospital in Spoleto to get my water baby checked out by a specialist.

"A magical exam? First you are ghost busting, now you have a magical exam?"

On the last day, Tanya strips off the bed and leaves her bedroom and bathroom clean and tidy. I get her to take all the carb full food with her on the next leg of her journey to Puglia, otherwise I will just eat it.

"This is much better," I say to Ronan. "It's so nice to have guests who are independent and do their own thing. I love that the house is also being used as a place for people to retreat to and work on their books and taking time to themselves. It's really what Anam Cara should be, not just a general BnB."

34

I go to the hospital prepared with my folder of scans, MRI, and all the reports I have so far.

I have written down what I am to say: I have an appointment.

It's easy enough. I have also come prepared with words I might need to recognise, such as liver, cyst, operation, surgery, cut, major, minor, die, better write your will—that sort of thing.

I have never had surgery and the thought of having surgery in a country with a language I am not fluent in and an alien health system, has taken up a lot of my head space since Doctor Chicken suggested the eleven centimetre water balloon attached to my liver, may need to be removed.

It's the perfect opportunity to try the translation gadget I bought for Ronan in case of emergencies, such as this. A small device the same length, but half the width of a cell phone. You choose the language you want to translate to, speak what you want to say, press the button and it says it back in that language.

It does it in reverse too—translating back for you and can do it in any language of the world. It could be the solution I need to calm my fears about not being able to speak Italian fluently enough in a hospital situation. And here I am. Time to put it to the test.

It's pouring rain. And we rush past two elderly nuns talking at the entrance. Rosary beads hanging from their waist, sneakers on, hair completely covered.

The hospital is built over two floors with an all glass entrance, spanning the height of the two floors. We go up to the first floor and realise we need to go back down to the ground floor. Descending the escalator, you can see why they gave the hospital entrance a glass front. Beyond the two huge, ornamental, terracotta urns on the first floor, the spectacular view of the Umbrian hills, dotted with different coloured fields and greens, makes you take deep healing breaths and perhaps gives hope to those in need of something to live for.

"I think the hospital in Castiglione del Lago has competition for the hospital with the best view in the world," I say to Ronan, fondly reminiscing of our times we have rushed to our local hospital in the past, when Ronan nearly died of pancreatitis and our son nearly bled to death.

I go to the desk and whip out the translation gadget and say confidently into it. "Can you direct me to this department?" I press the button and hold it out for the man to hear.

"Jeoleul i buseolo annaehae jusil su issnayo?" says the recorded voice. He looks at me blankly. It takes me a moment to realise it didn't sound anything like Italian.

Bloody hell, it has switched into Korean. While I am pressing buttons to try to get it back onto Italian, the guy checks my appointment sheet and tells me the outpatient department I need is in the basement, in Italian, which I understand perfectly.

The two nuns go into the elevator, so we take the stairs down and find the waiting area.

"Jezuz, that's not a lift, that's a magic box. Look at the nuns now," Ronan says as a young woman with a two-year-old steps out of the elevator the nuns went into.

I find the administration desk. A cheerful woman about the same age as me is behind the counter and a young guy in his twenties is chatting to her near the door, both wearing the same hospital uniform.

Shet takes my appointment sheet in hand. "I have an appointment," I say in my most perfectly rehearsed Italian.

"Dublino? Irlandese?" she smiles.

"Sì."

I am doing well. She hands me back my sheet with the number eighty-five stapled to it.

"You need to come when this arrives." She says loudly in English with lots of clear mouth movement, as if I am in need of lip reading. "Do you speak English?" she asks the young guy in Italian. He shrugs, "A little".

"Come si dici ottantacinque in inglese?" [How do you say eighty-five in English?] She says to him.

"Eighty-five," I say to her.

"Eighty-five," her co-worker echoes me.

"You need to come when they call," she says to me in Italian, "Eighty-five," she says in English.

"My friend who speaks English will call you when eighty-five is called," she says in Italian. I am glad there are other people who get as confused as me when trying to talk two different languages.

We take seats in the waiting area while I try to fix my translation gadget. But in the hospital basement, there is no wi-fi. The translation gadget needs wi-fi. I will need to use my brain. I begin to sweat and revise my words in Italian; Liver, cyst, surgery, die.

Soon a doctor comes out of a room in the hallway and calls out eighty-five in Italian. There is no sign of the guy who was to be my number translator.

The doctor looks over my files and asks if I speak Italian. Instead of saying my usual 'no' and just hearing white noise for the rest of the meeting, I say "Yes, a little". She speaks to me in Italian clearly and I understand the gist of what she is saying. I have let go of trying to understand every word. Being able to see their expression and mouth helps so much when you are trying to learn a language. Covid masks made that part hugely difficult.

"Do you have pain?"

"No."

"Did you have pain?"

"No."

"What brought you to your doctor to discover it?"

"A regular check-up." I do not mention he had got a new ultrasound machine and I wanted a go of it.

"There is nothing we need to do. If it causes you pain, come back. In twelve months get an echograph again."

"Is that it? No surgery?"

"No need."

Walking back to the car, my focus goes away from my water baby for the first time in months and I realise I am walking pain free. My back is no longer hurting. When did that happen? When I think about it, I have been getting out of bed with ease, no crunching. I am walking up and down the stairs quicker. I've been literally bouncing around the place. Is it the HRT? My regular Qi Gong practice? Perhaps a combination of both. Whatever it is, it's working.

A clump of invisible stress is shed with every step through the car park that has the most stunning view of the Umbrian countryside. I am no longer in pain, I am no longer worried about surgery, I got by in hospital in Italian. Life is good and is looking a whole lot brighter.

35

"Okay, tell me, should I start packing boxes for a move country?"

Ronan knows me too well. I've just arrived in Barcelona for a writing retreat and it is fabulous. It would just take me to say, "yes start packing," and he would go along with it.

"I don't know yet. I'll give you a call and let you know."

The first word I see graffitied on a wall in Barcelona is 'Burro'. My mind flashes back to way back when our moving abroad idea kicked off—learning Spanish dancing around the kitchen with my sister and the guy from South America. I can't remember his name. The only words I still remember are 'El burro es Malo'. The donkey is bad. Whereas 'il burro' in Italian is butter.

I arrive two days early for the retreat and book a hotel on La Rambla in the centre of the city near the Gothic quarter. I haven't travelled on my own in years and I need to get my nerve back.

First port of call is the Gothic quarter. A labyrinth of rambling alleyways with gargoyles galore. I love gargoyles. I need to get some for the garden. I haven't researched what to see—I prefer to be surprised and discover stuff. Such as 'stumbling' on the Cathedral of the Holy Cross and Saint Eulalia. Having not done research, I have no expectations. This way it feels like travelling in my early twenties with just a couple of paragraphs to follow torn out of an out of date "Europe by Train" book I had.

Within a few steps of entering the cathedral, my breath is literally taken away by the awesomeness of the vaulted brick ceilings and stone pillars lit by golden up-lighting. Slowly, I move through the cathedral and find an exit. But I am not back out onto the street, I am in a cloister with an enclosed ornamental garden of palm and orange trees, a large pond and fountain.

A weird honking noise is in the distance. It gets louder as I follow the cloister walls, trying to find my way back to the street. Instead of the street, I find a gaggle of geese in the enclosed garden. I don't know how long I stand taking in the scene. Thirteen white geese stretching their necks waddling around after each other in a lush garden of ferns and orange trees overlooked by gargoyles, cloistered in a square of medieval arches and pillars lit by the golden light of the setting sun while the sky above is still blue.

There is an information board about why the geese are here. Like so many other wonders, attached to something beautiful there is a sad story.

Saint Eulalia, the patron of Barcelona, was a goose herder who at the young age of thirteen, openly professed her Christian faith, despite the Roman authorities' attempts to suppress Christianity in the region. In the year 303, she went to the governor, and demanded the cease of hostilities against Christians. The governor, instead, sentenced her to thirteen tortures, including crucifixion and decapitation—one for each year she had lived as a Christian.

She was stripped, flogged, and tortured in an attempt to have her renounce her faith.

Her remains are buried in a crypt dedicated to her in the cathedral and since then, thirteen geese are kept in a designated area in the cloister of the cathedral, as homage to the young goose herder.

 It said that after her death, a sudden snowstorm covered her mostly nude body like a garment, hence white geese.

I eventually find my way back into the streets of the Quarter and make my way to the Passeig de Gràcia; the street with the houses that look like something out of a fantasy.

The people who lived along this street one hundred years previously had expensive butts. The tiled public benches running down the centre of the street have a chamber under them where someone was employed to place hot coals each day to create heated benches for the rich people to sit on.

A tour of Casa Amatller, the home of the rich chocolatier, satisfies my love of everything Art Nouveau. Just up the street, I get my first dollop of Gaudi with a tour of the house designed by him; Casa Batilo—the house with no straight lines—instead there are waves and curves, elongated windows, undulating ceilings, roof tiles like dragon scales and curved doorways. Nothing is straight because nothing in nature is straight and everything is colourful.

Two gorgeous houses full of ideas to tickle your mind like a psychedelic trip. I like the way the rooms in the houses each told a story.

I make my way back towards my hotel and wander into La Boqueria, the food market. With stalls full of freshly cut fruit, cured meats and delicious offerings, it reminds me of the food market in Florence, but with more variety of cultures. I get a Buddha bowl of lots of tasty stuff and go back to my room at the hotel with its balcony to eat and people watch late into the night.

The following day I am up early. I'm keen to see the still unfinished Gaudi masterpiece La Sagrada Familia or 'Cathedral of the Poor' as Gaudi called it.

Gaudi was nicknamed 'God's architect' and was well paid and famous for his work before he died. As he got older, he became more and more religious, attending mass and confession every day. He spent the rest of his time in his workshop, which he moved into in the Cathedral of the Poor, eating only lettuce and milk for lunch and fasting. He was so desperate to finish the cathedral, he went as far as begging for alms to continue the work on it.

It's because of this I find it ironic that the end of his life came sooner than perhaps necessary because people thought he was a beggar. He was going to church for his daily confession and got hit by a tram, which left him unconscious.

Because people thought he was 'just' a beggar without papers and old worn clothes, and not their iconic architect, he wasn't rescued immediately, as taxis wouldn't take a beggar to hospital.

When he eventually was taken to hospital by a police officer, he only got the rudimentary care a pauper would get. It wasn't until the following day a priest from the cathedral recognised the beggar as the city's most loved and famed architect, but it was too late. Gaudi died two days later. The whole of Barcelona snaked the streets for his funeral procession to the unfinished colossal cathedral where he lies in a crypt. Had the same church-going people cared for the man they thought was a beggar, their mourning may not have been needed so soon.

The work on La Sagrada Familia is due to be finished one hundred years after his death in 2026. From a distance, the eighteen spires look like they are melting with dripping stone.

I do my usual eaves-dropping in on tours, picking up bits about how the church has three facades: The Nativity, The Passion Facade and the yet to be finished Glory Facade.

The facade depicting The Nativity, has rich ornate intricate carvings: birds nestle in delicate folds of stone, while vines and flowers spill outward as if they had grown naturally from the walls. The Holy Family at its centre, surrounded by angels and shepherds. The columns twist like tree trunks, their textures mimicking bark, while animals—frogs, snakes, turtles—are hidden among the ornamentation. Above it all, the Star of Bethlehem. To me it all looks heavy, too much.

The Passion Facade is more stark and angular, reflecting the somber theme of the crucifixion. The figures are gaunt and I overhear a guide say the columns are shaped like the bones of Christ, supporting the weight of the basilica. "Together the facades, form a cathedral of emotions, a story of faith carved into the very bones of Barcelona."

In stark contrast, the interior feels empty, even though there are a lot of tourists walking around. It is clean and modern without pillars in the way. The pillars along the sides are inspired by a forest, features columns branching out like trees. Some are bathed in colourful light from the massive, modern stained-glass windows. Each column has its turn of being the receiver of projected colourful light as the sun does its daily commute.

While the design is fantastical and combines two of my favourite styles, Gothic and Art Nouveau, with nature-inspired elements, it doesn't do it for me. It's too big and vast and all too much. I much more prefer the Gothic cathedral with the geese. There, I could fall to my knees and pray if I felt the urge, but here I don't feel it. Although I do feel a sense of awe as I sit and enjoy the details of every crevice and the changing light through the windows. My feeling of awe is interrupted by the voices of two English tourists asking a miffed tour guide, "Is this all there is? Is there anything else we can see?"

I am not sure what they were expecting. They probably researched it too much.

I take a taxi to Park Güell. From the bustling streets of Barcelona, the taxi weaves up hill heading towards the enchanting Park Güell. I haven't researched it; I prefer to just turn up and be surprised by experiences rather than be possibly disappointed by expectations like the English couple in the cathedral.

Gaudí's plan was to create a modern housing estate away from the smog and chaos of the city below, on an empty plot of land on a hill to the south of Barcelona owned by Eusebi Güell.

Gaudí's original residential project was abandoned and the park transformed into a public space in 1926. Right in front of the main entrance a familiar lizard greets me, it was on the cover of a notebook Jamsie gave me as a kid—I didn't know it was one of Barcelona's most famous symbols and here he was in front of me. A hat tip greeting from my brother.

Together, Gaudi and Güell planned to build sixty houses with modern conveniences such as running water as well as facilities: a market, a laundry room, a church, and a public square. But the construction costs soared and only two houses and the park were completed.

I have time to kill before I go to the meeting spot for the retreat, so I spend time wandering around the colourful mosaiced structures and life-sized gingerbread like houses. The sound of children playing spills from a schoolyard in the middle of the park. What a wonderful place to have a school, where they are surrounded by colour and art and nature and their walk to school takes them through a world of fantasy every day.

I sit and have a glass of wine and think how I had forgotten how much inspiration travel can give. Barcelona has given me heaps and I have only been here for forty-eight hours so far.

My phone has realised I am in the city and as I was recently looking at tattoo artists, it is showing me tattoo studios close by, in case I want to nip in and mark myself for life during my lunch break. When I was growing up, the only place you could get a tattoo was in prison. But there is a tattoo I do want to get: a painting my brother James did. It's a cartoon guy with wiggly arms and legs running through a field. James called it Ecstatically Happy. I went to a tattoo artist in Italy, and she sketched it on my arm with a pen. Ecstatically Happy Man's arms and legs enwrapping my arm like a sleeve. "That is the smallest I can do it." It is not what I had in mind. I want it about two inches high and wide.

My phone's algorithm has its wicked way and shows me the Instagram page of a tattoo artist in Barcelona who specialises in small, detailed tattoos. I book an appointment for the day after the retreat ends. Another opportunity for Ronan to sell me off to the circus as the Tattooed Lady.

36

W hen I meet the other participants, most in their early thirties, it strikes me I am one of the oldest participants, which is a new experience for me and feels strange. I am also the only one who has finished writing a book and the only Irish one. There are women from England, the US and Finland, but most participants are originally from Russia and Ukraine. Most have been displaced because of the war, making me wonder how this is going to play out.

We are staying in an Airbnb in the city, and camp beds have been set up in every available room. I'm sharing a closed off entrance room with Brenda, the American, and luckily, we don't have to share a poo bag. There is a door straight into the kitchen on one side and a front door on the other side, which is no longer used. This was once the servants' entrance. We're effectively in the servants' cloak room.

The head of my camp bed is under the curtained window into the stairwell of the apartment block. I'm not impressed, but it gives me heart that people are okay with this, so what I offer should be very acceptable. The apartment has a nice big kitchen, a sitting area and a dining area. A cook comes each day to create delicious meals—Toasted bread rubbed with ripe tomatoes, drizzled with olive oil, and sprinkled with salt or a slice of Spanish omelette made with eggs and potatoes for breakfast, and paella or tasty tapas for dinner. Other meals we get ourselves when out.

The first evening after dinner, our group of ten are on the subway to a spa in town. It's the same chain as the one Izzy sent me to in London, with a similar underground feel. After two hours of floating, getting pounded by massage jets, boiled in steam rooms, saunas and plunging into ice cold water, we are left to our own devices to get back to the apartment. Again, this gives me confidence as no one else sees this as unusual; whereas I was thinking guests on a retreat should be handheld and be transferred and picked up to any activities outside the retreat's location.

Trying to sleep in the entrance hall with a complete stranger is interesting. She needs a noise machine to get her to sleep. The fuzzy sound is like an out of tune TV in the seventies and is as irritating as hell to my preference for silent nod off. But there is no fear of having that with the stairwell outside. Several drunk Spanish have a loud, jokey conversation above my head at about three in the morning. When I do eventually fall asleep, I fall so deeply that I keep my room mate awake with my snoring. But even though we both have had a crap sleep, we are up before dawn and getting taxis to the beach to watch the sunrise with the rest of the group.

We are not the only ones on the beach at the crack of dawn. There are the joggers and walkers. A barefoot, bearded man walking in the water with a well-groomed dog. They don't match. I can tell it's not his dog and my mind, given a moment of peace, is already filling the void with a story of whose dog it is and why he is walking it. A group of yogis standing silhouetted like mermaid purses against the peach sky while the sun does its thing.

As the sun climbs, our group stays in silence and I pick sea glass from the area around me. Sea glass brings memories of the first time we took the kids to the Amalfi Coast flooding back. How chaotic my life had been before that period. And how chaotic it became after I returned to Ireland.

Chaos breeds chaos. I stepped away from it and it stopped, but then returned and stepped back into it. I wonder what would have happened if I hadn't returned to Ireland, if we had stayed in Italy. What would have happened and what wouldn't have happened? Izzy would not have had the break she got into her acting career, that is for sure. Maybe that was the reason the Universe pushed us back to Ireland at that time. Who knows? I feel her career was the only good thing that came of going back that time. But who knows?

Our first retreat task is to think of ten things we are grateful for.

1. The sunrise: it took effort to get out of bed and get here, but I am glad to be alive to see it.

2. Sea glass: I am grateful for the memories it brought back.

3. The women I am with and the new friends I have already made.

4. Freedom to travel.

5. My back is pain free.

6. An understanding roommate about my snoring.

I look around and see homeless people sleeping under the steps down to the beach.

7. I'm grateful for a safe and warm place to sleep last night-even though it was an entrance hallway on a camp bed.

8. A beautiful, meaningful start to the day.

9. I am grateful for seeing people on the beach enjoying and appreciating the day, their bodies and each other. They are the type of people who get up early. They give me hope for humanity.

10. My ability to express myself in writing.

The beach here is different from the beaches in Italy. I think Italy's beach culture is unique to Italy. It is the classic seaside image of colourful umbrellas and beach loungers in orderly lines. Each beach club is designated by its unique umbrella colour or pattern and each offers its own set of amenities, which can include lifeguards, towels, showers, changing rooms, restaurants, and activities like paddle boarding or kayaking. Italians seem to use it as an opportunity to socialise and relax. Some beach goers rent a favourite spot for the entire summer season.

I didn't like it at first. It was too orderly for someone who enjoys beach walks and isolation. But it does mean you do not have to haul beach gear around-not that I ever did. Here in Barcelona the long beach is a free for all, like the ones in Ireland.

Our group walks in silence across the sand to a trendy beach side cafe and sit around the large wooden table big enough for all twelve of us. We are to write the things we are grateful for I add my breakfast of French toast and the chai tea to my list. You can't get breakfasts like this in Italy. I'd like to offer nice breakfasts to my guests—but unless I do an extensive health certification, I will be in breach of Italian law, I'll have to think of something else.

The writing sessions we do are more exercises in journaling than what I would normally do writing wise. My idea of writing is setting a timer for twenty-five minute sprints and using the sprints to stay focused long enough to get one thousand words written each day.

But doing something different is good. We are to note five things we see, four things we hear, three things we touch, two things we can smell and one taste in the present moment.

Grain of the wood, Russian lettering, juice waves in the juice machine, stack of tarot cards on someone's table near us, a paper cup. Clink of cups, rattle of cutlery, good music, guy laughing. My hair touching against my face, pen damp and warmth in my belly. I can smell shampooed hair and hot spicy chai is the taste.

I can see how doing this exercise regularly could improve my writing, thinking about descriptions of a moment in time.

Next, a card deck of seventy different tree photos is spread jumbled on the table in front of us. We are to pick one that we are drawn to and symbolises yourself. I surprise myself at the one I pick: a tree with no leaves on its branches, but on its trunk hangs a bird house. I am to describe it. "It is well weathered and aged, bare of its previous leaf beauty, but the beauty is now in the texture of the tree itself. I picked it because home is where I am, where my family gather. I am the bird box."

Identifying as a bird box is a new experience for me.

Continuing on with the tree theme our final task of the leisurely lovely morning in the beach cafe is to draw a tree with roots that each symbolise what is grounding us, the branches are what we want more of in our lives and the trunk is what the tree needs. It's an interesting exercise.

What is grounding me: my kids—each get a root. Belief in myself gets a root, my garden, writing, Qi Gong each get a root. But the deepest tap root is Dad and Jamsie. I want more love, joy, me-time, a strong body, health, retreats, enjoy my age and then I have a branch with leaves blowing off it—shedding the past.

We have the afternoon to ourselves to enjoy the beach or the city.

"Tomorrow we go to 'Els Encants' the famous lice market of Barcelona," Ella, our retreat leader, a woman in her mid thirties with short pink hair, tells us. English is not her first language and I know from experience translation apps don't always get it right. In this case, she has been given an alternative to the word 'flea' that doesn't quite work. "Buy something that represents you and tell us a story about it when we return."

I love this idea and the suggestion of the excursion to the Barcelona flea market reminds me of the old dream I had of having a house filled with memorable things I have brought at markets around the world. I drift off to sleep, trying to figure out how I am going to cart all the stuff I will want to buy back to Italy. I finally fall asleep after I text Ronan. Is the van still working? How long would it take you to drive to Barcelona in the van?

37

The ten of us leave the apartment early, a little groggy from the flowing cava of the night before. But the humour lifts quickly and the bonding of new friendships continues as we make our way by Metro to the famous 'Els Encants' market.

Italy doesn't have flea markets like these, their markets are more organised, like the antique market in Arrezzo, which takes over the streets of the old town every first Sunday of the month and previous Saturday. I have been to it a few times. The first visit was exciting, the second has a lot of the same stuff as the first and the third was a distraction when the interior doors had been taken from the house, the weekend after we placed the deposit down to buy it.

We were on the verge of pulling out of the sale as the previous owners denied they took the doors, but I lived in hope a miracle would happen and bought a set of ornate brass door handles at the market confirming to the Universe that I still wanted the house. Minutes later we got the call; the doors had been returned. It was a miracle.

The ornate handles still lie in a box. I haven't found a home on a door for them yet. They will be perfect for my secret door behind a library shelf into the converted attic room when I can afford to get it done.

The flea market in Barcelona is in a fabulous old structure, with a mirrored canopy, reflecting treasures of over five hundred vendors ready for a good haggle spread out below, in a kaleidoscopic view of the colourful tapestry of life and history beneath.

"This marketplace has been operating since the fourteenth century, making it one of Europe's oldest markets," Ella says standing at the spot we designate as our meeting point in two hours' time before we all spill in different directions to find our story object.

The bazaar is an Aladdin's cave of antique furniture, knick-knacks, vintage clothes, vinyl records, china, kitsch ornaments.

"Look at this," Brenda says to me and some of the group who have migrated towards a large stall selling toys and other household objects I had as a child, now labelled as vintage. "An original laptop," she laughs, holding up a travel typewriter.

"I had one identical to that!" I say. "I wrote my first stories and book on one of them."

"No!" Brenda says in disbelief. "What was your first book about?"

"About travelling by train around America with my friend, Pipi. We had a budget of twenty dollars a week for food."

"Was this before mobile phones?"

"It was before the internet."

"How did you find your way around and book trains and stuff?"

"We had a fold out A4 Amtrak map and a few pages of a travel book to guide us. We planned our route, so we'd stay on the trains overnight. "

"I can't imagine travelling without my phone. What would you do all day on a train?"

"Have conversations with people. We met some characters. I wrote lots of detailed notes about the trip and people we met. I still have them somewhere, I think."

"You should write a prequel to your life in Italy," Brenda says before we drift in different directions.

Where to start? I decide at the top and work my way down.

The top floor gallery surrounding the inner structure is dedicated to fabrics and new shoes. Although I have no intention of buying fabric, I can't help but have a few minutes of indulgence and momentarily get lost amongst the reams of silk brocade, velvet, flannel, satin and lace.

Wrought iron steps lead down into the huge inner belly where hawkers have set up their tables in the middle. The permanent antique sellers around the perimeter have a more shop style feel, with their storage lockups open like a tightly packed treasure chest. I dare to walk around one sideways without turning, so not to knock over anything. A vintage black typewriter catches my eye for one hundred and twenty euro. How beautiful it would look somewhere in our house.

I schmooze up and down the central labyrinth of stalls. I want to find a goddess statue. Ideally a Guanyin statue to celebrate getting my Qi Gong instructor certification and also to remind myself of how lotuses grow from mud-like my life slowly starting again after grief. I'm coming out of the mud. If I can't find her, any goddess statue will do to show how I have recognised the power and positivity of women gathering together and that is what brought me on this retreat. That is the story I will tell about the object I buy.

There is so much interesting stuff; vintage custom jewellery, record collections, postcards, black and white pictures of someone's relatives, dongs and bongs, taxidermy and religious icons. I can't see any goddesses.

They sell everything but nothing. There is nothing I need. Nothing anyone needs really when I think about it. Such as the vintage typewriter—it's beautiful, but I wouldn't use it to write on. I have just got rid of a shed full of someone else's clutter. I need less clutter in my life, not more. Like Helga, I don't want my kids having to sort through my clutter in years to come or for me to have a heap of stuff to move if I ever decide to move again.

My phone bings with a message from Ronan. He has just woken up and seen the forgotten text I sent him the previous night. "The van needs a new battery. Why? Are we moving to Barcelona? Is it that good?"

I think about the last few days. It's a beautiful city, and if I was going to move to a city, Barcelona would definitely be a contender. Perhaps we would have ended up here if our plans to move to northern Spain had of happened all those years ago, when our kids were small and if...

Ifs...there is no point in them. The 'Ifs' didn't happen. The past is gone; I am here now and while it is wonderful, Barcelona is too busy for me. "I don't think I want to live in any city in the future. I prefer our little town of Passignano with our walks along the lake to watch the sunset with an Aperol Spritz or the sunrise with a cappuccino." I say to Ronan when I call him. The morning cappuccino doesn't happen very often, probably twice, but the possibility is always there as long as we live in the town.

"So, we are not moving to Barcelona?"

"No. I just got excited because we were going to a flea market."

"You wanted me to drive across three countries to carry your shopping home?"

"Yes, sorry... when you put it like that. Although there is a gargoyle for sale, which I'd really like, but I think it might even be too heavy for the van." I say stroking the snout of the granite gargoyle with bulging eyes and dragon like wings. His previously vicious features softened by years of weathering.

"We'll get one of those sketchy things instead of a gargoyle to protect the house."

I immediately know what Ronan is talking about. A scacciaguai. The Italian answer to gargoyles. Though, unlike gargoyles, they don't have the dual purpose of being a water drain. A scacciaguai has only one sole purpose: to scare evil away and I sort of already know how to do that with my new ghost busting skills.

The name literally means "dispelling trouble" and the plaque of a scary, or sometimes comical, face can be spotted on the corner of streets in Italian old towns, on village wells and carved into the mantels of old fireplaces. There is one in Passignano of a guy pulling his mouth back at the corners and his tongue sticking out.

They are more common in rural areas as they were seen as a protection for animals and crops, too. Often on the same wall, or in close proximity, there will be a shrine to Our Lady or a saint. The Italians, like the Irish, like to cover all their bases when it comes to protection.

Time spent rummaging passes quickly. I have fifteen minutes before meeting with the rest of the group. I see some of them walking around with bags and one has a framed picture under her arm of a ballerina. I have nothing.

I spot a hippy shop on the periphery of the market. The type that sells labelled gemstones, incense and sage bundles. There is nothing secondhand or flea-bitten in this shop. Everything shines new to the background playlist of whale song and Tibetan sound bowls.

I see a plastic gold statue of the Indian goddess with all her arms and fling it on the counter. Fifteen euros down and a not so handsome statue, I bundle her into my bag and head back across the sprawling market to our meeting point.

I pause at the typewriter and can't help but place my fingers momentarily on the keys. And then I see her—a statuette of a small girl hugging her knees with a cartoon line smile and dots for eyes moulded from a small cube of dark metal with soft edges. Lines marking her hair, split in the middle and running down her back. I lift her. She is solid and heavy. Perhaps it was someone's first effort of sculpture in college, or perhaps it was a simple paperweight made by a great artist.

The happy little girl immediately reminds me of me as a child, sitting the way I did in the nun's field behind our garden dreaming of how life would be when I would be an adult, the places I would go, the things I would do. She brings an immediate smile to my face. I am instantly in love with her.

I try to haggle. He won't budge, so I walk away. Two minutes later, I am back with a sense of panic. I don't want to leave behind the little girl full of dreams. I pay the asking price: Twenty euros.

"It also reminds me that all women are just little girls trying to figure out adulting." I say later when we are each explaining our purchases. "I will put her on my dressing table, beside the mirror and greet her every day and remind myself that the woman I am looking at in the mirror is still that little girl, and it is my duty as an adult to help that little girl to live her fullest life and still chase all her dreams."

Before the session I Google 'Durga' so I can sound like I know what I am talking about when I explain about the goddess statue I have bought. It's then I notice the statue is standing on a baby's head. "Why is she standing on a baby's head?" I Google, and eventually find the answer.

The statuette I have bought to start my goddess statue collection is not a goddess, it is Shiva. He is standing on a dwarf's head, which represents spiritual ignorance.

So the first statue I buy for my goddess collection is of a male dancing on spiritual ignorance. Very apt. I feel the gods are having a laugh at me.

Our group session is accompanied by wine tasting. We have to be creative with our wine descriptions. These get more creative with each glass.

Touch of fossils. Sweat. Asbestos. Paint. Wet cardboard. A shit smelling rose.

What I learn on this trip: Spanish wine is not as good as Italian.

38

O ver lunch on the last day at a trendy tapas bar in the Gothic Quarter, one of the women on the retreat shows me a picture of her fluffy ragdoll cats she brought with her to London. "They are being looked after by pet sitters I found on a website for international house and pet sitters."

I recognise the name of the site, it was the one I used back in Ireland when we first stayed at La Dogana what seemed a lifetime ago. Was it really only seven years ago? So much has happened since: a pandemic, the death of my dad and brother, my mam in a nursing home, my two kids living their own lives in a different country to me, an almost-full villa renovation, Ronan retired, my wedding planning business becoming a distant memory and my dream of being a full-time author come true and ten published books realised.

"Is that petsitter website still going?"

"Yes, I use it at least five times a year so I can travel."

A plan forms. After lunch, I find a quiet corner and load a description, and some photos the house and our pets, on the website before joining the retreat group for our last exercise.

"Write your story of how you got to where you are at this moment," Ella says, sitting at the communal table we have found in a gorgeous bookshop with a courtyard and extensive English section. I miss bookshops so much. "It could be your full life story or just the bus trip you took this morning, but whichever section of your memoir you choose to write, you have to write it all in just three hours. It could be a poem, or just a couple of sentences or a full essay. Keep it to a maximum of two thousand words."

The women get to work, but I am at a loss for what to write.

"I've written a series of five books about where I got to where I am now." I say to Ella.

"Perhaps write about the first time you said 'We are off to Italy'."

Music suddenly triggers in my head and a story rises. But not the one in my books.

Pounding in my head are the words of a song that came out in Ireland when I was 19-years-old. The song, 'Put 'Em Under Pressure', had a catchy chorus of 'Olé, Olé' repeated over and over, along with a pulsating video, featuring footage from soccer matches and the Irish soccer team in Windmill Lane studios in Dublin, recording the chorus with Larry Mullen from U2. It stayed number one for thirteen weeks.

It was 1990, the year of one of the most momentous occasions in recent Irish history—Ireland qualifying for the World Cup. Italy was the host of the final matches. Like the time of hearing when Kennedy was shot, Elvis was dead, or a man walked on the moon, everyone old enough in Ireland, remembers where they were when Ireland beat Romania at a penalty shoot-out and qualified for the World Cup.

Having just finished my final school year exams, my attention was focused on collecting enough money for an InterRail ticket; a train pass entitling under 26-year-olds to travel by train in twenty-one European countries during any one month. It was sixty pounds—a veritable fortune to a teenager like myself at the time.

Collecting enough money did not involve a job, as there were none to be had in Ireland at the time—Even a job in one of the few fast-food places needed a glowing CV. It wasn't because of a recession, it was just the way Ireland was, we were a nation of potential emigrants. America, London or Germany were our career choices after school, there was never a mention of any of us going to college or university—a secretarial course or a trade apprenticeship perhaps.

So I collected aluminium cans from the field across the road where lads went drinking at the weekends because they were too young to get into pubs, leaving all their littered cans behind. Each week I'd collect two or three bags full and sell them to the charity Rehab, which paid 50p per bag. My mam, collected cans for me too when she walked our dog, Teddy—a border collie like all our family dogs before him.

Prince was coming to Ireland that year, so I got my sewing machine out and made Raspberry Berets and a shop in Temple Bar took them from me on a sale or return basis. They were a flop.

However, I made the most money for my train ticket on the day of the World Cup qualifier match with fan badges my mother and my friend Denise helped me make. Using an egg cup as a template, we traced circles on cereal boxes, cut them out and then painted with acrylic paint the word 'Olé'.

Thin strips of florist ribbon, curled with scissors, were crudely stapled on to the back of each cardboard Olé circle. Then we stuck a safety pin to the back of each one with sticky tape and priced them at 60p each.

We also had specials. These were giant badges made from stiff cardboard cutouts of the faces of the team being sold in petrol stations in Ireland. I bought twenty of them for one pound each. Stapling some of the looped green and yellow ribbon around them, and a sturdy safety pin on the back, turned each face into a rosette nearly a foot long; probably making them the gaudiest souvenir of the World Cup. These were valued at two pounds.

From one night's work we had enough to fill a suitcase—one of those heavy old ones with no wheels—and the next day my friend Denise took it to O'Connell Bridge in the centre of Dublin City, opened the case and started shouting "Get your Olé Olé badges here." The rough, gaudy badges made people laugh and sold like hotcakes.

"Have you any Packie Bonners or Paul McGraths?" These were the two most popular players requested and were in short supply.

"I've a Steve Staunton or Kevin Sheedy? How about a Niall Quinn?"

We didn't have a hawker's licence so when we saw police coming; we zipped up our wares pronto and walked away from the spot; just like the other illegal hawkers selling jewellery and pirated cassette tapes.

Once we were too slow, so we just stood there with our zipped up suitcase and said we were going on holiday. The foot patrol police knew what we were at but they just smiled at our response, and walked on by. We would not normally have been so brazen but the whole country, even the police, were in good humour that day.

I made one hundred and thirty pounds before kickoff. When Ireland scored the final deciding penalty shot, the crowds poured out from the pubs onto O'Connell Street—the main street in Dublin—and every street around it. The entire country was vibrating with joy, pride, and Guinness.

Denise and I had not seen the penalty shoot-out; we were heading down to the Garden of Remembrance with our empty suitcase to join a march for the release of the Birmingham Six. Bad timing on the organisers' part, but like the rest of Ireland, they were not expecting Ireland to get so far in the World Cup.

O'Connell Street, was flooded with people in green singing 'Olé Olé'. A group of lads promptly picked me up and threw me into the Anna Livia Fountain—I remember my head under water, the smell of fairy washing up liquid and a plastic bottle cap floating by with bubbles before my head resurfaced.

I was laughing with the rest of them before climbing out, dripping wet and continuing on down the road with the suitcase and soggy bank notes in my pocket. I think the march was postponed.

I got the train home and met up with my brothers and their friends in our local pub, The Beachcomber, to continue the celebrations. I have never experienced an atmosphere of a full day of widespread joy like it since.

The following week, I bought my train pass for Europe.

Irish people in any large group still sporadically break into the 'olé, olé' chant chorus when anything of significance happens in Ireland, such as Taylor Swift concerts, funerals, weddings, that sort of thing. Or in our case, when we were driving to Italy for the first time. Somewhere across The Alps, Ronan, myself, and the kids gave the song a blast as one line in the chorus is; 'We're all off to Italy."

My flight home from Barcelona does not leave until the evening after the retreat ends. But first, I have a date with a tattoo artist.

Of course, the studio entrance is down a dark alley behind a large intimidating metal door. I had a glass or two of wine at lunch to calm my nerves, and it is the want of needing to use their bathroom that stops me from backing out of the booking. It's a relief when the door doesn't lead to a dungeon but a bright, white, modern, open plan warehouse studio with four tattoo artists working at different stations.

I expected the sting of getting the memory of my brother etched into my arm forever to be worse than it was. After two and a half hours of work, there he was; Jamsie's cartoon guy Ecstatically Happy Man on my arm. A little part of Jamsie with me always to make me smile, until the day I, too, die.

The arrival time of my flight to Rome is too late for the last train, so Ronan kindly comes to collect me. I'm surprised to see him waiting at our usual airport meet up spot in Shelly's car. "Is our car not back from the repair shop yet?"

"They say another week," Ronan grumbles.

The car trouble began months ago when it started to shudder and drag, and a constant beep-beep alarm was going off as a warning. We brought it to the mechanic who does our annual car service—a broken sensor was the diagnosis. Two hundred euros later, the sensor was replaced, but by the time we get home, the car feels much the same. "Ah yes, there is another problem with the gearbox," the mechanic says. "We can't fix it. You need to go to a gear box specialist."

After several attempts, Ronan found a gearbox specialist in a town nearby. "There is a sensor that needs to be replaced and then we need to plug it into the software from the car company. It will be expensive."

Nearly thirteen hundred euros and four days later, we got the car back. It was okay, but not completely better. The alarm was going off again. We called the mechanics.

"Ah yes, there is another problem with the gearbox. It will take a lot longer to fix."

"Why didn't you do it?"

"Because we could not know about this problem until the other problem was fixed."

"Can we take it back to you and get it fixed?"

"Not until after August."

"You are booked up for the entire month?"

"No, it is Ferragosto. We are closed, but the car will not blow up. It is okay to drive it like this."

"But the alarm is going off. I have to have the radio blasting to stop it from driving us insane." Ronan said, exasperated.

"Ah, you found a good solution!" the mechanic said with glee. "See you after August!"

About a month later, after a lot of loud music being played on the car radio, Ronan got a text from the repair shop; "Good news. The boss mechanic thinks he can fix it in one day. You can bring it to us on Monday."

Ronan researched the problem and read the oil needs to be run through the system four times to ensure there are no air pockets or something. "I bet that is all that needs to be done. That is why he can do it in the day."

We dropped the car off on the Monday and waited.

At 6.15PM there was still no word. We were aware the car shop closed at 7PM. Ronan had texted and tried to call, but no response, so we decided to drive out there. And just as we were close, the woman in the office texts; "They need to run some more checks, I will update you tomorrow."

The following day, there was no update.

By day three of them having the car, I was getting worried. And angry. "What if they give us another massive bill for doing unauthorised work on the car? The car itself is not worth three thousand euros."

That evening we were out with Alex and his wife for dinner and, of course, we talk about our car trouble. "We can't get a straight answer from the mechanic about what is happening and how much it will be," Ronan said. Alex felt our frustration. "That is not right. I will go with you tomorrow Roman and together we fix the guy."

I was not sure what 'fix the guy' meant. I just wanted my car back without a big bill attached. I waited anxiously until Ronan called after the intervention at the car shop with Alex.

"You are not going to believe what happened," Ronan said when he called after their meeting.

"Oh no. Don't tell me I have to bail you both out of jail or something."

"Nooo. Alex and the head mechanic are old friends. They were hugging each other and joking. Basically, the guy explained he's waiting for a new part to arrive from the car manufacturer in UK. They sent a part, and the guy fitted it, but it was faulty, so they had to return it to be checked and now they are waiting for a new one to arrive. But due to Brexit, everything takes longer."

The guy showed Alex and Ronan all the emails he had sent to the car manufacturer. "The good news is that the cost is covered by the guarantee of the last payment we made, so it isn't going to cost us anymore. The bad news is we just have to wait for the part to arrive from the UK."

That was months ago. We had a hire car we were extending from week to week and the cost was adding up, but then Shelly offered us her car while she was away on business. We are so lucky we have such good friends.

"How was the retreat? I have to admit, I was jealous of your trip to the flea market. I miss rambling around markets, like we used to when we first met. Do you remember all those radios I bought at that market in Ireland?"

"The ones that burnt the caravan down?" I say recalling the sight of the smoke bellowing from what was left of our love shack caravan we had when we were dating. Ronan had left on his ingenious stereo system of five vintage radios—he bought at a market—wired together, while we went for a walk on the beach.

Ronan cringes. He knows it's still a contentious issue and quickly changes the subject.

"So it was an interesting place, Barcelona?" Ronan says, over taking an articulated truck on the motorway home.

"Actually, that is exactly what I took away from Barcelona; we should make the house and garden interesting. Like the way I once dreamed of having a house filled with meaningful things I have collected from markets around the world."

I'm about to tell Ronan the exciting surprise I have for him, when a cop car speeds past us on the motorway and weaves in front of the three lanes, slowing us, and the cars ahead of us, down. He is shouting out the window until the two cars ahead of us pull to the side. We follow their lead and park on the hard shoulder. Feeling curious and confused at the same time.

The cop car pulls across two lanes. All the traffic has come to a standstill behind us."What the hell is he doing?" Ronan says.

"I think he is after the person in the car ahead."

The cop jumps out of his car and runs to the car ahead of us and starts shouting, like a goalie trying to get the defence to do a better job during a soccer match. "I think he is he going to arrest them." I feel I should be panicking but instead I just feel I'm part of a movie set.

But no, he isn't arresting them, he is now shouting at the second car, too. The occupants of both cars leap out and run past our car. The cop is shouting at us and everyone behind us.

"Fuori dai piedi!" (clear out!) The cop roars, waving his arms back and forth, his adrenaline fuelled eyes wide.

"He's telling us to get out," I say to Ronan, "Come on!"

"There must be a bomb," Ronan says breathlessly, as we jog back to where a group of car evacuees are standing while others are scrambling up a grass bank.

"Why do you think that?"

"I don't know. It seems like something you'd have to do if there was a bomb."

"Why do you think the worst? Maybe it is just the road collapsing."

"Just the road collapsing? You think that is better than a bomb?"

We've reached the small bunch of about twenty car evacuees. The occupants of the rest of the queue of cars further back are safe behind the articulated truck, which the cop directed to manoeuvre across all the lanes as a barricade.

"Does anyone speak English? What is happening?" I say.

"Yes I do," a guy says. "Ehh, there is a baddy in a car coming the wrong way down the motorway."

"Oh, a car chase!" Ronan seems nearly as excited about this as he was about the bomb and lights a cigarette, while I scramble up the steep grass bank with the help of a girl with purple hair.

"Come on," I say to Ronan.

"I'm not going up there. I'm fine watching from here."

The articulated truck is blocking all the lanes except for one which our car is blocking. "Great. Our car is going to be smashed up and we won't have a way of getting home," I grumble to the woman with purple hair. "Don't worry, mine is in front of yours. It will hit my car first and I can do with a new one." We are both giddy and get our phones ready to video the high-speed drama we are about to encounter.

A woman near us, probably in her forties, is wailing, bending up and down crying but not crying. A young teenage boy scrambles up the grass bank after her, "Calma Mama, calma." His comforting arm around her.

"Guiseppe," she screams. "Guisseppeee." She is wailing loudly again. "Oh Dio, oh Dio, Guisepppeee."

We spot Guiseppee, her husband, strolling across the motorway and putting on his jacket. He joins Ronan for a cigarette, ignoring the dramatics of his wife.

"Jezzezz, he must be a very slow driver," Ronan says up in my direction, referring to the expected car chase.

With that, I spot headlights coming around the bend. "Here it is," says the woman with purple hair lifting her phone, ready for a video that could go viral and break the internet.

"Is that it?" I say as a white Fiat 500 creeps slowly into view.

"It must be back up?" she says.

"No, I think that is it." The car slows to a stop, and the cop runs over to it. He directs the driver to pull over in front of our cars on the hard shoulder and the cop climbs into the passenger seat.

"Yep, that was it. A guy in Fiat 500," I say, putting my phone in my pocket.

The dramatic woman suddenly stops wailing and starts laughing, as her son helps her down the grass bank. Both Guiseppe and Ronan have gone back to their cars, forgetting their wives. A guy holds out his hand to me and I take it before realising it's not to help me. This 30-something-year-old guy is using me as a support for himself to get down the grass bank so his trousers won't get dirty. I let him go, and he slides on his ass and doesn't look back. Instead, the girl with the purple hair and I help each other slide down on our arses and go back to our waiting cars.

The cop continues to give the guy a stern talking to. His hood is pulled up and I can't see his face, but I am guessing from his hoodie he is young - perhaps an inexperienced driver who just went down a feeder road the wrong way.

"Well, that was an exciting end to your year of trips," says Ronan.

"It's not over yet."

"You are going on another trip?"

"No, we are going on another trip. Together. I know what I want to do in regards to the retreats now, but I think we should both experience some BnBs and the best way to do it would be to take a road trip up through Europe."

"What about the pets?"

"I already have it sorted." I say, smiling. "Remember that site we used for pet sitters in Ireland? Well, it is still going. I put up an ad last night and within an hour, I had five applicants."

"Really? For our house?" Ronan seems to forget the house is no longer the derelict mess we bought.

"Ronan, we live in a restored stone villa beside a beautiful town and lake, with every convenience on its doorstep. Why do you think people would not want to stay? I have a German couple arriving at the end of the month. We are going on a road trip."

40

For the next two weeks, I dig and pull brambles from the front garden. Ronan does one of his usual Iron Man style challenges and drags the two 100-year-old metal doors from the illegal building at the end of the garden up to the garage. We had pledged to 'destroy' the illegal building as part of our house buying agreement, but it's definitely a project for another year. It will stay camouflaged as an ivy bramble mountain until then.

The doors perfectly fit the now empty garage. They look amazing. Together, we fit a wooden pergola structure inside the walls and fix a Perspex roof. This will be the tool shed.

I use old red bricks to create a Celtic spiral in the now cleared front garden. It is north facing and a narrow area, making it a difficult spot to grow anything. The two giant magnolia trees on either side of the ornate gate are enough of an attraction. So I have decided to create a Zen stone garden.

While Celtic patterns are not very Italian, we are Irish, and we are now part of the history of the house, so a Celtic pattern is fitting. Using the mound of tiny white stone left over from the foundation for the courtyard, I fill the brick pattern with one bucket of pebbles at a time.

Since I had my bone scan, and found out with great delight, I have no sign of osteoporosis; I want to keep it that way, and lifting buckets of stone to create something beautiful is much more enjoyable than sweating it out in a gym. I don't need a gym as long as I have my garden.

The great thing about stone, and solid structures like the old doors, is you don't have to wait five years to see the result. Within days, the front garden is looking much more respectable.

"I'm impressed, are you?" Ronan asks as we stand with our backs to the driveway gate and look at the result of our efforts.

"I am! We definitely deserve a holiday." Other than a holiday in Greece, all my travel up to this year had been visiting family or work oriented in the last ten years or more.

This year I gave myself permission to let myself go. To do whatever I wanted to do. I went on retreats for ghost busting, guru wisdom, energy flow, empowerment and journaling. Okay, so the ghost busting was a bit of a surprise, but interesting all the same. I have done workshops and courses in Qi Gong instruction, Tibetan sound bowl massage and baths, Menopause Coaching, Tarot reading, herbal teas and balms and every area of writing craft.

The retreats were not an indulgence, they were a necessity. The Me-Time I needed to get back to being Me. Stepping away from the norm gave me new energy and perspective. I gained inspiration for the house, ideas for books and insight into what I want to do with the second half of my life. I know who I am again-a new, improved version of the woman I wanted to be in my twenties.

"I hope the car is ready in time." Ronan says as we plot our route on the large Automobile Association map book of Europe I bought when the kids were small. For me, technology will never match the satisfaction of planning a road trip with a paper map.

"Of course it will be. They have had it for months."

With only days before our trip is due to begin, the mechanic texts; *I'm sorry your car won't be ready for another two weeks, the part has still not arrived.*

"We'll have to cancel," Ronan says disappointed.

"We can't cancel. The dog sitters have booked their flights and taken time from work. If you cancel, it's a big black mark against you on the website. We'll never get sitters again."

"Could we just hide on the ground floor?"

"No, I am not hiding in my own house so that two strangers can have a free holiday in it." I sigh, resigning myself to the fact that our trip is not going to happen. "We'll just go stay at Lucia's or something."

Ronan hands me a cup of tea. "I was really looking forward to doing a road trip, like the old days in the van."

Tea is magic. It makes everything better and makes solutions flow.

"That's it!" I say. "How about we take the van? It will be like the old days again."

"You mean the toolshed?"

"Don't refer to Old Betsy as a toolshed. She is a respectable, reliable old lady." I am referring to our 26-year-old Hiace van we bought from a bunch of nuns in Ireland about fifteen years ago, and then converted it into a small camper van. Old Betsy has got us back and forth to Ireland across the Alps several times. She brought us on holiday with the kids to France and our first trips to Italy.

She was the van we packed up with whatever we could fit in her, including two dogs and our 14-year-old son and drove to Italy across five countries six years ago. Since then she hasn't been driven much, other than to collect furniture we bought from time to time. Her main role in our lives at the moment is a storage unit until Ronan finishes the tool shed.

"I don't know if she'd make it. We haven't driven her any real distance for years," Ronan says, as we walk over and gaze at Betsy, her body blotched with sun bleached spots and patches of rust.

"I think she will be okay," I say. "She starts every time—and if she does stop working, we know how to fix her—it will either be oil, water, battery connection or a lack of fuel. Not like bloody stupid cars now with electric sensors. We'll be like the Joads in *The Grapes of Wrath*."

"She would need an oil change. I can't remember the last time she had a service."

"We are leaving in three days; We don't have time."

"I could change it."

"And what will you do with the old oil?" I say, already anticipating the mess.

"We could do what they used to do in Ireland-keep it until we are putting up fencing and use it to dip the end of the posts in order to save them from rotting."

"I don't see us having a need for a mile of fencing anytime soon, and I don't want a tub of dirty oil being moved around the garden for the next five years. We'll take our chances, and get it done by a mechanic when we get back, or along the way if she starts acting up. "

With the decision made to just go for it, I can sense the same feeling from Ronan that I am feeling, like electricity building in our bodies. Excitement of the unknown, taking a risk and a road trip. I can nearly feel it from Betsy, too.

"You are right. She won't let us down. As long as we are not going over any mountains." Ronan says. "I don't think her old heart would be able for them."

"Well, we can't avoid mountains. The whole of the northern Italian border is defined by mountains, but we have a choice: the Alps or the Dolomites."

"The Alps sound higher. We'll go with the Dolomites."

The next two days are intense preparations, brushing out and vacuuming three years of cobwebs and wasps nests from Betsy's insides and sprucing her up for her big journey. "How are bird droppings in here?" I ask as Ronan pulls out all the old broken tools he hasn't missed. They could have gone to the dump with Alessandro.

While I am polishing the dash, Ronan carries out two grape crates we found at the house, filled with random things; Duct tape, spray paint, a crowbar, four—no five—screwdrivers, nails and two hammers.

"Ronan, a hammer and nails? Are you planning to do some interior decorating and hanging some pictures while we drive?"

"A hammer is always handy."

"But why do you need two?"

"In case I can't find one of them."

From the unnecessary bulky crate, I allow him pack one hammer and a screwdriver before we go to the DIY store for some last bits and pieces. Ronan buys an expensive wheel jack, while I buy contact paper and paint to do up the cabinets, a rug for the chairs, air fresheners, some hippy stickers for the windows, a mat for the ground and some cushions.

I use the roll of dark green velvet I bought to upholster the chairs left in the house, but have never got around to doing, to cover the makeshift sofa bed in the back. We'd take it out all together if we could, as we never use it as a bed, but the van needs a bed in it to stay classed as a camper van.

"I just heard the weather forecast and there are warnings of flash flooding expected in Central Europe and the Dolomites for the next week," Ronan says, looking worried.

"Are there any sunny spells on your weather app for the next few days?"

"There's some over Switzerland," he says, checking his phone.

"Right then, we'll take that route instead." My spirit for an adventure has been reignited, and no flash flood is going to dampen it. "We'll go left across Europe through The Alps, Switzerland and Germany rather than right through the Dolomites, Austria and Central Europe."

"I just hope Betsy can do it."

41

The house sitters arrive and they are lovely. Juno and Paddy are excited to have visitors, but Looney looks depressed, like she always does when she sees me taking out my suitcase and senses I am leaving. Now that she is deaf, or just very good at ignoring me, and the bluish tint in her eyes is increasing, I have become her support human. I am tempted to take her with us, but she's getting on in years and I know she will be much more comfortable staying at home with Juno, Paddy, and Spooky. But my guilt is still massive.

There's a town called Carpi near Milan, I am dying to visit, as it is the backdrop to a book I want to write. This will be our first stopover and I have booked us into a BnB to start doing our investigation of what guests expect.

The BnB is nice. It seems to have about eight rooms to rent, but we are the only ones staying this evening. Our room has two single beds. "I guess that is what you have to do if you want any action in this room," I say, pointing at the painting of trapeze artists hanging on the wall between the two beds. It's the only bit of character to the room, which is otherwise fitted in grey kit furniture; two beds, a desk and a chair with shelves and a hanging rail for clothes. It's clean and functionally renovated, but dreary. I want my rooms to be clean too, of course, but also to have character and coziness.

I was expecting Carpi to be a little village, but to my surprise, it is a big vibrant town with one of the biggest central squares in Italy, surrounded by a dominating medieval palace, an orange and white cathedral and a long portico buzzing with high end boutiques and jewellery shops.

A wedding is just finished at the cathedral and the couple leaving are being showered with rice. Although I get PTSD symptoms now when someone asks me for advice on weddings, seeing weddings still makes me smile. I have told both our children, should they ever decide to get married, I am perfectly happy if they decide to elope rather than have a big wedding. I have also told them I am perfectly okay not becoming a grandmother should they choose to remain childless. They have no one else's dreams to fulfil other than their own.

The town of Carpi is hosting a philosophy festival, and about one thousand people are seated in ticketed seats in the square listening to a guy on stage who is talking nonstop.

We visit the palace which has free entry and the exhibits are set up with both English and Italian audio presentations. Magnificently preserved, every available space within the palace is adorned with colourful story-telling frescoes. A time of colour and feasts. It feeds my hunger to write the historical fiction book I am dying to write.

Stepping back into the sixteenth century of frescoed walls and ceilings makes time pass quickly. When I leave the time machine building, the guy on the stage is still talking at the same fast speed he was speaking when we entered the palace two hours ago. The audience is still enwrapped in his words. He's either fascinating or no one wants to feel unintelligent or insulting by getting up and leaving in broad daylight. I will never know the Italian language well enough to understand someone speaking his speed. But that is okay. I'd have trouble following someone speaking in English that fast.

The two rows of shuttered apartment windows above the portico walkway are painted in tasteful tones of oranges and creams with grey and blue shutters. As daylight is fading fast, the chandeliers within come on, illuminating ceilings of colourful frescoes.

The town is packed, and we struggle to find a restaurant ready to serve food at 7.30PM, other than cheap takeaways of crispy chicken and kebab shops on side streets. They are still too busy serving aperitivos. I have never seen so many bars along one street in Italy, and they are all full of chattering gorgeous people.

"Everyone seems dressed up to the nines. Maybe it's because of the philosophy festival, or maybe it's because it is Saturday night?" I say to Ronan as we stroll hand in hand, people watching under the golden glow of the old-fashioned street-lights. The streets are alive with people walking their designer dogs; mostly toy versions of toy dogs. One mini chihuahua, on the end of a pink jewel encrusted lead, is viciously shredding a free supermarket-specials flyer. She's moving so fast with it in her mouth, her owner can't catch her.

"Or perhaps it is just because they are Italian. They seem very wealthy in this part of Italy," Ronan says, before stopping and looking around. "Why does this town remind me of France rather than Italy?"

I get what he means. "It's the blue shutters. In Tuscany and Umbria we have green, but it's the blue shutters against the plastered walls, rather than stone that gives it the French feel. Ugh. You've reminded me I still need to paint the shutters."

The menu prices reflect the expected wealth to hang out in this town, but that doesn't stop us enjoying plates of truffle laden pasta and bruschetta.

The following morning, after a breakfast adhering to the Italian laws with plastic wrapped croissants, fruit and yogurt at the owner's kitchen table, we head north, out of Modena towards Switzerland.

The roads gradually climb higher and the air gets thinner. Betsy belches black fumes in protest of the decreased oxygen.

"They look like alien insects," I say as a colony of Lamborghinis speed by."Do Lamborghini owners go around in clusters, like Harley Davidson gangs?" I'm not expecting Ronan to answer; For one, his hearing is bad enough without the loud puttering rumble of Betsy's engine stopping any effort of normal conversation, and two, it was a stupid question.

We are heading towards the Gotthard Base Tunnel that runs beneath the Swiss Alps between Italy and Switzerland. At fifty-seven kilometers (about thirty-five miles) in length, it is the longest tunnel in the world.

It is not only the longest, but also the deepest traffic tunnel in the world, reaching depths of up to 2,300 meters (7,500 feet) below the mountain peaks. Similar to when we were going through the Channel Tunnel, between England and France, I try not to think about depth.

The longest tunnel also has what seems to be the longest tail-back to get into it. Only a specified number of vehicles are allowed into the tunnel at any one time, so a traffic light system operates the flow of traffic in and out of the tunnel. After an hour, we are still moving along super slow.

"I'm glad we filled up the petrol tank this morning," I say as we edge closer to the tunnel's mouth after nearly two hours of stop and crawl. We pass a Mercedes pulled to the side with its bonnet up. Five hundred yards on and there is another new looking Mercedes with its bonnet up. Old Betsy trundles past them, not a bother on her. The tail back also means we have caught up with the Lamborghinis. The fable of the hare and the tortoise springs to mind.

42

S even hours of driving through beautiful scenery and we are out the other side of Switzerland and stopping over in one of my favourite towns in France: Colmar. Its colourful, half-timbered houses ooze with flowering window boxes, canals and cobbled streets, making it look like it fell off the page from a book of fairytales.

In the past, the colour of the houses in the town illustrated the owner's profession: white was for bakers, yellow for cheese-makers, blue for fishermen and fishmongers and green for gardeners. It makes me want to write a fairytale.

I add it to the list of books to write someday when I get my roll-top desk. It's then the realisation strikes. "Ronan, we have the van with us." I don't say anything else. I just gleam at him because I forgot he can't read my mind. Well, not all the time.

"Yes," he says, cautiously confirming what I said, wondering where I am going with this.

"We have space. On our way back, we could drive back down through France and visit flea markets like we said we always wanted to do. And if we see a roll-top desk at one of the markets, we could buy it."

"We could." He smiles. "Let's make it our mission to find one, but first let's stick to our plan and get to The Netherlands."

After a morning of exploring Colmar—taking photos we'll probably never look at again and eating pastries—we set off to drive through Germany towards The Netherlands. We swear to each other never to do that again—it is the most boring country to drive through-there isn't even a petrol station to stop at to break the boredom of the journey. We have fallen into our usual comfortable pattern of Ronan doing all the driving and me doing the route planning and accommodation booking.

Eventually we get to Ronan's brother's house in The Netherlands and spend a fabulous few days catching up with family and going shopping in secondhand market shops that sell everything from Lederhosen, furniture, glass, ceramics and ornaments. But no roll-top desks. I buy a pair of oak nest tables for fourteen euros and I end up with six clear glass, wine decanters of different shapes ranging from six euros to thirteen. They look like large potion bottles.

"They will look great in our kitchen. They'd look even better on a witchy style dresser if I had one."

"There's no chance of us bringing one of those back. Even if we saw the perfect one, it would not fit in Betsy, and they cost a fortune."

Ronan is right—I'll focus on finding a roll-top desk and when I write all my best sellers on the said desk, I will then be able to afford the witchy dresser for my potion bottles and rows of mason jars filled with teas to share with the wonderful women and writers who come to stay at Casa Anam Cara.

I plot and plan our return trip, timing it so we are in the town of Metz just across the French border for Saturday morning, home to one of France's biggest weekend flea markets. Both of us can hardly wait to get out of the van. "Okay, the rules are; nothing big except for a roll-top desk, and whoever can find the weirdest thing for sale wins lunch. Just take a photo, don't buy it. Meet you back at the entrance in two hours."

Like the market in Barcelona, the Metz Market has everything, but nothing at the same time. Ronan wins the weirdest thing with two left prosthetic legs being sold as a pair, whereas my taxidermy cat with the bowler hat comes in at a close second.

"I didn't see any roll-top desks," Ronan says over his victory lunch of a kebab at a food stall.

"Neither did I, but I was looking at the map of French flea markets and if you are on for a five-hour drive, we could get to Lyon this evening and go to its market in the morning. It's only on, on Sundays. It's massive and seems to specialise in antique furniture."

"Sounds like a plan, and it will be a day closer to Italy, so less distance for Betsy to travel with a heavy load."

"Okay, decision made. I'll book somewhere really nice for tonight on the outskirts of Lyon. We'll have a nice dinner, an early night and hit the market early tomorrow."

I scroll through Lyon options on my accommodation booking app. There is a nice hotel for seventy-four euros for the night, but as we don't get away together often, I instead choose a boutique maison for double the price. It looks like the perfect bed-and-breakfast, with beautiful gardens and an outdoor pool. Restaurant. Free parking. I click and book.

"The last time we were in Lyon we were travelling in Betsy, too. Do you remember?" I reminisce. "Luca and Izzy were with us. It must have been fifteen years ago."

"God, you are right! I think that must have been the first trip we did in this van. We stayed overnight with that Aussie friend of yours, Pipi. Do you remember?"

"I do," I say, remembering my dear pal. Pipi and I met as camp Counsellors in America when we were both twenty. After camp, we travelled the States together for a month by Amtrak and then she came back and lived with me in Ireland for a while. We both had similar big dreams for the future of travelling and writing. It was Pipi I was going to go and stay with in Australia thirty years ago, and it was her who I was going to have a boho-life of travelling the world with. Then I met Ronan, and the rest is history.

"It was amazing you hadn't seen each other for fifteen years, and then in Lyon, it was like as if you had only seen each other the day before. That's a sign of true friends. Do you ever hear from her?" Ronan asks.

"No. We used to write to each other before the internet ruined the art of letter writing. That is how we stayed in touch and met up with her in Lyon. It wasn't by accident. She was going to Cambodia after Lyon and we lost touch."

I gaze out the window of France's pretty villages in the distance, surrounded by lush fields, deciduous trees, peach and mustard maisons, chateaux and chapels. The things that make France distinct from Italy.

"I wonder where Pipi is now. I hope she is happy." But I say it too low for Ronan to hear. It's more of a wish and a prayer for my old friend.

43

"This guest house sounds amazing. It will be a good one for us to aspire to be like," I say, reading the description to Ronan. The description says their restaurant serves a buffet of local organic produce. As Ronan had a kebab for lunch and I only had a croissant, we are looking forward to dinner.

We follow the GPS to the outskirts of Lyon, up a desolate hill to a laneway, and from there I switch over to the instructions the owner has texted. Arriving at big ornate gates. Once elegant in their day, the chipped paint adds to the charm and mystery of what lies beyond. The bell does not seem to be working, so I call the owner.

"You need to open the gate manually and please close it after you. I am waiting to get it fixed." That's fine by me. I might have to ask our guests to do the same as we are waiting to get our own electric gates at home fixed too. These things take time.

The driveway looks disheveled, the cypress trees could do with some trimming and we stop near the pool where a woman with a bottle of spray cleaner in one hand and a cigarette in the other waves at us.

"That must be the owner," I say, noting to myself not to let Ronan greet the guests while he is smoking a cigarette or carrying disinfectant or doing both at the same time. Nor should either of us be wearing yellow crocs and a sweater with burn holes in it. Also, we should brush our hair at least once during the two days before guests arrive. But the warmth of her smile and greeting surpass all the instant first four seconds of negative thoughts I just had. "Welcome! You can park just up there to the right of my chateau and I will give you the tour."

We park at the side of the house in front of what must have been a beautiful terrace, but now weeds have grown between the joins of paving and the AWOL topiary trees remind me I'll need to trim Looney back into the shape of a dog when I get home.

"This Maison has been in my family for two generations. The grounds I keep eco diverse with nature," she says, explaining the weeds growing out of the walls and through the tarmac in the sad-looking tennis court.

But I note her clever use of words. They could come useful should we not get the gardens finished before our first guests arrive. *They are not unkept or abandoned, they are eco diverse*, I imagine myself saying to guests if Ronan's tractor mower ever stops working.

She shows us around the ground-floor rooms, explaining she likes shabby chic. They are definitely more shabby than chic. As we walk, we tell her we are going to the market the next morning. "Ah, the market, yes I have many antique dealers come to stay here from the UK and all over Europe for the market. The professionals go very early because, as we say in France; 'L'avenir appartient à ceux qui se lèvent tôt.' You know this saying? The early bird catches the worm?"

"Yes we do. How early do you recommend we go?"

"Oh, by 8AM at least to get the bargains, the really good items will be gone by 9AM."

She leads us up the wooden curved ornamental staircase to our bedroom on the second floor. It's nothing special. Like a cheaply done-up bedsit in an old house. The heavy original door without a keyhole or lock has years of layered gloss paint, as has the 60s style light switch and wires running up the wall— making the outdated wiring a feature. She leads us across the landing of creaking boards to the bathroom. "You are the only ones staying here tonight. I am going to have a shower and I am going out, so it is all yours. Don't go into any rooms with the doors closed please."

I'm regretting not packing my wiggle rod.

The bathroom has a bath that was designed to have a panelled side, but the panelling has been removed, and the outside of the bath is painted bright pink; to match the bright pink plastic toilet seat and plastic bin.

"Where is the restaurant?" I say, when we are back out on the landing and she is heading towards the stairs. I'm hoping there is another building on the estate we just haven't seen yet.

"You want to eat?" She looks back at me with an element of shock.

"Yes, I texted to say we would like to eat here tonight? And you responded with a restaurant buffet option?" I say, in an effort to jog her memory. "We have been driving for over five hours and want to just have dinner and have an early night."

"Of course. There are restaurants in town. But, I do have a very special buffet of local produce of meats and cheeses, bread, jams and wines. All organic and local from the markets. I will prepare two plates for you, yes?"

I look at Ronan, he looks as tired as I am feeling. "That sounds okay, doesn't it?"

"Yeah sure. I don't want to have to drive another inch today." We are all still standing on the landing, us outside the door of our room and herself holding the bannister at the top of the stairs.

"Ah, you are tired from driving. Do you want a coffee?"

"Not now, thanks, but later, when we come down for dinner."

"What time do you want dinner? I will go out to dinner myself tonight and I need to have a shower and get ready."

"Would seven fit with your plans?" I ask.

"Yes, perfect. So I will prepare two plates for seven. See you downstairs in an hour." And she trots down two steps before stopping and asking, "Are you vegetarian?"

"I am. He isn't." It's getting gloomy so I flick the switch for landing light but it's not working.

"Okay, I will put on some extra cheese, and some fruits, some strawberries!" Her excitement about this is distracting. "They are grown locally. There is a magical farmer close by who still has them, even though they are out of season. And you like goat cheese I hope?" She says, now halfway down the stairs.

"I'm okay with goat cheese," I call after her.

"Good, because I only have goat cheese today from the market. Everything I source is local." She laughs and continues downstairs before we can ask anything else, such as the wi-fi code.

I can't get online, but I did take a screenshot of the directions she sent, as well as the details of the food her guesthouse has available.

'A wide range of local organic beers and wines and platters of local meats, fruits, breads and cheeses. The cost is €25 per person. Bottles of wine start at €25. A carafe of wine is €10.'

"So if I am not eating the meat or the bread, and she only has goats cheese... Is she going to charge me twenty-five euros for just goat cheese and magically grown strawberries?" I'm tired and really hungry.

"Sounds like it. I'm not that big into goat cheese, so if we just get one plate then I'll have the meat and you can have the cheese. I'll fill up on bread. Let's go for a walk around the grounds and stretch our legs before dinner. Although it sounds like we shouldn't work up too much of an appetite."

We walk the outskirts of the estate on a path marked with fallen branches haphazardly laid to mark some kind of path border. Everything is overgrown or looking dilapidated.

I get it, the upkeep on a big place is difficult, so I don't judge, even though it is the most expensive place we have stayed and the pool has a tinge of green. The path widens beside a pit scraped out by a bulldozer at some stage and the cheapest of plastic furniture set up as a place to dine. The mix mash of garden furniture is coated with a fine film of green moss.

"With our experience here so far, what has stood out for you as positive?" I ask Ronan.

"The way she welcomed us."

"Exactly! Being made to feel at home made everything else okay, like the eco diverse overgrown grounds, the greening pool and inaccessible tennis court—which we weren't going to use anyway, the cheap bedroom and the crap bathroom and the lack of a lock on the bedroom door. Her welcome made up for it. Even if she did tell us three times, she needed to shower."

I feel we are on a reality TV show marking BnB's out of ten.

"We are good at giving warm welcomes so we'll do okay, but I also think we can do way better than this," Ronan says. "Come on, let's go to the dining room. I'm dying for a coffee."

But Ronan's positivity is soon dashed.

44

"You are on time," she says with surprise as we wait in the hallway for her. "It will be ready soon." She ushers us to the set table in the dining room with left over Christmas paper napkins with holly and bells in the corners.

"Do you want wine? I have bottles starting at twenty-five euros."

"A carafe of the house wine is fine," I say, taking a seat, ready to relax.

"The house wine? I am not a vineyard. I do not have my own wines," she says defensively.

I am taken aback. I glance at Ronan to see if he has sensed the same from her response. But he hasn't really heard her. He's too focused on what he wants to ask her. "And can I have a coffee please?"

"I asked you if you wanted a coffee and you said no. I am going out. I have to have a shower, I don't have time to make you a coffee," she scoffs.

Ronan's eyes widen. I know that look. His need for coffee can't be challenged.

"I did say I wanted a coffee. Not when I arrived, but later at dinner." He's trying to keep his cool.

"But it is not included in the menu. There will be a charge," she states.

"How much?" Ronan bristles.

"Four euros."

Now he's not just bristling, he's starting to steam.

"Okay then, I will have it instead of the plate. We will just have one plate, a carafe of wine and a coffee, please."

"No, you ordered two plates. It is not possible to change now. What size cup do you want?"

"A double espresso with some hot water, so a big cup please," Ronan says holding up his hand with spread out finger and thumb to indicate a cup bigger than an espresso cup. He is still focused on coffee, so seems to have missed where she has said we can't reduce our order.

"I do Italian coffee. It is espresso, so a big cup like that is not possible. "

She's messing with Ronan's need for coffee again. This is not good.

"I know what Italian coffee is, I live there. I just want a double espresso with some hot water. Please." I can nearly feel how much he is biting his tongue, stopping himself saying, "Rosie, get into the van, I'll get the bags."

"You want hot water also? I will have to boil the kettle." She doesn't just roll her eyes, but her whole head, before she turns and marches out of the room.

Ronan and I can do nothing but stare at each other. It would just take one of us to say "let's go" and we'd be out of there. But we are both too tired. "Did you hear her say we can't cancel a plate? We have to have the two?" I whisper loudly across the table to Ronan.

"Did she?"

"I'm sure that's what she said. So much for her great welcome. That went downhill fast." I quiet when we hear her coming back down the hall, although it does take her about ten minutes, with the sound of the coffee machine going all that time.

"Good news," she says joyfully, "We don't need hot water because the double espresso fills the cup. Look." She holds out the full cup to Ronan. "The coffee is Arabic. Moroccan. It is the best. Morocco is known for its coffee, markets and its spices—"

"We've decided we'll just have one plate between two." Ronan interrupts her Wikipedia sharing of knowledge on the delights of Morocco.

"No, it is not possible to change now. You ordered two, and it is made."

"Oh, I didn't realise it was already made. Can you bring it to us," I say, my stomach is audibly grumbling. "We are very hungry."

"Yes, I bring it now." Her disappearance from the room is followed by the sound of chopping echoing down the hall from the kitchen for fifteen minutes. Ronan and I again stare at each other across the table. Our frustration has turned into amusement, "She hasn't brought the wine."

I go looking for her. I call towards the kitchen. "Hello?"

The chopping stops. Nothing is said. I return to the dining room.

Five minutes later, she swings through the door with two plates. One is a side plate size with four pieces of ham folded on it decorated with parsley. "This is from a local pig. They are ethically slaughtered and allowed to roam free during their lives." She again is very enthusiastic. The other is serving plate size with ten wedges of four different types of cheese, four plums, eight olives, and five magic strawberries. "This is the plate for two people. All the cheeses are locally produced and organic and wonderful. I have arranged them in their strength of taste. It is best to start with this one, which is the weakest. Then this one, this one, and finally this one is the strongest. The two on the edge are vegan cheeses because you are vegetarian."

Ronan and I are both lost for words, looking at the plate with the bits of cheese and fruit displayed in a circular pattern, like something from a 70s cocktail party.

"Is there a problem? What is wrong? You seemed happy earlier, but now you are not?" She says aggressively.

This woman is nuts.

It's dark outside and I really don't feel like trying to find somewhere else to stay, but I can't help but say something. I am too long on this earth to be chastised for the expression on my face, especially by someone I am paying to feed me and is taking the mick.

"In the description, it says there is a restaurant and there isn't. We were expecting more... choice for dinner."

"But I made it clear in the text what is included: local cheeses, fruits and meats. You know this is not a hotel, it is my home. You cannot expect it to be like a hotel." She's scoffing again. Yep, she is definitely nuts. I remember there is no lock on our door.

"Can I get the wine please?"

"Yes, you have to pay for the food now, cash."

"Now?"

"Yes now, because I go out now, and I will not be here in the morning, before you go."

"What about breakfast?" Ronan says.

"You said you are leaving early for the market at 8am? Breakfast is not served until 9am. You will have missed the best time to be at the market," she says with dismay. "While you get the money, I will bring your wine." And she swooshes out of the room.

Ronan has already started on the ham and has nearly finished a slice already. He's looking at me, I'm looking at him. I know he's waiting for me to take the lead in the emotional reaction spectrum and he will follow. But I am again lost for words. "I have some protein biscuits in the van," is all I can muster.

"This ham is really good," Ronan smirks, shoving a second slice in his mouth, while I eat the four raw slivers of courgette twirled around the sides.

"Here is the wine," she says coming into the room and placing a decent size carafe of white wine on the table. I will be drinking it all. "You wanted a carafe for ten euros, so this is the wine." She says, lifting up the empty bottle she is holding in her other hand. For all I know she could have taken the empty bottle out of the recycling bin. "It is a very good wine, made from a grape that grows locally."

If I hear the word locally again, I might just choke. "Oh you are eating the garnish!" And she starts to laugh. Loudly. At me.

"Can I get a glass please?"

"A glass?"

"Yes a wine glass to drink out of?" I'm beginning to think I have landed on a different planet.

"Of course. Did you get the money?"

"We will pay you after...this food." I can't bring myself to call it dinner, even though it is the most expensive meal we have had on this trip. Ronan starts to tremble. His cheeks bulging like a hamster's, full of the 'really good local' ham slices. His eyes are watering, he might just explode holding back his laughter. He pulls out his wallet and slaps a ten and fifty on the table and fishes the only two coins he has in his pocket. "Sixty-four euros" he says when there is enough room in his mouth to let the words pass.

She lifts the money and looks at it as if we have done her a big injustice. "But the total is sixty-eight euro?"

"Ten for the wine, fifty for the ten pieces of cheese and four slices of meat, and four euros for the coffee." I say in an effort to shame her about her prices, but it doesn't work.

"But it was a double coffee? That is eight euro."

I am chewing hard on my lip, trying not to let my glare at her be distracted by Ronan, who is practically doubled over. I am afraid he might choke, as he still hasn't had a chance to swallow the food in his mouth since being stricken by uncontrollable laughter.

"You can leave the other four euro on the table tonight, I will get it in the morning. If you hear a noise, I am sorry, it is my friend who stays here sometimes with his dog. Turn off the lights when you are going to bed—I'm going to have my shower and go out to dinner." And she is gone, leaving us in her family mansion alone for the night, with the possibility of some man coming in with his dog.

The wine is delicious. It tastes even better by the fourth glass on the terrace, overlooking the lights of Lyon reflecting on the Rhone, accompanied by a packet of protein biscuits.

"I can't believe you paid her for that," I say to Ronan, our eyes still damp from laughing.

"Are you serious? It was a French version of Fawlty Towers. Staying here was the best comedy I've experienced in a long time, well worth the money."

I look out at the lights and enjoy the warm air. "I'll tell you one thing, our experiences so far are giving me great hope for Casa Anam Cara."

45

We hardly sleep a wink. Not because of the man with the dog—he never arrived—we both had massive indigestion from eating so much bloody cheese. It was so expensive I couldn't leave it; except for the vegan cheese, which was awful, and the mildest cheese, which was so hard, I was afraid I might break a tooth.

Even with the lack of sleep, we are not slow in yanking ourselves out of bed early the next morning and leaving the abandoned-looking villa and head with great excitement to Les Puces—the market.

"First thing to buy?" Ronan says.

"A roll-top desk?"

"No. Breakfast."

"Absolutely, I am starving."

The large main carpark is already full, and we are ushered to the overflow car park. It's not even nine o'clock and the makeshift cafes are already packed. We find a seat in one with a bar and opt for cappuccinos and delicious French pain au chocolat pastries, while the French wheeler-dealers are drinking glasses of white wine and eating some local dish made from pigs innards. The whole place is buzzing with chat while showing each other the bargains they have already bought.

There is a whole warehouse divided into permanent antique seller units. The furniture is not cheap. I spot a magnificent apothecary cabinet. Too big for our house and too big for Betsy, and at seven thousand euros, it is way too big for our budget.

The smaller pop-up stalls are chock full of interesting stuff. So many memories of my childhood flood back with the sight of a Girl's World head, a yapping sausage dog toy just like the hand-me-down one I got from a neighbour-his legs no longer worked but it didn't stop me dragging him around on a piece of string and slapping his head to made him yap even without batteries.

A bundle of souvenir dolls in traditional dress lay on a stand, identical to the ones Eileen brought me back from her European bus tours when she was in her late teens; Greek, Dutch, Spanish, English, I take a photo of them. I don't know what I will do with the photo. But like Ecstatically Happy Man on my arm, they have made me smile and remember wonderful times; like Eileen putting on the Greek music record in the back room of our childhood home, and teaching me and Mam to do Greek dancing before she had even unpacked her blue leather suitcase from her last trip.

The only items she had taken out, were the traditional Greek, red, baggy pants and embroidered cotton shirt she couldn't wait to dress her adored little sister in, and the pair of dolls to add to my precious souvenir doll collection-just like the ones that are sitting in front of me here on a stall in France, forty-five years later.

I had forgotten that evening; looking up at my mam and sister laughing and Greek dancing together, Mam sampling the peach schnapps Eileen bought on the German leg of her trip. And me having a taste too.

Like the other markets we have been to, this one has everything but the one thing I want. A roll-top desk to write my novels at.

Some things tempt us, but we decide not, or can't find our way back to where we saw the item.

By noon, our feet are talking to us and the waft of fish and chips carries us to its place of origin. We sit and eat and look at our purchases. I have bought Ronan a tweed cap. It's new, not second hand and we discover from the label it is made in Italy. Ronan has bought a Beatles Album to play on the record player we never use.

"I saw a roll-top desk," says Ronan.

"The one for nearly four grand, over there?" I say, pointing in the direction of the warehouse.

"That's the one."

"Too big and too expensive."

"Yeah, my thoughts too. You will just have to make do with the bed tray for your laptop to write your books on for another while."

"It's fine. I'm glad we came to the markets anyway. Even if we didn't buy stuff to fill our house with, it's still been everything I expected and ticked the dream experience off my bucket list."

"Ready to start heading towards home?"

"Absolutely."

———

We have one more night in France staying in the Happy Birdy Hotel in Aux de Provence. The scenery in the region is gob smackingly gorgeous even though the hotel itself is in more of an industrial area. Another disastrous booking on my part, I think as we pull up outside what looks like an office building. But looks can be deceiving, as we have learnt by now.

Inside we are greeted by the friendliest reception staff, our room is very comfortable and we enjoy a fabulous dinner and breakfast all for half the price of the previous night's effort of a cheese board.

Instead of going through The Alps, I am taking us along the coastal route home from France into Italy. By late afternoon, we cross into Italy and soon the area starts to look familiar.

"My god this country where we live is beautiful," I say, peering down at the coastal towns below from the high highway. "It's like other countries are beige until you find their heart, but Italy is red and orange and azure; in your face in the scenery, people, pizza ovens, and earth."

A sense of pride creeps up—The same feeling when something happens that makes me proud to be Irish. I usually just ogle Italy from a distance as an outsider, but for the first time I feel like a little piece of Italy's spirit has allowed herself to come into me, or a little part my spirit has been allowed into hers. However, I don't have Italian blood running through my veins, nor will I ever be married or adopted into an Italian family.

I think being part of an Italian family and speaking Italian with them, would be the only way I could feel really part of Italy.

"Rosie, this is the route we took all those years ago! In Betsy, with the kids, do you remember?" Ronan exclaims, snapping me back into the moment.

"How could I forget?" I say, remembering the high hairpin bends down to the towns of Nervi and Sori as we traverse the Scalextric-style roads near Genoa.

"Try to find the hotel we stayed at in that town near the beach for tonight. Do you remember what the name of it was?" Ronan says. He didn't have to tell me. I am already scanning the map to find the town. Recco, that's it. I've often thought of that town as somewhere I'd like to check out a possible location if we ever decided to move to the coast.

"We could be home tomorrow, at this pace. A day early, if you are happy with that?" Ronan says.

"That's okay with me."

Ronan slows down when we approach the signs for Nervi and Sori, so I can take a photo to send to Izzy and Luca.

"It was about here Luca said he needed to pee and Izzy said she was starving," I say, recalling how anxious I felt the first time on this route with the kids in Betsy. Anxious to find somewhere to stop and look after our chicks after eight hours of driving. I miss my kids being small in one way, but the freedom I am feeling at the moment, travelling without having to take anyone else's bodily functions into account is amazing.

"The hotel seems to not be a hotel anymore," I say double checking the hotel's location against the map. It's now listed as an 'unpretentious' BnB."

"Another BnB for our research, then?"

"Unpretentious? Are they telling us not to expect too much? Maybe we should advertise our place as an unpretentious place to stay?"

"With an eco-diverse, re-wilding garden? Then we won't have to do anything else inside or out."

Our room is okay. It has a coffee machine and an electric kettle which is always a plus. I notice the bed does not have an actual headboard but a shape of one painted on the wall. Interesting. And it has a ceiling fan rather than air-con like a lot of places in Italy and all the BnBs we have stayed in on this trip. Our legal Italian breakfast is already in the room, in a box on the table: two small cartons of orange juice, a capsule for the coffee machine, two tea bags, a croissant in plastic, a tart in a box and pop tart style thing. There is nothing appetising. I would rather not do breakfast than offer this.

The best part of the room is the sea view stretching to the horizon. "I am going to the beach," I state.

We stroll into town along the road and find the small crescent-shaped beach we had arrived at fifteen years ago. Is she gone that long? Like the evening Italy first welcomed us across her border, the sun is setting against a blaze of oranges and pinks. Two kids skipping stones into the sea just like ours did.

Without needing to be asked, Ronan leaves me to walk down the beach alone to find the same spot I sat the first time we arrived here; just days after my sister's funeral. The little watch tower structure in the distance I sat facing is still there, marking the perfect spot I found to watch the sunset.

A flood of the emotions I felt then, begin to bubble again; Away from the chaos of sudden death, funeral preparations and burying my big sister. This spot was the first time I had a minute alone to think of her, to take a deep breath and fill my lungs with salty air. She was with me then. I could feel her walking beside me, whispering on the breeze, "everything is going to be all right."

Tears flow, like they did all those years ago, but seem so recent. I hadn't noticed the small stone stack, five stones high, when I first sat down. An earlier visitor to this spot must have built it with care and precision. The tide will soon take it, but at this moment it is perfect.

I feel her here again, beside me where the balanced stones stand. This time she's whispering; "See. I told you so."

———

"I've just realised, everything we see from now on, is within two hours of where we live," I say to Ronan the following morning as we drive past the towns around Carrara beaming whiteness in the morning light. They are in stark contrast to the burnt orange, mustard and splashes of candy pink we have come from on the coast, having slept well in our unpretentious BnB after a delicious dinner of yellowfin tuna with raspberry and balsamic vinaigrette and crusted with pistachio at a restaurant beside the crescent beach.

Sure enough, Betsy gets us home in two hours, having taken us three-thousand kilometres without a blip.

"Are we moving and you forgot to tell me?" Ronan asks, seeing a moving van outside as we approach our house. It's backdoors are open and I can see furniture and boxes piled inside covered in dust sheets.

"No!" My heart speeds up. "Bloody hell, the house sitters must be clearing us out! Where are the dogs?"

Betsy gives it all she has got and swerves in front of the truck, in case they try having a quick getaway. Helga hops out of the passenger seat.

"You are home a day early," she says, grinning. "I wanted to surprise you. We sold the house and we are heading back to Scotland."

"That's the surprise? You are leaving? You will come back to visit, won't you?"

"Yes, we'll be back to visit in a few months, but we wanted to drop this off."

Two guys are standing inside the gate, beside Helga's magnificent, antique, roll-top writing desk. "It needs to belong to a writer. We want you to have it."

I 'm sitting in the dappled light of old oaks, my head leaning back, face to the sun, my sunglasses on. I'm with a gorgeous looking man, brown eyes, short white hair and stubble just about long enough to be classed as a beard.

It's the last day of the Qi Gong weekend retreat. It's been a few months since my trip to Barcelona and this is the last retreat I have booked. I can't see myself going on another for a while, other than ones I run myself. I think I have retreat burnout, but I couldn't miss this one. It's my fourth Qi Gong retreat in the Sacred Wood and this time I have brought my set of Tibetan sound bowls-A gift to myself along with classes in my year of letting myself go.

This is the first time I have played them for a group. Thankfully, one of the other participants has brought his pan drum. He removes his wedding ring so not to interfere with the sound when he taps and slaps the curved metal drum.

He doesn't speak English. But we don't need words. Hand gestures and facial expressions are all we need as we make music together in the secluded spot we found in the sacred woods.

I met him yesterday, and like the others I have met this year, I may never see him again, but we have bonded over ethereal music, Qi Gong and the optional stress release exercises we have participated in. The rest of the group gradually join us, attracted by the shimmering sound of his pan drum, punctured by the rich deep pulsating hum of the metal bowls I have come to love.

The cocoon of relaxing sound is welcomed, having done breathing and optional scream therapy a couple of hours previously in the hotel conference room. I screamed the loudest I have ever screamed, and laughed hysterically, until I sobbed so hard I thought I would never stop, before screaming again, but more guttural with anger, because the dead told me to. They said let yourself go. You have been given permission.

We are the only guests staying at the hotel, and the staff had been warned of our screaming, but I wonder...did they warn the monastery a couple of hundred yards away? We screamed, and the Franciscan monks having mass were probably praying for the souls of the demented next door.

It's been a year since I first came to these sacred woods, a couple of weeks after Jamsie's funeral—my life has changed so much since then. I have changed so much since then. It's a year since I gave myself permission to have guilt free me-time, to find myself again, the girl in her twenties who got pushed into a dark corner and disappeared inside me when life-wrangling took over and the constant stress of surviving the next chapter in her life became the focus in no particular order as; mother, wife, boss, magazine editor, wedding planner, daughter, sister, woman, adult.

I am still a mother, wife, daughter, sister, adult woman, but in an altered state. A new improved version. I no longer crave the girl in her twenties who felt she needed to constantly fight for her own, and other people's survival, who worried what others thought of her. Instead, I embrace the new, improved version of myself.

I feel fully alive. This is what Italy has done to me.

———

Ronan collects me from the retreat, as I can't manage my bags of bowls on the train. Even though our car is running better than ever since the new part was installed, Ronan has rented an eight-seater minivan—because it's not just me he is collecting today.

"I checked and their flight will arrive on time," he says excitedly. Izzy, Luca and his girlfriend and Jamsie's three adult kids are all coming to stay for a week. I'm afraid I might burst with the excitement of having them all here in Italy, together at the same time.

Ciaran, my nephew, has never been to our house and Luca hasn't been back to Italy in eighteen months. "Wow, the courtyard, the sitting room, the place looks amazing!" Luca says. I had forgotten how much we had done since he had left.

"This place is gorgeous. How did you find it?" Ciaran asks.

"You don't know the story?" I say, as I lead Ciaran into the lounge with the big open fireplace and comfy sofa. "It was your dad that found it. Without him, we wouldn't be here."

Ciaran picks up the little metal wolf from the mantelpiece. I blink hard at his choice, to him it is just an ornament. "It all started when Ronan, your dad and I were driving past here four years ago. We saw the Vendesi sign and your dad asked how much would a place like this cost. We arranged a viewing, just to be nosey. Inside, it was like a dollhouse your Aunt Eileen had when we were little. Your dad found grapes and snakes in the garden—to him it was heaven. "

I don't cry saying his name anymore. Grief has become manageable.

We walk down the town and sit by the lake eating Perfumo-Sicilia gelato; a blend of pistachio, white chocolate and lemon, while watching the sunset cause yet another glorious colourful day finale and moon rise; calmly taking its place in the star studded sky.

———

Lucia joins us for dinner the following night along with Karen, John, and their son and daughter; like Jamsie's kids and ours, they are now in their twenties too. Strings of bulbs light the courtyard. The toads and cicadas are singing in unison and the bums of the fireflies are flickering. The lilt of music is coming down from the town, where the week-long festival preparations are starting.

We fall into the traditional role of the menfolk going hunting and the women gathering in the kitchen. Except our version of hunting is the collection of fifteen takeaway pizzas from the local pizzeria, and our womanly kitchen tasks involve Izzy and Lucia making a salad, while the rest of us drink Prosecco.

I don't need to look at my tattoo to remind myself to be ecstatically happy. At this moment, surrounded by complete love, I could not be happier.

"I bought you a present," Karen announces, pulling out a navy table cloth with stars all over it. "I thought it would be perfect for when you are doing tarot readings. You'll have to break it in and read all our cards on it tonight."

"It would take too long. But I could do a group reading before the lads get back with the pizzas."

Karen gathers all the girls around the table, and I take my cards out, shuffle and draw the cards. Turning them, I piece their meanings together.

"There are a lot of cups, so lots of love. There is a new home for someone. And someone will move countries...there's a wedding." I look up to get a hint who could it be. No one is moving a muscle.

And then I see a message from the cards as clear as day. It is not in the past. It is not in the future. It is now. But I can't say it.

The car pulls in through the gate, headlights hit the faces of everyone gathered. One face stands out like a startled rabbit caught in the headlights. She knows I know.

Juno barks excitedly. Spooky jumps up on the table, scattering the cards.

"The lads are back with the pizza. Let's clear these up and set the table for dinner."

By the time we are halfway through our pizzas, everyone is chattering except for me. Instead, I am enjoying just being here in this moment, watching the family around me; chatting with Lucia and Karen are Jamsie's three—all with elements of his personality—it makes me like feel he's here.

Sitting between Izzy and Luca are Karen's two, it doesn't seem long since the four of them were jumping on trampolines together, chasing firefly fairies and being amazed by the wonder of Italy.

I look at Ronan sitting at the end of the table in deep conversation with John. Tonight is the first time we extended the table in the courtyard. The expandable table I expected to fill regularly with family meals surrounded by twinkling fireflies and fairy lights with the sound of cicadas and toads like the night in La Dogana eight years ago for Mam and Dad's sixtieth wedding anniversary. It is happening in our back garden at last, but with a twist—Ronan and I are now the elders of the clan. And this, I hope, will be the first of many times we extend the table in the courtyard for laughter, good food and to raise glasses to those here in spirit.

Especially now that I have the website live offering BnC at our home; Bed and Creativity at Casa Anam Cara—for writers looking for a place to retreat to and solo female travellers to stay. I still haven't finished the shutters but I am not going to think about them at this moment.

Tonight the table is full.

Perhaps we will need an extension onto the extension as time goes on. We will definitely need a highchair added next year. Because the cards don't lie. Someone at this table is pregnant. And it's not me.

———

Book 7: What Rosie Did Next coming soon.

If you can't wait, subscribe to my blog on Substack (@rosieme-leady) to follow my story as it unfolds and develops into book 7.

If you liked this book, please leave a review where ever you bought it!

A NOTE FROM ROSIE

I have so many stories I want to write at my roll-top desk! Some are just fun (have you read my most recent book Tilly Fox's Fabulous Midlife Crisis?) but some are based on women in the past, who have never had a light shine on them.

I think it will be interesting for readers of this series to see how parts of my real-life experiences seep into my fiction. It happens with most authors, and it is only after I finish a work of fiction and doing rereads, I spot tiny elements of how my own story has snuck in unintentionally. Keep in mind when reading my fiction, I have a vivid imagination, so my fiction books are completely fiction. Especially the murder ones!

I'm loving running writing retreats here in Italy and watching others get their stories written. And, I am sure, welcoming guests into Casa Anam Cara is going to keep life interesting.

If you have read all six books in this series and enjoyed them, I hope you will some day come to one of my retreats or be a guest in my home and see the magical full-size doll's house that inspired the series.

To find out more about retreats:

www.rosiemeleady.com

To find out more about staying at the house: www.casaanamcara.com

In the meantime, if you have enjoyed this book, please leave a review where ever you bought it from!

Slán!

Xxx

Rosie

ABOUT THE AUTHOR

Dubliner Rosie Meleady was a magazine publisher and editor for twenty years. She won the International Women in Publishing Award 1996 at the ripe old age of 24. She couldn't attend the award ceremony in London as she decided it would also be a good day to give birth.

She lives happily ever after in Italy, running writers retreats, hosting creatives at her travel house and writing long into the night.

Follow Rosie on: www.rosiemeleady.com

ALSO BY ROSIE MELEADY

A Rosie Life In Italy Series

A Rosie Life In Italy - The Prequel (Published by Sourcebooks)

What Have We Done?

Should I Stay or Should I Go?

Potatoes, Pizza & Poteen

Romulus & Seamus

What Rosie Did Next

How to Have a Fabulous Midlife Crisis: A User's Guide to Dusting
Off Dreams and Making Them Happen

Womens Fiction:

Tilly Fox's Fabulous Midlife Crisis

Heroscope Series:

The Cosmo Club

Laura's Lion

Bell's Bull

Deadly Wedding Cozy Mystery series

A Nun-Holy Murder

A Brush With Death

Made in the USA
Las Vegas, NV
27 December 2025

37977902R00194